dixi
books

Joy Norstrom

Joy Norstrom is a Canadian writer and social worker residing in Treaty 7 territory. She enjoys sharing stories about the human experience, exploring the outdoors with her family, and reading late into the night when she should be asleep.

Whether Joy is enjoying a few minutes at the local coffee shop, working the 9 - 5 hustle, or discussing eyeshadow tips with her teenagers, she can generally be found in conversation. Why? She believes human connection and laughter keep her grounded in a muddled world.

Interested in other books by this author? Connect with Joy on social media or at www.joynorstrom.ca

Flying the Nest

Joy Norstrom

Dixi Books
Copyright © 2020 by Joy Norstrom
Copyright © 2020 Dixi Books
All rights reserved. No part of this book may be used or reproduced or transmitted to any form or by any means, electronic or mechanical, including photocopying, recording, or by any information and retrieval system, without written permission from the Publisher.

Flying the Nest
Joy Norstrom
Editor: Cherry Carlson
Proofreading: Andrea Bailey
Designer: Pablo Ulyanov
I. Edition: November 2020

Library of Congress Cataloging-in-Publication Data
Joy Norstrom - 1st ed.
ISBN: 978-1-913680-05-3
1. Literature 2. Humorous Fiction 3. Women Writers & Fiction 4. Family Life Fiction

© Dixi Books Publishing
293 Green Lanes, Palmers Green, London, England, N13 4XS
info@dixibooks.com
www.dixibooks.com

Flying the Nest

Joy Norstrom

dixi books

The Voice of the New Age

ACKNOWLEDGMENTS

I owe my deepest gratitude to Ayse Ozden at Dixi Books, without whom this book would not be sitting before you. Thank you for believing in this story and for seeing it to publication.

There were many generous people who assisted me during the development of this story. In particular I would like to thank Linda Noster for sharing about the occupation of a funeral director, to Carissa Koster for explaining the onion analogy and discussing her time working in long term care facilities. To Richie Brown for giving me the ins and outs of a call centre. And to Christine Lee, Frankie Hum, Long Lam, Sabrina Song and countless others who have shared their experiences bridging Canadian and Chinese culture, thank you for your openness, generosity of information and friendship. Any errors or inaccuracies are mine.

Thank you to my writing friends for your unwavering support. Jacqueline Aubin-Chornohus, Heidi Catherine, Janine Dilger, Don Owen, Dee Ann Evans, Theo Eystathioy, Gwynne Jackson and Robin Van Eck: I'm talking to you! Your willingness to commiserate, encourage, host writing retreats, and give frank feedback made this book better. Thank you also to my mother and Silvia Ross for your eagle eyes; your help was a true gift. And to Robyn Harding who first encouraged me to turn a short story about condoms into a full-on novel—I'm so glad I listened to you! I could not see the forest for the trees.

To my wonderful family who have made endless sacrifices, so I had space and time to write, thank you always. To readers and reviewers and bloggers of my first book, and to those friends who celebrated each step with me, I am humbled by your support. And last to my Grandmother who lived a second, (or maybe third) life in assisted living: this book is in memory of your fax machine, your sheer stockings, and your particular gentleman 'friend'—I am long inspired by your tenacious spirit. As the young kids say, #YOLT.

CONTENTS

PART ONE

Chad: Fire & Ice	13
Clara: Chess Match	21
Chad: Rebel in Love	33
Rosie: PET-ition Ambition	47
Quinn: Root Beer	51
Chad: Chaos	59
Martin: Power of the Herd	71
Chad: Time of Plenty	79
Rosie: A Trap	87
Lila: Precautionary Measures	91
Chad: Turning Tables	103

PART TWO

Chad: Postie One-Two	115
Quinn: Little White Lies	127
Clara: Heart on Fire	133
Rosie: Night Search	143
Quinn: Wedding Bells	153
Chad: Dinner Party	159
Martin: Distraction	171
Rosie: Aftermath	179
Chad: Respite	183
Chad: Small Steps	191
Felicity: Comfort and Joy	197
Martin: Reconciliation	205
Quinn: New Year	213
Chad: The Man Code	215
Chad: Supplies	223
Martin: Leather / Prelude	229

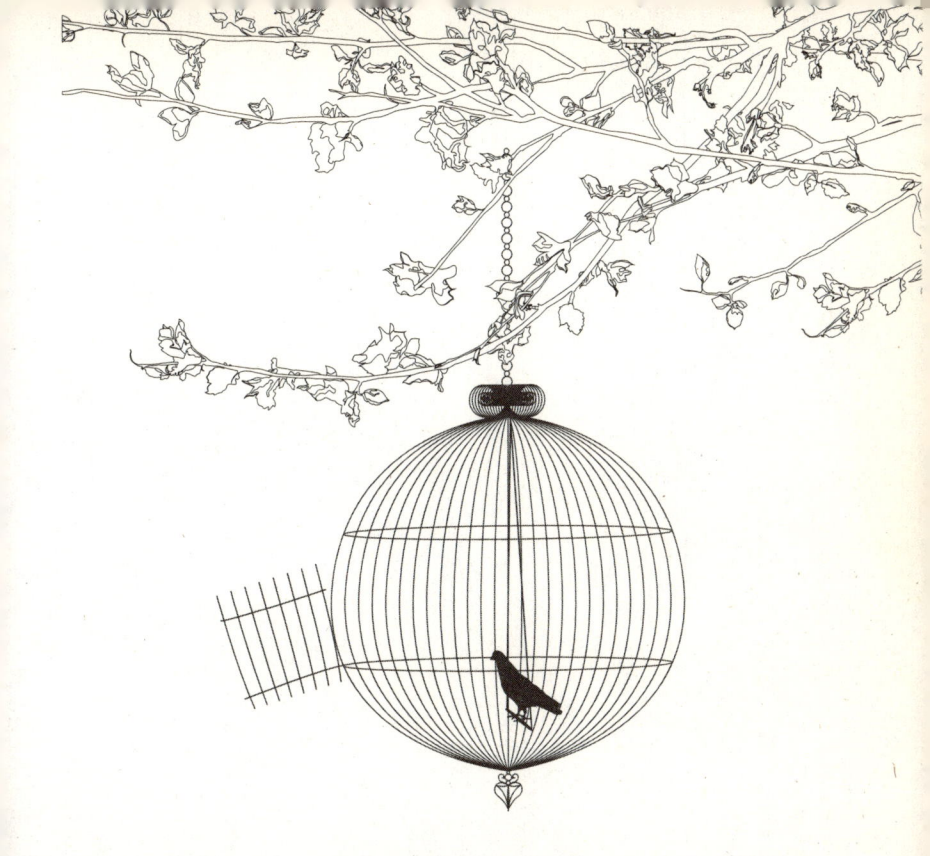

PART ONE

Chad: Fire & Ice

Uncle Martin traced his thumb over the embossed lettering on the package of disposable razors, the words a brilliant white against the emerald background. Quadruple Blades. Aloe strip for comfort. MEGA-PACK. By the way his mouth opened and closed I already knew he'd found fault in my shopping skills.

"Fifty-two friggin' razors. I'll be dead before I finish this pack, Chad."

I didn't let his comment rattle me. I'd heard it all before, besides he had more energy than most of his fellow residents at the Eldernest Assisted Living Lodge. He was a silver Lamborghini amid a collection of beige family sedans. Heck, he was a stallion; a living legend of masculinity.

Martin shook his head one last time and placed the razors beside the bottle of cologne and jar of hair pomade that rested on the cafeteria table between us. Jovan Musk aftershave, quadruple-blade razors, whey protein powder for his morning milk, and condoms. All items the onsite pharmacy didn't stock, yet Martin swore he could not live without. The man had priorities. And me? I was forever sheepish in his virile presence.

My uncle reached back into the shopping bag and pulled out a small metallic square and held it up toward the fluorescent lights.

"That one's not for the cafeteria, Uncle."

He wasn't listening. His attention was solely on the condom, turning it over in his hand, to look at the label.

"These aren't my usual brand."

13

"I know. The pharmacist threw it in. New product sample or something. But don't worry; there's a box of your regulars in the bag, too. Maybe you should put it away, okay?" The cafeteria was crawling with weekend visitors and I hoped the other patrons hadn't taken notice. The last thing we needed was another complaint about my uncle's moral compass. He was popular with his lady friends; he wasn't popular with their families.

Thankfully he took my advice and threw it back in the bag. I rubbed my nose, trying to block the smell of tuna casserole and industrial disinfectant, and casually looked around the cafeteria for a compact figure, black hair cut in a shining bob. She didn't seem to be working today.

"Things are moving in the right direction with Clara," Martin continued. "But I could keep things fresh with Felicity too. If I wanted. Time will tell, won't it, lad?"

I gave him a weak smile. I didn't wish Martin a life of solitude, it's just... how did he manage such a bountiful lifestyle? Whenever we walked the halls of the 'Nest, it seemed Uncle Martin had an admirer in every wing. Then there was me. I was less than half his age, yet couldn't seem to keep a single woman interested.

"Felicity... that's the one with the shapely—"

"You got it."

Felicity wore tennis skirts, shiny white runners and tight V-neck tops that displayed fleshy, tanned cleavage. Perhaps she did play tennis. Or had. Before the hip replacement.

"Decaf or regular?" At the sound of her voice adrenaline shot through my body. Where had she come from? I looked up to see a set of well-formed cheekbones and coal black hair. She held a carafe of coffee in each hand.

"Regular, please." We made eye contact and the old habit kicked in. Face on fire, I dropped my gaze.

She poured with practiced disregard. Coffee sloshed over the side of my ceramic mug and formed a puddle on the table. I took a deep breath and readied myself to thank her, but it was too late. She was off to the next table, and once again I'd blown my chance. What was wrong with me?

I made eye contact with my uncle, hoping my face wasn't as red as it felt. He ground his dentures together in a sort of jaw twisting action and immediately started rummaging through the shopping bag again. I was not talking to him about this. No way. Instead I cleared my throat and returned to his favourite subject. "So, this Clara. Is she the one you play chess with?"

"That's the one."

"She doesn't strike me as… well… one of your regulars."

Martin nodded. "She's a class act."

When I'd met Clara, she'd been sitting across the chess board from my uncle, confidently moving her pieces from one square to another. She'd looked more interested in the game than in Martin, but what did I know?

By this time my uncle's curiousity had got the better of him. He drew the sample condom back out of the bag, held it away from his face as far as his arm would stretch and squinted his eyes. "Damn small print on this. Do you think it's lubricated?"

"Oh gawd. Let's talk about that later."

"You know, Chad, lubrication is pretty necessary at this stage of life. A little extra help in the moisture department isn't going to go amiss, especially as a woman ages." Martin tapped the table with his forefinger to emphasize his point. "You should be taking notes. You and the Missus aren't getting any younger."

I rolled my eyes. "I'm only thirty."

And as for the "Missus," Kate was no longer around. Hadn't been for several months. Not that I'd told Martin. We talked about his love life, not mine.

Anyway I couldn't blame Kate for leaving. As the lonely weeks turned into solitary months, it became clear she'd made the right choice. I had nothing to offer. It was unlikely lubricated condoms could make up for my inadequacies.

I took a sip of my coffee and looked across the dining room at the attendant's slender form. Christ, I timed my visits with my uncle to align with her damn shifts, but I lacked Martin's balls. Martin's way with women.

That gene had passed me by.

Uncle Martin called a short three days later. My phone vibrated on my desk and recognizing my uncle's number I decided to answer it. Martin did not, after all, text.

He didn't even email. If I didn't answer now, he would only

call back.

"Hi, Martin, I'm at work. I'll call—"

"I need more supplies." My uncle's plea reverberated through the phone. "That there new brand. You know, the sample you brought?"

I smiled politely as my colleague popped her big head over the half cubicle wall separating us. Janice was insufferable; she let nothing slip. I already knew I'd be getting an ear-full for breaking the unwritten code: Thou shalt not conduct personal phone calls in the office unless they involved your child's next dental appointment. I turned my back to her. "Alright. I'll bring them when I visit on—"

"No. *Tonight.*" Martin's voice cracked in a burst of excitement. "It's got to be tonight. Harold's on."

"Harold?"

"You know, the night nurse. Turns a blind eye, remember? Don't forget: that new brand. Might as well get me a big box."

So he'd tried the sample. "Are they actually better?"

"Like fire and ice, lad. Fire and ice."

I laughed, picturing the suave Martin making his way from room to room at the 'Nest. "Ha! Well I'm glad the condom met your high expectations."

I heard an in-drawn breath and turned in time to see Janice glaring at me, her eyes saying a hell of a lot more than her tightly pressed lips. I had the decency to flush. As Martin got into details better shared outside of cubicle-land, I covered the receiver. "Sorry. It's my uncle...he's quite lonely at times..."

"Whatever you think is important," Janice hissed. "Me, I would think office culture, respectful workplace—or God knows monthly sales—but what do I know?"

"But...we're the Complaints Department."

Janice narrowed her eyes. "You could at least try." She sat back on her chair, the hydraulics huffing in righteous indignation.

I returned to the phone in time to hear my uncle say farewell. "I've got to go. Walking group's starting in a few minutes and I promised Felicity I'd be there. See you tonight."

"Alright," I agreed. "See you tonight."

I stopped at the pharmacy after work to purchase Martin's

condoms. As I stood in line waiting to pay, I couldn't escape the sweet and bitter taste of random recollections that always dogged me while I waited at that till. It was a hole in the wall kind of place; nothing special. Laminate flooring, bad light. But it was where I'd picked up my mother's medications when she was too sick to come herself. I'd waited countless times in this very line, staring at magazines and waiting my turn to pay. Now, it seemed one of my only connections to her and I couldn't bring myself to stop shopping there.

Is this what Mom had meant, that I should buy her brother condoms? I shook my head at the ridiculousness of it. She hadn't left very specific instructions. Only that I should visit her brother and help him out because he wouldn't have anyone else after she was gone.

It turned out to be me who had no one else.

I paid for Martin's purchase and went home. There was no point eating out—I hated eating in public by myself and I was not interested in the visitor's special at the 'Nest. No way. So home it was to change, make some macaroni or maybe one of those instant dinners that Kate hated before taking the condoms to Martin.

It wasn't until I was washing my solitary dinner plate when I heard the key in the doorknob. It startled me with its jangling and turning, and in seconds the door traitorously gave way to her gentle pressure.

"Hello?" Her voice floated through the air.

I looked down at the old sweatpants and t-shirt I'd changed into. My work clothes were in a pile on my bed and there was no time to put them back on. She was already walking down the hall.

Kate rounded the corner and took in my pitiful joggers, my soapy hands.

"Well hello, Chad. It's good to see you." I was flooded with the awareness—both sudden and acute—of the thick layer of silence that had grown in the apartment, undisturbed, for several months.

Her hair had recently been cut and I could tell she had taken the time to apply a shimmering lip gloss. I cleared my throat. "That's a nice dress." How easily I fell back into an attempt to please.

"Why, thank you." Kate performed a quick turn on her heel, the dress flaring out from her toned legs. "I'm here for the waffle iron."

"Right." She'd emailed last week about it. I turned to look at the cupboards behind me. "Where is it?"

"Up here, silly." She reached up and withdrew the little appliance from one of the top cupboards. The sight of the iron's aged patina brought back lazy Sunday mornings with Kate, and my chest tightened.

"I'll bring it back."

She'd bring it back? I'd heard that before. Last time it was my copy of Dark Souls 3. It stung to think of my game in his Xbox—my Kate in his bed—and somehow the loss of both seemed a deeper betrayal than either one alone.

"It's fine. I'll never use it. Besides, I'm cutting out carbs." I chuckled, as though my lie were funny and attempted a relaxed smile.

Not that it mattered. Her eyes had fastened on something behind me and she broke into a grin. "Hey, what's that?"

I turned to see the glossy box of fire and ice on the table. "Oh, those aren't for me."

Her eyebrows shot up.

"Really. They're for Martin," I said. "You remember my uncle? I've started visiting him on weekends. With my mom gone...well, he doesn't have anyone else. Anyway, these are supposed to be great. Like 'fire and ice' he says." A genuine smile stretched across my face thinking of what a character my uncle was.

Kate fiddled with the waffle iron cord. "You can tell me if you're with someone else."

"No, really. I'm not. It's—"

"Stop, Chad. I'm happy for you. Honestly." She reached over and squeezed my shoulder. "I've been worried about you. About you being alone. But here you've been busy all along." The grin spread up into her eyes and wreathed her face in happiness. "See? Moving on was the right decision. You were never frisky before... and now look at you! Packets of condoms just waiting to be ripped open."

I thought back to those final nights lying beside Kate. Wanting to touch but not touching. Maintaining as civil a distance as the queen-sized mattress would allow. Distance fueled by my inadequacies and her charismatic colleague.

She gave me an exaggerated wink. "Have fun!"

I walked Kate, the waffle iron and her misconception to the door.

She had everything she needed and would not be back.

***

Martin was waiting for me on the bench out front of the Eldernest when I arrived. I collapsed down beside him and thrust the bag with the requested condoms into his lap.

"Here you go, old man."

He cuffed my shoulder in one of those improvised man-hugs before taking a quick look inside the bag. "You've done well, lad."

"Not as well as you."

"Trouble with the missus?" He gave me the once over, his eyes settling on my Star Wars T-shirt. "You've just got to get on your 'A' game. Dress the part. Act the part." He straightened his shirt collar, the indigo button-down looking vivid against his trim, white hair. I wondered who kept his shirts ironed.

I cleared my throat and changed the subject by pointing at the box of condoms now in Martin's hands. "So, are you sure these are necessary? I mean…"

Martin's eyebrows nearly hit his hairline. "Are you kidding? This place has more clap than an Allied trench in 1917. Perhaps you can rest on your laurels—you're in a committed relationship—but me?" Martin paused and looked around. Satisfied we wouldn't be overheard, he continued. "Nathan got it from Sarah, but Sarah claims she only slept with Edgar the once."

"Wait. Hold on. Isn't Edgar that guy with the two canes? At his age?"

"Sure. He's only seven years older than I am. Anyway, Herbert—the one who blares the American football in the social room—he says he got it from either Maggie or Felicity, but he's not sure which one. I've got to be careful."

"*Your* Felicity…the tennis clothes one?"

"You got it. But it's Clara I need the fire and ice for." Martin tapped the box of condoms. "Thanks again, lad."

"If you don't mind me asking, how did you…convince her?"

"Convince? If you've got to convince someone you're doing

it wrong, aren't you? It's like back in my postal service days. No one's convincing a person to send mail, but we posties were ready and willing if you wanted to."

What? I didn't quite understand the link to mail delivery, but somehow Martin was able to link nearly everything back to his days in the postal service. He leaned in. "I told Clara we didn't have to. Told her we could just go on playing chess."

I nodded over my confusion. What good would it do to admit I didn't understand? I wished him well and set off for the bus stop. With nothing to do and no one to talk to, it was hard not to dwell on the emptiness in my life. My brain twisted between Kate's happiness and my uncle's prowess. I sat on the metal bench inside the bus shelter and knew my life was as solitary as the setting sun.

That's when she walked into the Plexiglas enclosure. I looked up as she pushed her coal-black hair behind the curve of her ear.

"This seat," she pointed at the bench beside me. "It's free?"

"Yes," I stammered. A rush of colour hit my face and my heart hammered behind Yoda's silhouette. I inched over to make room for her.

The last golden rays of sunlight streamed through the enclosure and I closed my eyes. I would stand up when the bus arrived. I would get on the bus. I would sit by myself and I would probably never have breakfast on a Saturday morning with this beautiful woman.

Unless I could say something. Say anything.

"My name. It's Chad." The words rushed out and it was too late to choke them back.

She tilted her head and looked at me. Looked at me for what seemed the first time.

Clara: Chess Match

"Do you want to stay over?" There. She'd said it.

Clara had found enough courage to ask, but not quite enough to look Martin in the eye. Instead, she kept her gaze on the battlefield. Picking up her ivory knight (what a silly game this was) she knocked his castle over and placed her little horse in its place.

"Stay over? If you think you can tempt me into an all-night chess tournament, you're dead wrong. I give up now." Picking up his queen, Martin casually moved it forward on the board. "Check."

Clara looked around the social hall. Would anyone overhear? For once they appeared to be alone. Alone, except for Linus.

Linus sat where he'd been left. In his wheelchair, by the window overlooking the manicured lawns of the Eldernest Assisted Living Lodge. Even if Linus were listening, he certainly wasn't talking. The stroke had taken everything from him but his life.

Clara straightened her shoulders. Her heart was a staccato beat in her throat, but she swallowed it down. Picking up her one remaining pawn, she slid it forward in a half-hearted effort at protecting her king from Martin's advance. "Actually, I had something else in mind."

"Checkers? Please not checkers."

He was goading her. Of that she was certain. But why he enjoyed making it difficult, Clara wasn't sure. This had surely been on the table as clearly as the checkered squares of the chessboard. Looking up, she met the challenge in his eyes. "You know what I'm talking about."

Martin grinned, "Of course I do, darling. I wasn't born

yesterday." He reached across the board and moved his queen one last time. "Checkmate."

***

Martin had been adamant they wait until Thursday night as Harold would be working the evening shift. Of all the night staff, Harold was known for minding his own business when it came to discrete liaisons between Eldernest inhabitants. That left Clara two days, nearly forty-eight hours, to prepare. Prepare and vacillate.

In all her seven decades Clara had never experienced a physical relationship with anyone other than her husband. For most of her life she'd not questioned this. It was the way it was supposed to be. The way God had intended.

But had the good Lord intended Clara to feel desperately alone in her last years? Children, housework, wifely duties. All that was behind her now. Her husband was gone yet she wasn't.

So why shouldn't she live out the days she had left? Really live? Was it not time to put herself first?

Besides, she couldn't back out now. What would Martin think? Proper women did not lead men on, and Clara was proper. A woman of her word.

Opening her nightstand drawer Clara withdrew her nail file, then remembered and placed it back in its drawer. The whites of her nails had already been chewed clean off.

***

Like any other Thursday morning, Clara was waiting outside the sliding front doors of the Eldernest five minutes before the shopping bus was scheduled to arrive. The bus transported Eldernest residents to the closest mall on a weekly basis, barring—of course—major holidays and inclement weather.

It was always women on the bus. Women with their hair done up in stiff curls, or cut into sharp, straight angles. The short hair rained, in silvers and salt and peppers and brass dye jobs Clara did not at all fancy. She kept her own white hair long and tied back.

"Clara? Yoo-hoo!" She grit her teeth and turned in the direction of Rosie's chipper voice. Rosie was standing just inside the doorway, her arms flapping in an attempt to gain Clara's attention.

"Oh good! You've heard me."

Clara stiffened. Why Rosie thought she couldn't hear was

beyond her. A person would have to be two blocks away not to hear the woman. "Don't let the bus leave without me! I've got to take my blood thinners. Alright, Clara? Did you hear me?"

"Alrig—"

"I've got to get my blood thinners!" Rosie's eyes were huge, making her look like a nervous bug. She had large, thick framed glasses, the type that made a person's eyeballs look larger than they were.

"Yes. I'll save you a seat." Clara waved Rosie back into the building and turned her attention to the flowers growing in the cement planters either side of the entrance.

Out of the corner of her eye, Clara could see Felicity sitting on the bench with her lackey, Marg. An amused expression twisted Felicity's fuchsia lips. Clara couldn't see the top half of Felicity's face, but she imagined Felicity's eyes were narrow and hateful behind the new Jackie O sunglasses she wore.

The oversized lenses sat atop Felicity's flawlessly made-up face and Clara couldn't help but covet them. They were real sunglasses, and not the kind worn over-top prescription lenses.

Felicity and Marg were twittering like magpies, enjoying a laugh at Rosie's—and perhaps her—expense. Rosie could be exasperating, there was no arguing that. But had these women no manners? Clara thought not.

The shuttlebus pulled up and Rosie hustled out of the Eldernest, her glasses askew. Single file, the women boarded the bus and sat down. Clara and Rosie sat together, choosing a row near the driver.

"I thought I might miss the bus!" Rosie said, starting in on Clara as soon as they sat down. "What a busy morning. I barely had time to comb my hair." Clara smiled politely and didn't let her eyes wander to the other woman's untidy hair. Then she turned to the window in an effort not to encourage Rosie into more conversation. The woman could be an energy drain and today was not a day Clara intended to waste energy.

She had plans. Exciting plans! She could feel a nervous tingling in her fingertips and a spark in her chest. Not even Felicity's chic Jackie O sunglasses or Marg's look of contempt could bring Clara down.

"Shall we visit the bookstore first?" Rosie continued. "I'd like to take a look-see at the sale table. But I won't be buying anything there, not on your life. I've my holds at the library." As Rosie yammered on about books then discount sweaters then the food court, it began to dawn on Clara she might have a hitch in her plan.

She had an errand to do. An errand she did not intend to have an audience for. No. That would not do. She'd somehow have to give Rosie the slip.

But how? Clara wouldn't be able to walk faster and 'accidentally' out-pace the woman. Rosie was a member of the Eldernest walking group and set a quicker pace than she did.

As the bus pulled up to the mall, Clara glanced at her watch. 10:30. She had exactly two and a half hours to shake Rosie and complete her errand before the return trip. It was possible. It had to be.

The Eldernest women disembarked from the bus, one by one by one. They set off in their little groups with their lists and walkers and pension cheques. For many, it was the social highlight of the week. It had been for Clara too...until she'd started playing chess with Martin.

"The bookstore then—oh my word! Just look at that little dog!"

Clara sighed. They hadn't even gotten into the mall yet. Not that this was unusual. Rosie was an absolute animal lover and couldn't manage to pass one without stopping.

As Clara waited, Rosie and the dog owner chatted about the labradoodle's parentage. His sleep schedule. His eating habits. Clara's gut twisted with anxiety. It was just nerves; nothing serious. But maybe it could be her ticket?

When the women finally made their way inside the mall doors, Clara rested her hand against the back of the nearest bench.

"Do you know, Rose, I'm not feeling altogether well." She rubbed her tummy. "The eggs, I think. At breakfast."

Rosie gasped and clutched at Clara's arm "Haven't I told you— don't eat the eggs. They are laced with Metamucil! Absolutely *laced*. For goodness sake, Clara." Rosie flapped her arms and looked around wildly as though a solution might appear to Clara's gastrointestinal problem. "We'll have to go back. I'll call a cab. No,

I'll go chat with the bus driver."

"No, no. You should shop, Rosie. Go to the bookstore; enjoy yourself. I think I'll just sit here for a bit. I'm sure it will pass."

"It'll pass alright!" Rosie turned and was off like a rocket, her back-end moving energetically in her polyester slacks. "I'll find help! Hold on, Clara!"

"Er...Rosie?" Clara called after her, "I'll just sit for a bit. Don't be silly! Go to the bookstore, won't you?" But Rosie could not be stopped. She was already making her way across the parking lot to where the driver sat in his vehicle.

Perhaps that had worked too well? There was nothing for it now. Clara stood up and hustled to the department store at the far end of the mall.

The lingerie department was not hard to find. Clara wandered through the clothing racks and chose two nightgowns that seemed just about right.

The first was a vibrant turquoise. The silk fabric slipped smoothly through her fingers like sand. The second nightie was a dove's gray with a neckline trimmed in cream lace. It seemed, perhaps, more appropriate; more expected for a woman her age. But the turquoise...it sang to Clara like the first brilliant days of spring.

"Can I help you with anything?" A young saleswoman smiled sweetly up at Clara. She hadn't noticed her approaching.

"Do you think...the colour?"

"Oh, it's absolutely darling. Your husband will love it."

Clara's face stiffened but she didn't bother to correct her. "I'll take it."

Paying for her purchase was an excruciatingly slow process. Clara was acutely aware of how many Eldernest busybodies were peppered throughout the mall. Anyone might see her. The worst would be Felicity. Or Marg. And what about Rosie? She must be in hysterics, unable to find Clara on the bench where she'd left her. She felt an overwhelming urge to chew on the end of her thumb nail.

"Receipt in the bag?"

"Yes, thanks." The young saleswoman took her time, stapling the debit receipt to the sales receipt.

"We've a survey right now. If you go online, just here—" she highlighted a web address on the stapled receipts in neon yellow. "—do you know how to use a computer?"

Clara grit her teeth. "Yes. I know how to get online." What did this have to do with anything? Clara needed to get out of sight. Leaning over the counter she snatched both the receipt and shopping bag out of the startled saleswoman's hands. "Have a good day, Miss," and with that Clara turned and raced out of the department store.

Now she had a new problem: what to do with the bag? If she arrived back at the bus with it, she'd have some explaining to do. And with the volume of Rosie's voice…Lordy, that wouldn't do. Not at all.

But clearly she couldn't hide it in her purse. These days Clara carried a very small handbag so the weight of it wouldn't pain her sore shoulders.

Clara headed to the nearest washroom. Thankfully, she found it empty. Choosing the handicap stall for extra maneuvering room, she locked the door before sliding the new nightie out of the plastic bag.

With the help of the folding scissors on her keychain, Clara cut off the price tags and shoved them into the metal garbage bin attached to the stall wall. In went the plastic bag after the tags. Easy.

Harder was taking off her sweater while sitting on the edge of the toilet, but she managed it. The nightie slid over her shoulders and down her body, the fabric the softest whisper against her skin. It was perfect; softer than Clara had even imagined.

She tucked the extra fabric in the waist of her slacks and began to maneuver her arms back through her sweater sleeves. It was then the washroom door banged open.

"Clara! Are you in here, Clara?" Rosie's frantic voice bounced off the hard bathroom fixtures.

Clara froze behind her partition, left arm half in and half out of her sweater. "I'm here. I'll be out in a minute."

"Oh my Woooord! I've been searching everywhere! I thought you may've found yourself in a compromising situation. I was just about to contact security!"

She'd gotten away with it. Relief sprang through Clara's body.

All she needed to do was push her arm through the tight sleeve of her sweater, and there, she'd done it!

She exited the toilet stall to find Rosie flustered and sweaty, leaning against the countertop for support.

"The bus driver *refused* to take us home early. Absolutely refused! Said he wasn't authorized to make a second trip. Can you believe that?"

Rosie cupped her hands under the faucet, catching cold water in her hands. She slapped it on the back of her neck, letting it trickle over her flushed skin. "Now that I've found you, we'll call a taxi. Get you back home in a jiffy, alright?"

"Honestly, I'm fine now. I just…well I'm fine. I'm feeling much better." Clara turned away from Rosie's sweaty hairline and pink cheeks and washed her hands under the automatic faucet. "Shall we visit that bookstore now?"

***

It was after 9:00 pm, and Clara's heart pattered with nervous anticipation. Waiting these last few minutes for Martin was maddening. There was nothing left to do but worry. For the hundredth time she fiddled with the neckline of her nightie. Would Martin like it? And her hair. Would he like that? She always wore it tied back in the social room, but tonight she'd left it down. The long white strands had been brushed till they were gleaming.

Clara's heart stopped.

She hadn't expected the door knock to be so loud. Or so soon.

He was here. Clara took a deep inhalation, as deep as her aging lungs would allow, and let the air out in a quick puff. Using her hands for leverage she pushed herself up from the standard issue, twin-sized bed and walked to the door. Her heart was pounding in her chest enough to make her want to pass out. *Could she do this? Could she really and truly do this?*

She placed her hand on the levered doorknob, ready to turn the handle, when a second tap, tap, tap caused her to freeze.

"Mrs. Cardinal?"

Clara gasped. It wasn't Martin. Wasn't even the night nurse, Harold. She recognized the voice of one of the female caregivers who helped the more invalid residents with grooming, eating and the like.

Clara cracked the door open a few inches and peeked out. "Hello?"

"Good evening, Mrs. Cardinal. I was wondering if you might be up for a cup of tea with Linus? He seems a bit agitated tonight." The caregiver leaned in, causing the silver crucifix on her necklace to swing forward then come back to rest against her uniform. "I think he's lonely."

"Oh." Clara swallowed, trying to keep her body hidden behind the door. She hoped the woman wouldn't catch sight of her aquamarine nightie. If she did, it would certainly draw questions. "It's rather late. Um…sorry. I—not tonight."

The caregiver's forehead wrinkled. "Alright. Are you feeling okay? You look a bit flushed."

"I'm fine." Clara said, forcing a smile. "Just tired. Goodnight."

Clara closed the door, and took several panting breaths trying to calm herself.

She listened to the caregiver's receding footsteps as she walked down the polished linoleum hallway. Would she be back to check on her? It was several minutes before Clara could make her way back to her bed.

Perched on the edge of her mattress she tried to think of something else. Anything else. Her eyes were drawn to the only other living thing in the room: the African violet on her windowsill. Its woolly leaves drooped over the yellow foil pot and the blossoms, a brilliant spark of magenta, thrust up from the center of the foliage in a showy and defiant manner.

Felicity's violets weren't nearly as perky. The trick was to not over-water. And then, once a month, an infusion of cold tea.

It was just as her mother had taught her. Her mother, that distant woman who, it seemed to Clara, had obeyed all the rules with a content and quiet heart.

It occurred to Clara she had never liked violets.

She stood up, walked to the windowsill, picked up the offending plant and dropped it in the garbage bin.

This was Clara's life, and not her mother's.

Again Clara heard someone tapping on her door. Could this be him? For the second time that night she walked to the door, opening it a fraction of an inch and peeking out.

Martin stood with his hands clasped together. He was still wearing his khaki slacks and collared golf shirt. What had she been expecting? A housecoat? Boxers and a t-shirt?

She was underdressed.

Decidedly underdressed.

"Good evening, darling." Martin smiled, shifted his weight and then looked nervously down the women's hallway. It was silent, except for Rosie's steady snores from the next room over. "Er, are you going to let me in?"

"Oh, yes." Clara opened the door a foot wider. The cooler breeze from the hallway slipped into her room and sent a shiver up Clara's loose nightgown, instantly reminding her of her unbound breasts, loose and floating under the slippery turquoise silk.

Her skin was covered in a thick sheen of dread as Martin wedged himself around the half open door. He maneuvered around the door jam, pulling his shirt away from its metallic edges until he'd managed to sneak his whole body inside Clara's room.

Clara was terrified. She had to shut the door. She'd have to turn around and face Martin. With all the courage she had left, Clara clicked the door latch into place, took another fortifying breath and turned around.

Her room was dimly lit; the emergency call button bathed everything in a rosy glow. Her eyes were already adjusted, but were Martin's? The hallway had been much brighter. She felt a nervous giggle threaten in her chest.

"Clara, dear. You look an absolute dream." Clara heard the catch in his voice and felt instant pleasure spread across her face and heart. It freed her to take three quick steps in his direction and suddenly, wonderfully, she was in Martin's arms.

He gently kissed her with a sweetness she had long imagined. Her breath caught in her throat. It was magic. If she closed her eyes, she could be sixteen again.

In time, Martin removed his shoes. His socks. His slacks and his shirt. He folded them carefully and piled them neatly on her chair. With no small effort, they maneuvered onto Clara's twin bed. Laying side-by-side it was a tight squeeze, but it had its advantages over any of the other options available.

His hands gently explored her body—something no one had

done in a very long time—and Clara tried to relax. It wasn't easy. She wondered what he might be thinking as her parts slid sideways into the firm, institutional mattress.

Forget it, she chided herself. At seventy-two was she really going to spend one more minute worried about her waistline?

She ran her hands gently over his back, feeling his skin soft and warm under her fingertips. It was nice feeling this close to someone again.

Clip. Clip. Clip. Clara froze at the sound of hard-sole shoes walking down the linoleum hallway. Could that woman be back?

"Who's that?" she hissed in Martin's ear.

Martin reluctantly moved his hand away from the space between Clara's waist and hip and attempted to adjust his hearing-aid. "Sounds like Nurse Harold, but I can't be sure."

"What if he walks in?"

"Does anyone ever walk into your room uninvited?"

"Only when I press the emergency-call button."

"Have you pressed it tonight?"

"Well, no!" Clara swallowed. Should she tell Martin about her earlier visitor? She didn't want to. She didn't want to dwell on it. Not tonight. Thankfully, the footsteps receded down the hall and Clara's shoulders relaxed.

"Well then, let's not worry. Besides, I put a sock on the door, so no one will bother us."

"Martin! You did not!"

He chuckled and traced his fingertips along the curve of Clara's hip, but she couldn't relax. Martin removed his hand and kissed her lightly on the forehead. "We don't have to, you know. We could just go on playing chess."

With what confidence she could muster Clara pressed her body against his. "And let Felicity get her claws into you? Forget it." She tried to laugh so he understood it was a joke. She could be funny. She could be lighthearted.

Clara reached down and grasped Martin in her hand. Was she doing it the right way? It was like riding a bicycle, wasn't it? In the red glow she gazed up into his eyes. "I'm glad you're here."

"So am I. But be careful with my hip, honey. It's still being worn in."

***

Rolling onto her side, Clara curled up against Martin. After so long sleeping alone the feel of his skin behind her knees and against her back sent a shiver of pleasure through her limbs. She didn't know how long he could stay, but for now he was right here beside her. His breathing heavy and slow and comforting.

She felt a familiar twinge but swallowed it down. There was nothing to feel guilty about. The kids were busy with their own lives. And why shouldn't she follow her heart? The Eldernest could be a lonely place, but it didn't have to be. Clara closed her eyes and drifted off listening to the sound of Martin's slow, steady breathing.

***

If it were up to Clara, she would gladly give up the Thursday shopping trips to spend more time with Martin. Yet here she was, just one week later, sitting beside Rosie on the outbound journey. As Rosie discussed the price of birdseed for her outdoor feeder, Clara replayed the short exchange she'd had with Martin after breakfast.

"Shall we play some chess this morning?" she'd asked eagerly. "It will be quiet in the social room today."

"Oh shoot, darling, I've made plans. Got to check-in on that nephew of mine. See that he's staying out of trouble. Rain check?" He'd placed a kiss on her forehead and quickly maneuvered to the cafeteria door so he could help one of the young and pretty workers who had her hands full pushing a woman in a wheelchair.

Clara was brought abruptly to the present by Rosie. Rosie was looking at her, waiting for an answer, but Clara had missed what she'd been asked. "I'm sorry. What did you say?"

"I said, I don't know why you do that. It's not good for the nail bed. Surely you know?"

Clara hadn't even realized she was chewing her nails. Face flushing, she lowered her hand.

"It's just...I'm just thinking about something. Can I ask you something, Rosie? What do you think about—" Clara dropped her voice but carefully enunciated so she wouldn't have to repeat herself, "Martin?"

"Martin?"

"Shhh!"

"Alright, alright," Rosie dropped her voice to a whisper. "He's with Felicity. You do know that, right? Everyone knows. They do the walking group together most afternoons. She can't keep her hands off him.

"Anyway, you don't need his attention; you've got Linus. He adores you. Can't stop watching you. If I had a husband as smitten as yours—"

Clara snorted. "You'd what? He can't do anything but sit in his chair and breathe."

Rosie's eyes opened wide behind her magnifying lenses. "But…he's your husband, Clara." Her blue irises were obscenely large, and Clara had to look away from their raw depths.

It had been a long four months playing chess. But they had been full of a sweet anticipation Clara had hardly recognized. The bus jolted to a stop; the brakes hammering into Clara's heart.

"You've got Linus—"

"He's not enough."

Chad: Rebel in Love

With only seconds to make a choice, I did what any lonely and desperate man would do. I got on the bus. Not my bus; her bus.

It wasn't a hard choice. I'd first noticed her meandering around the 'Nest cafeteria tables weeks ago. Since then, I'd been gathering and storing every piece of information about her that I could. Granted, my knowledge was limited: I hadn't the courage to actually speak with her. Still, I'd observed a few things: she wore colourful socks under her Eldernest Assisted Living Lodge uniform; rainbows and goldfish and bats peeked out as she stopped at various tables. They were easy to spot for people who kept their eyes down.

She overlooked the repeated demands of the surlier seniors and took her time with the quieter ones. Helped pour cream and add sugar when shaky hands made it difficult. From what I'd observed she never blushed or got flustered; that made us practically polar opposites. That was okay with me. Her thoughtful expression and killer stare were the magic most manga artists tried to pull off but couldn't always manage.

She also seemed to work every Sunday afternoon, and that's why I'd made it a priority to visit Uncle Martin every Sunday at exactly one o'clock. If it hadn't been for Martin's frantic request for fire and ice condoms, I'd never have made an unscheduled Friday night trip. And if I hadn't made the unscheduled trip, I would never have crossed paths with the colourful sock wearing cafeteria worker at the bus stop. It was dumb luck, but I was a believer in dumb luck. I trusted it in a way I didn't trust myself.

Being the only other person at the bus stop made it easy. We'd exchanged words ("Warm out tonight." "Sure is.") and even shared a bench in the Plexiglas shelter (my palms sweating rivers). When the number six pulled up, she stood up. So did I. Then she boarded the bus. And I, heart pounding, did the same.

I'd no bloody clue where the number six was going, and I didn't care. All that waited for me at home was a cold bowl of Shreddies and the television.

She chose an empty seat in the middle of the bus and sat down. *Screw it, why try playing cool? I might never get a chance like this again.* I took the empty seat right in front of her. My heart pattered a mile a minute. I was all in.

I turned sideways; my back pressed against the wall of the bus instead of my backrest so I could see her face in my periphery. Then, with a nervous half-cough-half-throat-clearing I turned my head to look her full-on and went for it. "I didn't, uh, catch your name."

Her eyes opened wider as her hands stilled. She'd been in the process of plugging her headphones into her phone. "I'm Lila."

"Nice to meet you. Officially. You know, after so long seeing you...around."

She eyed my flushing face, then gave a curt nod. Quickly losing interest, Lila dropped her gaze and began scrolling through her phone. I had to push on before she popped her ear buds in. After that it would be game over. "I've not met many Lilas. Is it, er, a family name?" The old-lady words stumbled out. Dumb, Chad. Dumb. Had I really no skill?

She glanced up and gave me the same level gaze she dished out when I stumbled over my request for a coffee refill. "It's from a Harlequin. Number 234. Rebel in Love." Anyone with a shred of self-respect would've dropped the conversation, but I had none of that. Heat flooded my chest as I threw out the only thing that came to mind.

"Your mom's a reader?"

"Nope. There were five books in the hospital waiting room and Rebel in Love was one of them. My dad believed an English name would bring better opportunities. At least that's how the story goes."

"Wow." What else was there to say? I tried channeling Uncle Martin. He was a crack in any social situation, especially when it came to women. "It's lovely. A really…lovely…name."

"You don't blink a lot."

"Er, ya. I do that. You know. Forget to blink. When I hear something interesting."

"Creepy."

I was officially shit at this. I nodded, making sure to blink. "Right. Nice to meet you."

I had at least tried. I reached into my pocket and pulled my own phone out. Now seemed a great time to check my emails. My Facebook. My non-existent follower list on Twitter.

"The body's like that. Works in very creepy, random ways."

A lifeline? I was not about to turn down dumb luck. "Totally." My voice rose as though I were asking a question rather than making a statement.

Lila shrugged. "That's what I love about embalming."

I put my phone back in my pocket. "Pardon?"

"Embalming. It's fascinating." Lila leaned in. "I'm studying for my license. Well, my Funeral Director license too; it's kind of a two-part deal these days."

My eyelids didn't want to, but I forced them to blink. Twice. "And you work in a senior's lodge. Are these two interests… related?" Maybe she served people coffee one week and was preparing their cold, dead bodies the next?

"Heck, no. The 'Nest is a paycheck. The other's a *passion*. Do your eyes get dry a lot?"

"Sorry." I blinked with a rapidness I didn't know I had. "It's just…like you said…incredibly fascinating." I had never known anyone who worked with dead bodies. It wasn't like a job at the grocery store or the dentist's office or the insurance company where Kate worked. Everyone visited those places, was easy to find something to say about them. But embalming? My experience was limited.

Lila tucked her chin down and began tapping on her phone screen. A few wisps of her jet-black hair fell in front on her face and I surreptitiously watched as she slipped it behind her ear.

Man, I loved watching her. I tried not to stare, tried not to commit the dreaded male gaze by keeping my head tilted toward the window across from me. It was a battle keeping my eyes from wandering back to her. Every movement she made seemed graceful and elegant. I'd watched from afar for weeks yet had barely been able to maintain eye contact when she filled my coffee cup. And now here I was. Sitting nearly beside her on the number six bus.

A strange warmth filled me. Optimism? Hope? Who the hell knew, but what was certain: I was not about to waste this opportunity.

Should I suggest going for a drink? Ask if she might text me a link to some dead people podcasts so I'd have her number? As I tried to work up the courage, I found myself distracted by the way she bit her lower lip while thumb-typing into her phone.

I could practically feel her tongue tracing a line along my clavicle. Kate had once said mine looked just like Jake Gyllenhaal's and I reminded myself of that every time I got out of the shower and caught my reflection in the bathroom mirror. It was, perhaps, the kindest gift she'd given me.

Lila reached over to the chrome rail and pushed the button to indicate she wanted the bus driver to pull over at the next stop. "It was nice to meet you, Chuck."

"Er…Chad."

"Oh right. Chad. See ya' around."

I barely got out a "Goodbye, Lila" before she ambled up to the front and got off. The bus pulled away and she didn't look back. Not once. I know because I watched as she turned and walked down Seventeenth Avenue, the bus rumbling away.

***

Seventeenth Ave was home to a number of restaurants and storefront businesses, none of which I was familiar with. What I couldn't determine, even with the help of Google Earth, was where Lila might have been walking to. There were stacks of apartments intermixed with older houses within the vicinity. Any of them could be hers. Or maybe Lila had walked for several blocks before turning into one of the surrounding communities?

I accepted, before even stepping into my own apartment, that Lila was probably not going straight home. She'd been in street clothes at the bus shelter. That meant she'd changed out of the standard-issue uniform worn by the cafeteria attendants before leaving the Eldernest.

A woman like Lila could be doing anything. A woman, who could easily speak to a stranger at a bus shelter, had a social life. Had places to be. She was likely out for drinks with a friend. Or worse, I gulped, dinner with a lover.

I pulled a beer out of the fridge and took both it and my laptop to bed. Just me, some Bud and the old Mac. It wasn't the first time around for this particular threesome. Heck, it had been a regular occurrence in the weeks after Kate left.

But tonight was different. I plugged a few words into the search engine and pressed enter. I shook my head, still a bit baffled. I was damn sure nothing like this particular search had crossed my screen before. Embalming. Morticians. Funeral Service courses in a 50 km radius. I was signed up for Preparing the Human Body for its Final Rest e-newsletter before I finished my beer.

My mother's body was the only one I'd ever seen, well, not living. After watching several episodes of Morticians of Orange County it seemed only natural I'd dream of her. Mom hadn't been embalmed. She'd been cremated, as per her wishes, but in my dream her decedent (I'd learned the technical term for dead body just that night) lay in a casket ready for burial.

She was wearing her favourite chocolate brown dress, the one with the large pink roses. It was the same dress she'd worn to my university convocation so long ago.

At the ceremony she'd sat in the stands beside her brother, Martin. He'd been sporting a deep tan from his recent bachelor's vacation in Puerto Vallarta. While Martin scanned the audience for lonely women of a certain age, Mom had kept her hands clasped tightly against her chest, her face giddy with pride. I could see her beaming all the way from where I sat, in the centre of the auditorium with the other graduates.

Her son had completed his Bachelor of Arts degree. For her this seemed the ultimate proof raising me as a single parent hadn't been a mistake. I'd succeeded; hadn't been held back in any significant way.

Heck, at that time even I was a believer. I sat straight with a cocky mix of pride and assured future success. I *knew* my university education would propel me far above my current telecommunications customer service position. It was a given.

In truth, I hadn't moved far. I hadn't even moved up.

I was given a new desk down one floor in the Complaints Department. Management felt my psych degree would come in useful for handling distraught customers. I'd hung my degree on my cubicle wall pretty sure it would be a short stop-over, but there it had stayed.

I'd let Mom believe I was now managing my own team of staff. Providing leadership to the masses. She used to say, "I knew it. Knew all those years of hard work would pay off. I wanted the best for you, you know?"

In my dream Mom looked peaceful, and yet I felt deeply troubled. I couldn't remember if she liked coffee. What son doesn't know if his mother likes coffee? "Do you drink coffee, Mom? Why don't I know if you like coffee?"

Of course, she didn't answer.

***

I was a nervous ball of energy when I arrived for my next weekly visit to the Eldernest. As agreed, I met Uncle Martin at our regular table in the cafeteria.

"I see you've taken my advice." Martin winked and gave me a knowing look.

"Pardon?" I pulled my attention back to the conversation. I was trying not to make it obvious I was searching for Lila. She usually circled the tables, carrying carafes of both regular and decaf coffee, or a plastic bin for gathering dirty dishes. Today I didn't see her. The fluorescent lights glared off the surfaces of dozens of bifocals and reading glasses but they did not illuminate a head of shiny black hair.

"Your shirt. You've taken my advice." I self-consciously touched my chest. I was wearing a short-sleeved plaid dress shirt, un-ironed. Untucked. Still, it was a step-up from my usual graphic tee. "Dress the part, act the part. That's my motto." Martin leaned over the table, careful not to crease his own linen button-down. "Making some effort with the Missus, I presume?"

"Actually, about that..." I cleared my throat. "Kate and I have gone our separate ways. It's for the best, you know?" Finally. I'd managed to tell him. To tell someone.

My uncle leaned back in his chair, arms crossed as he assessed both me and my new relationship status. "Gonna be a load of legalities, getting out of that marriage. I sure wish you would've listened before going on that Jamaican Mistaken."

Gawd. Not this again. "It was just a trip. With friends. And it felt right at the time." It was hard not to cringe remembering the abrupt and unplanned elopement. The shame at how hurt mom had been to not be there. For Mom to find out over the phone that we'd gotten married. "Besides, like I've said *many times* before, it's not legal in Canada. And as far as paperwork, Kate's already organized everything. We are done." My voice trailed off. She couldn't have finished us faster if she'd tried. "Anyway, I thought you were the one who says never regret anything?"

My uncle tilted his head to the side. Then, after several moments of frowning, gave a nod of approval. "The long and short of it is you're a free agent, right?"

"Yes."

"Best way to be, I say."

A burden lifted and I smiled. "I'm a free agent." For months I'd felt a failure in my uncle's virile shadow, but why hadn't I considered it from this angle? I was an unrestricted player. Unhampered. With room for new opportunities. An opportunity like Lila.

And there she was. Lila pushed her way through the swinging double doors leading from the kitchen into the cafeteria. She carried a gray plastic bin for collecting dirty dishes; her face was both beautiful and remote.

Was she as aware of me as I was of her? I took a deep breath and exhaled, trying to hide my nervous energy from my uncle by fiddling with the handle on my coffee cup. "So tell me, how goes your social situation? Any new developments with the ladies?"

"It's funny you should ask. I've got a feeling my days with the walking group may have come to an end."

"Oh? And why is that?"

My uncle didn't have a chance to answer before a woman in chunky gold jewelry and a tight-fitting navy and white striped sweater sat down at our table. She nodded a greeting in my direction then turned on my uncle.

"Martin."

"Hello, Felicity."

"We need to talk."

"My apologies," was that a quaver in my uncle's voice? "I've my nephew visiting at present. Raincheck?"

Felicity didn't respond. Her face was as frozen and unmoving as her coiffed hair.

My uncle grimaced and pressed on. "This evening, perchance?"

Felicity's eyes narrowed like a gun ready to go off. I felt for my uncle; I really did. My guess was Felicity had found out that he'd moved his attentions to Clara, the woman he'd been wooing over the chessboard. It was a tangled web my uncle had woven, and yet I had my own pressing concerns to consider. Lila was now only a few tables away.

"Oh. Hey. Don't let me hold you back. Please, be my guest." I made a sweeping arm gesture as my uncle's jaw hung open. My lack of brotherhood was appalling, but a man had to do what a man had to do. I stood up and helped him along his way by easing his chair back from the table. "I'll wait for you in the social room, Uncle. Have a nice chat."

Martin shot me a panicked look as he was being hustled out to the garden by Felicity.

I sat back down, my heart racing as Lila neared my table. She was diligently gathering cups and saucers as she maneuvered around circular tables, wheelchairs and breathing apparatus.

I rubbed my palms on my jeans under the table. I could do this. I was a free agent. A player.

As soon as she reached my table I spoke. "Hi, there. It's Lila, right?"

We made the briefest eye contact. Was that a smile lurking at the corner of her mouth? I wondered if I looked as nervous as I felt, and firmly blinked trying to strike a balance between interested but not creepy.

"Chad, right?" *She'd recognized me! She'd remembered my name.*

"That's me. Hey, did you hear the one about the mortician who brought her child to 'take your kid to work day'?"

Lila frowned, resting the bin of dirty dishes against the table, she looked around before shrugging her shoulders.

"It was a grave mistake."

Lila continued to frown.

"Get it?" She gave me an odd look and didn't return my smile. My own faded. Had I said something wrong? "Never mind. Just a joke. I, uh, have a good day."

"You too."

She turned and walked briskly to the next table.

***

I wasn't a stalker.

I wasn't spying on Lila through un-curtained windows. And I definitely wasn't manhandling myself in the shrubbery outside her home.

I was just taking leisurely rides along her bus route. Repeatedly. Window-shopping on seventeenth. Frequently. I was being what Uncle Martin would call proactive.

Even so, I wasn't proud. A more confident man would approach the person they were interested in directly. They'd make it clear they were interested and then get busy living a confident and full life, knowing if it was meant to be it would happen. But here I was, for the fifth time in two weeks, walking up and down Seventeenth Avenue.

I had eaten in four restaurants. Drank coffee in two shops. Browsed second-hand books, read real estate posters and once received an offer for services of an adult nature. I'd blushed, stammered, walked quickly in the other direction.

It wasn't until I was walking back to the bus stop on a Friday, seriously contemplating registering for a night class in mortuary science, that I saw Lila exiting the One Spirit Dojo. She held the door open for a child in a white gi. As the child followed Lila out the door, he grabbed her free hand in his.

In a complete panic I sprinted into the nearest shop and watched them walk by on the sidewalk. I was unprepared. A kid. Why I hadn't thought about the possibility of a kid.

"Chicken on sale. Good price."

I turned to see a short, stern-looking woman dressed in a white apron. She was standing behind a refrigerated display case filled with various cuts of meat. She gazed back at me, a suspicious look on her unsmiling face.

"Oh. Sorry. I'm just looking."

"Come. Look. Meat over here; not out the window. You like sausage? Sausage on sale too."

"It's alright, I'm just—"

"No loitering! You buy."

I glanced back at the street. Lila had stopped outside the next store to tie the boy's shoe. I could go out now, but what would I say? I hadn't thought about what I would say if I actually ran into her. And if I walked out of the meat shop without buying anything, what would that indicate? That I'd been following her? That I'd been trying to create an opportunity to run into her? I did not want her to think I was some kind of weirdo.

"I'll buy some sausages."

"Bavarian or Italian?"

"Uh…Bavarian?"

"How many?"

"Two." I kept my eyes on Lila while the butcher wrapped the sausages up. When Lila finished tying the boy's shoelace, they continued walking down the street. Okay, I had to move quickly. Whether I was ready or not, this was my chance. "How much for the sausages?"

"Thirty dollars."

"For TWO sausages?" I turned away from the window to look at the butcher incredulously.

"We sell by the dozen."

"Fine. But can we be quick?" Arguing would only waste time. I plunked my cash down on top of the display case and she handed over two brown paper wrapped parcels then slowly counted my change. I was sweating bullets, could practically hear the clock ticking out the seconds. She set my change on the counter and I shifted the packages into one hand and grabbed at my money with the other. The packages felt soft, like playdough wrapped in paper. How did stuff like this happen to me?

"Can I have a bag?"

"No bags left. You carry it like this."

"Right. That's great."

I hastily left the store in time to see Lila rounding the corner up ahead. I had proof I was shopping and not stalking. That was much less creepy.

And I didn't even have to hurry in order to catch up. The kid was taking three small steps for each of my long strides.

For once my timing was perfect. They were waiting at the intersection for the lights to change when I stepped up beside them. I waited for a split-second then said, "Oh! Hey. Funny seeing you here." I was pleased with the surprised tone in my voice.

Lila turned and looked up. Her eyebrows arched in disbelief. "Chad." Her eyes trailed down to the boy, then the paper-wrapped packages in my hand. "Shopping?"

"Exactly!" I'd never been so happy for sausages. "There's a sale on. At the butchers. And you?"

"We're going to the park," said the boy. He pointed to the fenced-off treed area across the street. In the distance I could see a play structure. The kind with monkey bars for climbing and tire-swings and curvy slides.

"It's pretty warm out," I said. "Do you recommend anywhere nearby for a drink?" Lila looked down at the boy who looked up at me.

"You can buy a Slurpee at the 7-Eleven," said the kid. "Or a bubble tea over there." He pointed at a restaurant not far away.

"Right. Um. Thanks." The silence stretched. What should I do when the light changed to green? Continue following them down the street? Go into the restaurant? This wasn't going to work. I had two packages of raw meat and she was busy with a kid.

I hadn't expected a child. I looked back down at him, looking for similarities. He had dark hair; not as dark as Lila's. "And what's your name?"

"I'm Quinn."

"Quinn?"

"That's right."

The light changed and we all crossed the street; me for the 7-Eleven and Lila and the boy for the park. We arrived first at the entrance to the park. "I'll be seeing you," I said, feeling like this was failed attempt number eight hundred and one. "Would you, um, like some sausage? I've got more than I need." My face

43

coloured. But really, what was I going to do with this much?

"Thanks, but we don't eat meat."

"The body is sacred," interjected the boy.

"We just don't eat meat," Lila said. "It's the whole mortuary thing, you know?"

"Right. Exactly." I nodded vigorously, as if in complete understanding. "So, is this your son?"

Lila's face froze at about the same time the kid snapped, "I'm a girl."

I just about lost my guts right there on the street. After all my proactive activity I'd ruined my chances in one moment. "I'm sorry. I'm like a complete idiot. I don't know anything about kids. Or fashion."

Both Quinn and Lila looked at my shirt and then down at my shoes.

"Are you coming?" Quinn pointed into the park.

"What? Me?" I looked at Lila to see what she thought. A small smile played at the corner of her mouth and she shrugged. "Oh. Sure," I squeaked. "That would be nice." I couldn't believe my luck. Couldn't believe the graciousness of kids. We stopped at a bench and sat down, Quinn in the middle and Lila and me on either side.

Quinn looked up at me. "Who are you?"

"I'm Chad. I know your mom from the Eldernest."

"You know my mom?"

"Well, I mean *recognize*. We don't know, know each other." Gawd. When I got home I was going to immediately sign myself up for Toastmasters.

"Ma says the Eldernest is full of rich, snobby geriatrics."

"I didn't say that—" Lila's eyes opened wide and she gave me a nervous smile.

"You always say that," cut in Quinn.

I cleared my throat. I hadn't given much thought to the income level of the average 'Nest inhabitant, but I suppose that was probably true. Especially the Garden Wing. "Geriatrics. That's a pretty big word."

Quinn's forehead scrunched up. "I'm in grade *three*."

"Right. Of course. I can tell you're very…"

"Ma says only the Eldernest visitors have manners and that's because they want a big inheritance. Do you want a big inheritance?"

"I definitely didn't say *everyone*." Lila put her hand on Quinn's knee. I'd never seen her flustered before. For the first time I wondered how Lila felt about working at the 'Nest. What was it really like? I'd never considered before; had only seen her slim figure and confident posture.

"You said *everyone*." Quinn turned her attention back to me. "So? Are you hoping to get lots of moolah?"

I cleared my throat and thought about what to say. I could smell garlic and wondered if raw meat juices were going to start dripping from the corners of the folded paper. I couldn't imagine how this could get any worse. "I think my uncle should use his money to enjoy life right now."

Quinn, thank God, nodded. "Can I go play?"

"Yes. Five minutes," said Lila. The child catapulted herself off the bench and ran across the grass toward the playground structure. It was now just Lila, me, and several pounds of ground meat packed into sausage casing.

"Look, I'm sorry about that." Lila bit her lip.. "Sometimes, after work, I'm just frustrated."

"Of course. You shouldn't worry—you should hear what I say about *my* work." I decided to change the subject before having to admit to being on the complaints line. It was a less than impressive job. "Quinn's your daughter?"

"Yes. Named for Harlequin."

"Ah. Family tradition."

Lila smiled. "Right. Parents always want the best for their kids."

"Absolutely." We sat in silence, before I finally got my courage together. "Look, I don't know if my uncle has ever been rude to you. I seriously hope he hasn't been. It's probably not easy, all those cranky old people."

She shrugged but didn't say anything. Instead she closed her eyes and raised her face to the sun.

"And I'm really sorry about that boy thing."

"She wanted her hair cut. I wasn't sure it was a good idea, but she *really* wanted to do it." Lila's hand rose and tugged twice on the end of her own hair which hung just below her jawline. "It's just...now she desperately wishes she hadn't done it. And there's nothing I can do but tell her it'll grow."

"Yes. I understand." I cleared my throat, trying to find the right words. "When I was young, I thought it would be a good idea to get one of those perms. It was...an awful way to start junior high."

Lila snickered. So did I. Finally, after all those years, *something* good had come out of that homemade perm. Lila watched as her daughter climbed the metal slide. I found myself following suit as I tried to work out the best way to ask Lila if she were in a relationship. Would it be creepy? To come straight out and ask?

"So..." Lila said, glancing at me then back at her daughter. "Do you want to grab a drink sometime? Maybe somewhere other than 7-Eleven?"

My heart seized then started beating double-time. I remembered to blink in case she looked over. "Sure. Absolutely." More than anything I wanted to pull my phone out and ask for her number, but my hands were full of meat and it seemed wrong to place the sacred remains of a body down on the bench. Instead we sat and watched Quinn swing across the monkey bars, hand over hand over hand, a feeling of extreme joy bursting inside me.

Rosie: PET-ition Ambition

"Can I level with you, Mrs. Dylan? We're surprised a woman in your position would do something like this. It's rather subversive, don't you think?"

Rosie could feel her hands shaking and she hoped the schmuck wouldn't notice. She was angry, not scared, but he would interpret the shaking as fear, Rosie was sure of it. "A woman in *my* position?"

Director Knightly inclined his head and smiled at her as though she weren't following along. She was following alright; she knew what he meant.

One of the residents on subsidy.

Filling their quota so the Eldernest received the government grant, that was why she was here. She wondered if he'd the balls to say it.

"Housing is a very precarious market. Very precarious indeed, especially for those without a substantial depth of resources to dip into. I'd hate for this little—what do you call this?" Director Knightly taped his forefinger on the list of signatures Rosie had placed on his desk.

"A petition. PET-ition. It's more of a request though. Pet companionship. Lowers blood pressure. Reduced anxiety and dep—"

"—Yes, how creative. A PET-ition. I'd hate for this petition to be misunderstood. To cause anyone to question your *suitability* for our facility." He paused to pick up the papers, then pushed them across the desk toward Rosie. They caught on his shiny brass name plate—*Thomas Knightly, Director*—and he let go of the offending

47

documents in order to straighten it. "Have you considered fish? We've got the tank in the lobby. Perhaps some neon tetras? Or what about those little fish who look like Nemo! The grandchildren would love that, wouldn't they? And it would sure brighten the space." His smile was the kind you gave nervous kindergartners when you dropped them off at school on the first day.

"But we've already got brightly coloured stuff swimming out of Felicity's closet—"

"Rose."

It's *Rosie*. She could correct him, but where would that get her? "I'm not sure we need to brighten the place. What we need is something warm and affectionate for residents to hold." Something that wouldn't leave a person feeling so damn alone.

Fish could not help with that. They swam about in their cold water, cold blood flowing through their cold veins. Rosie couldn't name a less emotive animal. "It's *touch* everyone at the Eldernest is starving for. You can't pet a fish."

"We've got the psychologist on Tuesdays if people are feeling lonely, Mrs. Dylan. I highly encourage anyone feeling lonely"— he paused and raised his eyebrows suggestively at Rosie— "to make an appointment with the psychologist. Besides, no one else is asking for a companion pet. They may have signed on your list, but that's only because of your incessant prompting."

"It could be the ones who most need a pet companion can't speak. Take Linus—"

"Let's not name names, Mrs. Dylan. It would be highly inappropriate for me to speak with you about the health needs of other residents, wouldn't it?"

Rosie's cheeks flamed. She picked up her PET-ition and rolled it into a tight bat. She imagined whacking Director Knightly about the ears with it. Or, better yet, she could get one of those sledgehammers from her nephew's costume shop and smack it down on Knightly's lollipop head. That probably wouldn't help the situation though. Instead Rosie took a deep breath and changed tactics.

"My PET-ition, Mr. Knightly, is not a subversive act. It's my democratic right to organize. But I can see you find yourself in a conflict of interest. Perhaps we need to involve other people in this conversation. Not to worry. I'll take this up with the board, thank you very much." Rosie stood up in one swift movement that belied her years and marched out of the office. She didn't have time for this anyway. She had a job to get to.

Rosie might be one of the only Eldernest inhabitants with a job, but she loved it. Two shifts a week at her nephew's costume shop, and sometimes more if anyone called in sick. She got the worst shifts, the shifts no one else wanted, but Rosie was happy for them. She loved interacting with the customers and getting out of the stifling and rule-bound Eldernest facility.

Back in her assigned room, Rosie placed the PET-ition on her nightstand then dragged her standard-issue chair over to her closed door and anchored the backrest under the knob. That should do it; there was no sense being surprised by housekeeping. Opening her window, Rosie undid the clips holding the screen in place and set the screen against her bed.

On the sill sat a plastic dish. It was empty; not one crumb left over. Terry must have been hungry.

It had taken weeks for the shaggy ginger to trust Rosie enough to cross the windowsill into her room. But just like any man, food had worked to draw Terry in. He wasn't feral, Rosie suspected, or at least he hadn't always been. He just seemed nervous. Distrustful, yet hopeful.

He reminded Rosie of her old friend, Mr. Terrance. So similar, the way he looked up at her with his wide eyes, and how he stretched out straight as a nail on her rug when he slept, that she'd given him the name Terry.

He still didn't allow Rosie to pick him up, but that would come, especially if Terry were able to roam the halls and get used to being around people. Rosie re-filled his food dish from the container she kept in her underwear drawer, then placed it back on the windowsill.

She decided not to replace the screen, at least not yet. Maybe Terry would pay her a visit before she had to leave for work. Instead, she sat on the edge of her bed and rehashed the afternoon. Her meeting with the Director had not gone well. It was almost as though he had been given a heads-up about her project. But who would have done that?

Rosie's stomach tightened. Felicity. She was the only one who'd been excessively hostile toward the idea of a companion animal at the Eldernest. When Rosie had shown her the PET-ition, and had suggested a cat as a hypothetical example, Felicity had tapped her brightly painted fuchsia nails annoyingly on the list of signatures and spoken to Rosie as though she were a child.

"They need veterinary care, *Rosie*. I think you've underestimated the cost, and my monthly fee is high enough without factoring in some mongrel cat. So no, I won't sign."

Clara had reached across the scratched social room table and pulled the petition toward herself. "I believe mongrel is the term for a mixed-breed dog, Felicity, not a cat." She signed her name in clean, even strokes and Rosie's heart soared.

Still, Felicity would not let it go. "A cat will track in germs. Disease. Maybe even dead mice! I've heard of cats doing that. Leaving carcasses on doorways as little presents. No way. I'll not support it."

"They're very clean animals," Rosie called after her, but it was no use. Felicity had left, probably to spread her anti-cat rhetoric in the hearing aids of other Eldernest residents and maybe even to Director Knightly himself.

Rosie massaged her stiff knuckles, still looking out her bedroom window incase Terry appeared. She had assumed the hard work was over—gaining Terry's trust, convincing the other residents to sign the PET-ition—but she had underestimated that darn stick-in-the-mud gatekeeper, Director Knightly.

She wouldn't give up that easily though. She would just have to by-pass him and present her PET-ition directly to the board of directors. Until then this was her room, wasn't it? Rosie stood up and gently replaced the screen on her window. She put her good walking shoes on, grabbed her canvas purse and closed the door behind her. She'd do what she wanted in her own room.

Quinn: Root Beer

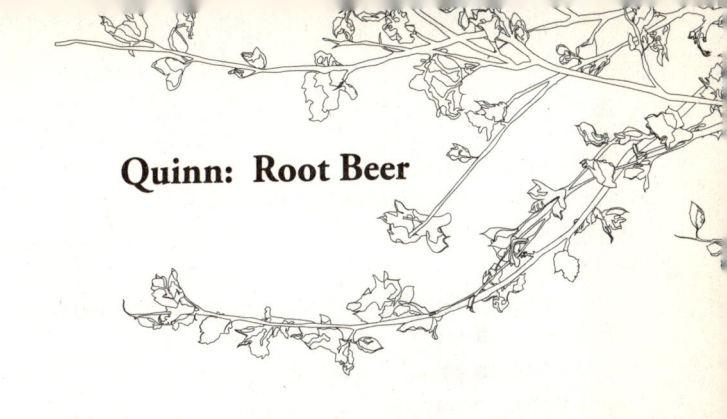

The best part of Quinn's school day happened after the dismissal bell rang. Her coat was zipped, her backpack between her shoulder blades, and she was ready to shuffle over to the after-school program next door to the school. But there was Ma, leaning against the school's rough brick wall.

"Surprise, kiddo!"

Quinn wrapped her arms around her mother, a smile across her face. In a matter of moments it had officially become a good day. Walking home with Ma meant not having to fill two hours of time playing games she didn't want to play. It might even include a quick stop at the park or at the bubble tea shop if Ma was in the mood. Best of all, it meant not having to try and fit-in.

"How was school?"

"Fine."

"Just fine? It's Friday. The best day of the week."

They'd started to walk away from the school, where no one would overhear them, so Quinn answered truthfully. "Fine except gym."

Ma stopped walking and took Quinn's backpack from off her shoulders, loosened the shoulder straps, and put it on her own back. She withdrew a little plastic bag of dried mango strips from her coat pocket and handed them to Quinn as they left the school yard.

Quinn loved the sugary and chewy strips, her mouth watered as she opened the bag and popped one of the bright orange pieces into her mouth.

"Floor hockey again?"

Chewing the fruit, Quinn took her time answering. "Mrs. Chou made us pair up, but there's twenty-one kids in the class."

"And?"

"That's an uneven number. Why didn't she just make it groups of three? Three goes into twenty-one perfectly and no one would be left out."

"So true." Ma folded Quinn's hand in her own and squeezed. "Who was left out?"

Quinn shrugged. "Maybe me."

"I think it was a test," Ma said.

"You *always* say that."

"I say it because it's true. Life is made up of little tests so we can practice being strong. That's great preparation for real life, Quinn, a test like that."

Quinn could easily point out a test wouldn't be needed if she hadn't changed schools. She hated having to start over, hated having to find new friends. But saying that would just make her mom feel guilty. Ma had switched Quinn to the new school because this one had the after-school program nearby. Without it, her mother couldn't juggle school and work and picking Quinn up on time.

So instead, Quinn bit her lip and changed the subject. "Who do you want to be tonight? Mrs. White or Colonel Mustard?" There was no point saying she would be Ms. Scarlett. Quinn was always Ms. Scarlett when it came to Clue. It was their favourite game, and Ms. Scarlett was her lucky character. They played every Friday night and Quinn could sometimes beat Ma fair and square.

"Actually kiddo, that's something I wanted to chat with you about. Do you remember that guy we met? That time after karate?"

How could Quinn forget? They didn't 'meet guys' ever, unless you counted Wai Gong. "Of course I remember. He was carrying all that meat. In the brown paper."

"That's right. Chad. I think I might go and meet him tonight. Wai Gong will stay with you, okay?"

Quinn narrowed her eyes. "Friday's our night."

"Right. That's right. It's just I was thinking maybe this once I would meet this Chad, and then we could play Clue and throw a pizza in the oven when I get home from work on Saturday. What do you think?"

Quinn knew why Ma worked at the old people home on

weekends. If Ma didn't, there would be no way to pay for things. Still, it meant she only got to see her mother in the evenings. It didn't seem fair. Especially if Ma skipped out on their Friday night. That meant Quinn would have to wait all day Saturday before her mother got home before they could have their special time together.

"Friday's *our* night."

"Yes, I know. I promise, it won't happen again. I'm just kind of interested to see what this guy, this Chad, is like."

Quinn remembered the time they'd run into Chad. He had a red face and he seemed a bit twitchy, although he had a nice way of smiling. There didn't seem anything altogether wrong with him, but there didn't seem anything very interesting either. "Why do you want to know what he's like?"

Ma ran a hand through her hair and laughed softly. "Good question. I suppose I'm curious."

Was being curious the same as liking? Quinn didn't want to ask. She peered into stores and read sale signs in the store windows. 50% off. Buy One Get One Free. Why Pay Now?

What would it mean if her mother liked this guy, this guy named Chad? Would things change? Would Friday night Clue be over, just like that? She stopped walking and looked up at her mother. "What are you curious about?"

Ma smiled. "Oh, I'm not sure, really. Maybe it's because he visits the old people a lot."

That didn't make sense. Quinn visited her grandparents all the time. What was special about that? "He visits old people?"

"Sure. And I like how he kind of walks slowly beside the old people without making it look like he is walking slowly, you know? He's got those long legs. He could walk a lot faster, but he doesn't."

How old were these people? Wai Gong was the oldest person Quinn knew and he could walk just as fast as her. They started walking again, but this time Quinn kept her hands scrunched in her pockets. The mango strips were gone; the plastic bag was a tight ball inside her fist.

Her mother continued. "I like how he knows everyone's name, too."

"Chad knows everyone's name?"

"Ya. People say hi and he says 'Hello, Grant.' Stuff like that. He even smiles at the weirder ones. You know, the older people who are starting to go."

Quinn scrunched her nose. Knowing people's names, hanging out with old people...that would make the worst Disney movie. On tv people liked someone because they were smart, funny, attractive or rich. Take a classic, like Cinderella. She liked the Prince, because he was *The Prince*. Rich, famous. No mention of old people or knowing people's names.

"Have you noticed this Chad is missing some hair? About here?" Quinn touched both sides of her head, her fingertips pressing a few inches back from her forehead. It was where Quinn imagined antlers growing on a moose.

Her mother looked at Quinn's hands and bit her lip. "Would you like to stop at the park? We've got a few minutes."

Ma didn't need to ask twice.

***

The little white house with the blue shutters and the rusty red mailbox had two doors. One was smack in the middle of the front of the house. It led to Wai Po and Wai Gong's home. The second door was on the side of the house, behind the wooden gate with the blue paint that Quinn liked to peel off in thin strips when Ma wasn't watching. It was the second door that led down the stairs to Ma and Quinn's home.

Quinn liked having her grandparents upstairs because that meant she got to see them every day and listen to Wai Gong's stories about growing up in China, or she could help herself to the foil-wrapped candies her Wai Po kept in a glass bowl on the counter. They ate dinner together almost every night, which Wai Po made. Ma and Quinn only used their downstairs kitchen for cereal and popcorn.

Sometimes Ma got calls in the night for her apprenticeship— Ma said apprenticeships were about practicing for your future career—and she had to go no matter what time it was. Bodies needed to be 'transferred into our care'—that's what her mother called it—both day and night. When that happened her Wai Gong would come down the stairs and sleep on their couch, his big snores filling their basement apartment, and Quinn was never worried about being alone.

Tonight, her grandfather was only resting on the couch. She didn't think he'd meant to fall asleep, and maybe it was because they had already watched The Jungle Book many times before and you could miss parts and still know what was going on. Even though Quinn was getting a little old for the move, she still liked to watch it. She liked how Mowglie's friends watched out for him. It reminded her the world could be a friendly place.

But tonight the movie wasn't working. Maybe it was because she was thinking about standing alone in the school gym when no one wanted to be her partner. Or maybe it was because she'd been looking forward to hanging out with Ma and playing Clue. If they were playing Clue Quinn's mind would be too busy thinking and she wouldn't have room in her head to remember gym class.

She didn't feel well. She never felt well when she worried. Her stomach was flipping and dipping and would only get worse. Shouldn't her mother be home if she were sick? But she didn't know Quinn was sick.

Quinn eyed Wai Gong where he rested on the couch. If Quinn were ill, she should tell him and not worry Ma unless it was serious. Still, wouldn't Ma want to know if Quinn were feeling sick? Even if it was only kind of sick? Of course she would. That was the kind of thing all moms wanted to know.

Quinn tiptoed out of the TV room, picking up the cordless telephone on her way to the bathroom and shut the door behind her. She didn't want to wake her grandfather when he was resting so peacefully.

Her mother answered on the third ring. Quinn could hear music in the background. "Hello? Ba ba?" her mother yelled over the noise.

"I think I'm sick."

"You're sick?"

"I'm pretty sure."

"What's wrong?"

"My stomach. It's awful. I think it could be…may…my appendix."

Ma didn't say anything. Quinn wondered if she was thinking

about that kid in Quinn's class last year. The one who had his appendix removed. Jack's parents had taken him to the hospital and the doctors had taken it out. But what if they hadn't? Jack said he could've died!

Her mother was probably thinking about death. Maybe she was even panicking a bit on the inside. Maybe a whole bunch of stuff was flashing through Ma's mind like what it would be like to receive her own daughter's body into her care. And maybe she would always feel guilty she hadn't been at home when it happened. When Quinn's appendix burst. Quinn let the worry sink in. Life was short. It could be over—

"Where does it hurt?"

"All over my belly."

"Have you tried using the toilet?"

What? "I don't have to go to the bathroom! I think you should come home. You need to check on me. There was that boy in my class last year, remember? Jack. His appendix burst and they said it could've killed him."

Quinn waited for her mother to say she was coming home, but her mother didn't say anything. Instead she heard music and the jumbled sounds of people laughing and talking.

"Can you come home? I really want you to come home."

Ma huffed air into the phone. "Okay."

"I think you should pick up some ginger ale on your way home too," Quinn suggested. "To help my stomach."

***

The side door shuddered as it was pulled open. Ma thumped down the stairs and into the basement apartment with a loudness that woke Wai Gong right in the middle of one of his soft snores. He looked around, surprise on his face. Quinn stayed seated in the comfy chair, her blanket wrapped around her, but she could see Ma in the kitchen. She pulled a bottle of root beer out of a plastic shopping bag and put it on the table.

Root beer? Ginger ale was what white moms brought their kids when they were sick. They don't feed them tripe like Wai Po wanted Quinn to eat whenever she had a sore stomach. Wai Po believed a person should eat some of whatever hurt when a person was sick but that didn't make any sense to Quinn. Anyway, her grandmother should know Quinn wouldn't eat body parts. Body parts were meat!

The white moms Quinn saw on TV didn't give their sick children root beer or tripe. No way. Ma mostly got things like this right. She was born here, not in China like Wai Po.

Quinn's grandfather rubbed his eyes, then stood up and walked over to Quinn and gave her a kiss on the forehead. He said goodnight to her mother and then quietly left their basement apartment.

"Scoot over, kid." Quinn moved over so Ma could squeeze into the comfy chair beside her. Their hips pressed together in a comfortable way. They watched the rest of The Jungle Book together, cheering when Shere Khan got the beat down.

When the credits came on Quinn glanced at Ma, took a deep breath and asked what she really wanted to know. "How was this Chad?"

"Chad? I was only there ten minutes. I'm still finding out."

Ten minutes. It felt much longer than that. "Sorry."

Ma smiled and ruffled Quinn's hair, pushing the flyaway pieces back behind her ear. "It's okay. You always come first. And maybe it's good, like a test, you know?"

"A pop quiz for Chad?"

"Something like that."

It made Quinn wonder what kind of boy Chad had been in gym class. Had he been the kind who always had friends or the kind who sometimes got left out? "Did he pass?"

Ma tilted her head to the side, and Quinn waited patiently to see what she would say. She could tell her mother was thinking hard because even though it seemed like she was looking right at Quinn, Ma was looking somewhere far away. There was no use rushing Ma when she was looking far away. If Quinn did, Ma lost her idea and changed the subject. The only thing to do was wait.

At last Ma nodded. "Ya, he passed. Shall we have some root beer?"

Quinn smiled, feeling much better already. They even had time for Clue.

Chad: Chaos

Today was the day. I was officially going on a date with Lila Leung. On the outside I was identical to every other 'bot on the complaint line, but on the inside I was the male version of Elizabeth Shue from the opening scene of that 90s flick, Adventures in Babysitting. If I'd been at home, and not at work, I'd be lip-syncing to radio love songs one after the other. As it was, my irritable colleague, Janice, was mere feet away and I made do with counting down the minutes until I would meet up with Lila. I was on top of the freakin' world.

I hung up with my latest caller to see Imran sauntering down the aisle toward my cubicle. He still wore his headset, but the mouthpiece was pushed up by his ear. "Chad, my man. Any chance you're free tonight?"

"No chance at all, I'm afraid." I leaned back in my swivel chair, raised my arms and crossed my fingers behind my head. "I've got plans."

"Real plans? I know you like that gaming place, but we could really use another guy down on the court."

I pushed my own headset away from my mouth. "I've got a date." I was half nervous, half excited and completely stoked he'd asked so I had an excuse to talk about Lila. "She's dope. Really laid back. Super hot."

Imran's eye's widened. "Yaas! Where'd you meet?"

"She works at this senior's place where my uncle lives. We've chatted a few times." A rolling drum started churning in my stomach. "Two times, I guess."

"Cool." Imran leaned up against the half wall of my cubicle. "Where are you going to meet up?"

"Oh, you know. A pub near her place."

Imran sucked air in through pursed lips. "Duuude. You should suggest somewhere special. You do like her, amright?"

I rubbed the back of my neck. "Definitely. It's just...the pub was her suggestion." Was I doing this wrong? Had I failed some secret test before we'd even begun?

"She's checking you out, man. Seeing what you're like. That's why she picked somewhere public; a place she's familiar with. That way she can escape if she doesn't want to stay."

My mental self was no longer lip-syncing sweet love ballads. Instead it was slipping on the wood floor, arms flailing in wild arcs as I fought to maintain my balance. This wasn't a date. It was *just* drinks. Lila had intentionally picked something where she could keep it short. Maybe she wouldn't want to stay after the first drink? *Of course she wasn't going to want to stay.*

I'd always liked Imran, but at that moment a bitter taste burned my throat just looking at him. He hung on my cubicle partition, hands resting under his chin and elbows folded on top of the half wall. His life was a cake walk. He was a man who knew what to do on dates. Who knew if things didn't work out with one woman, there was always another as equally interesting waiting in the wing.

I almost asked for advice. A younger me would've. But thirty-year-old me—wasn't I supposed to know how to do this on my own by now?

I tried to rally. It was still drinks. With a woman I'd already sustained conversation with. Twice. I didn't need advice. Well, maybe I did, but I wasn't going to swallow what pride I had when it was easier to deflect. "What was it you needed help with tonight anyway?"

"Oh right. It's this volunteer thing with a bunch of kids. A basketball program at the community centre by my place. We could use another adult to help out. Maybe next week? Think about it, Chad; you'd slay it."

"I don't know 'bout that."

"Sure you would. You're..." Imran paused and gave me the

once over. "You've played basketball before, right?"

"I'm king on NBA Live. Xbox."

Imran nodded. "Right. What we really need is another warm body for ratios, so you'd be great. Anyway, think about it. It's once a week and the best part," he paused and leaned in. "it gives you something to impress the ladies with. Women love guys who volunteer with underprivileged youth, you know what I'm saying?"

I heard the wheeze of Janice's chair as she swiveled toward us. "I didn't realize it was break time."

Imran pulled himself off the partition wall. "Next time, my friend. And good luck!"

"Thanks," I said. Imran left and I yanked open my desk drawer, pulled out a bottle of antacids and popped two tablets into my mouth.

I was not the male version of Elizabeth Shue. I was the big brother of that little kid she was hired to babysit. The brother with the acne problem and confidence issues and a crush on the woman totally out of his league.

***

The pub Lila suggested was called Chaos. Despite the name she assured me it wasn't a nightclub, but more a neighbourhood pub with wing specials, (not that she ate those) cheap draft and a small selection of half decent craft beer. I knew it was close to her home because she'd told me it was; as to her actual address I was still in the dark. If Imran were right (and let's face it, *of course Imran was right*) this was a convenient location for her to escape from.

I caught the number six with only one thought on my mind: *don't screw up, MacEwan. Don't screw this up.* As the bus inched forward along its route, it stopped and started, picking up passengers and letting others off along the way. I stared out the window, not really seeing anything. I was planning what to say if the conversation between Lila and I lulled into awkward silence when I heard someone clear their throat above me. I looked up. An elderly woman was grinning down at me through sturdy, round glasses.

"Sorry." I blushed and immediately moved over to make room for her on the seat. I hadn't even realized I was sprawling across two seats causing old people to stand in the aisle. I glanced back at the woman when she didn't immediately sit down. Instead she stood there nodding and smiling as though she'd just received confirmation of something. "Do I know—"

"Yes! I believe you do know me." The smile stretched across her happy face causing her eyes to nearly close behind her generous cheeks before she finally lowered herself onto the seat beside me and arranging her cloth shopping bag and canvas purse on her lap. "I'm Rosie, from the Eldernest Senior's Lodge. I believe you visit Martin quite often?"

"That's right," I said and nodded. "I'm Chad. Martin's nephew."

"How lovely." Rosie offered her hand and I shook her frail hand gently. It felt like a small bird, hollow bones held together by a thin layer of skin. "I was sure I recognized you. I've seen you plenty of times in the cafeteria pining over that young waitress."

I choked on my own air intake. "Pardon me?"

"You should smile more." She elbowed me in the ribs. "It works wonders, although no doubt it's a challenge. Martin is, well, he is what he is, isn't that so? A bit of a handful, but well meaning. Anyway, a smile might help you look a bit more approachable when it comes to the young waitress you keep your eye on." She lowered her voice. "You've excellent taste. She's a diamond, she is. Just lovely."

I managed an odd sound that was more mumble than words and moved my head in a jerky motion. I wasn't quite sure I understood what the hell I was trying to convey, but Rosie seemed to take it as thanks for her advice. "My pleasure, Chad. No trouble at all sharing a bit of advice. You seem a nice sort yourself." I had to physically turn my head and stare straight ahead. My confidence may have been shaken after my chat with Imran, but it had now been annihilated by a little old woman in a lilac coat.

If this woman, (this woman who seemed not entirely 'with-it') said I was pining over Lila, then what on earth did Lila (a very astute, very with-it kind of person) think?

I glanced back at Rosie. She was *still* smiling up at me.

"And where are you off to this evening, young man?"

Nope. Not doing it. I cleared my throat. "Meeting a friend."

"Friends! How lovely."

"And how about you?"

"I'm working the evening shift at my nephew's costume shop. I do just a few hours here and there. Keeps me young." She patted my arm. "It's just such a treat to have someone to travel with."

The quiet bus ride I'd imagined, the one with me trying to pretend I was neither nervous nor overly excited, became an educational session. It started with the best costumes for comic con, which lead neatly into popular costumes for pets, before finally settling on the power of animals.

"Did you know animals can also help memory recall? I saw a memo on it."

"A memo?"

"Yes. On Facebook."

"Maybe a meme?"

"A meme? Never heard of it."

"It's a, well...never mind. Basically, a short memo but colourful."

For the whole ride I was struck by how Martin's existence seemed to be completely invading mine. Was that even possible? Were the cosmos or some higher power conspiring to have a good laugh at my expense?

And so it came as no surprise that just before my intended stop Rosie broke off from her animal facts and said, "Press the button, won't you dear?" She pointed at the button that would indicate to the bus driver a passenger wanted to get off at the next stop. I did as I was bidden.

With me sitting by the window and Rosie by the aisle, I had to wait until Rosie got moving before I could stand up. She waited patiently until the bus came to a complete stop. In what seemed like slow motion Rosie stood up, adjusted her glasses, leaned down for her purse and shopping bag, attempted to offer *me* a hand in getting up, before finally walking toward the front of the bus. I could see the driver watching in his rear-view mirror as we made our slow progress forward. There was no rushing Rosie. She set a steady pace and I sheepishly followed her down the aisle, trying my best not to look at the smiles on middle aged faces and the bored looks on the younger ones.

At last we reached the front of the bus. "Have a nice evening, you two," said the driver.

Rosie beamed, clutching her bag and purse in front of her.

I cleared my throat. "Would you like help with the stairs, Rosie?"

"Help with the stairs? My land! I don't need help. You sound like you're taking lessons from your uncle's playbook."

She ambled down the stairs slow but sure, me on her tail trying not to blush. Martin's playbook. Is that all it took? Offering help that was not needed? As soon as my feet touched solid ground the doors snapped shut and the bus took off.

I pulled out my phone to check the GPS location of Chaos. "It looks like the place I'm going is just a few blocks south of here, so see you—"

"Me too!"

"Are you sure? I'm going to a place called Chaos. Probably a little loud—"

"That's right by the costume shop!"

"You're not serious."

"Darn tootin' I'm serious. This is great! We can walk together."

Right. Rosie's face glowed with happiness. How did a person get out of something like this? I looked back at my phone and checked the time. There was twenty minutes before I was to meet Lila. I should be able to drop Rosie off and be at the pub before Lila arrived. Maybe this was a good idea. What was I going to do if I arrived early but sit alone sweating bullets and stressing myself out?

As we walked Rosie talked, and I listened. "We lived right down there." She pointed to a side street then proceeded to tell me the history behind each store we passed. "Jack Parson's owned the bakery when it first opened. He thought his son would run it, but no, his son had bigger plans. Car dealership. The bakery was sold off. Broke Jack's heart when it turned into one of those adult sexuality shops."

Many of the stores had seen better days. Crumbling foundations. Dirty glass and more than enough payday loan vendors for an entire city, never mind a small suburb. The neighbourhood was a bit rougher than I was used to. I kicked an empty chip bag off the sidewalk and wondered if Lila would move once she'd completed her schooling.

"And this shop right here—I used to love getting my hair done at Betty's Beauty Parlor. I'm not sure when it turned its focus to massages." Rosie had stopped and was looking at some of the signage. I tried to hurry her along by not stopping myself. It seemed to work as she turned her attention away from the establishment.

"How long would you say you lived around here, Rosie?"

"My land. Years and years. It was a nice little community; everyone knew everyone else back then. Raised our family here. Me and the husband and our daughter, Kathy. Always a four-legged friend or two around. What's a home without a furry friend, right?"

I nodded although I'd never had pets growing up and I'd not been interested in getting one in the years I'd been on my own either.

"Here we are." Rosie stopped in front of a strip mall that didn't look much different from the others we'd passed. I could see a black sign with crisp white capital letters spelling CHAOS a few doors down. The pub's windows were mirrored, and I couldn't see into the establishment. A quick look at my phone told me I had five minutes to spare.

The store nearest us sold secondhand furniture and in between it and Chaos was a store with a large window display showcasing a line of mannequins dressed in various fantasy garb and superhero costumes. I pointed to it. "That must be your nephew's shop. I've some friends who'd like this place."

"Hold this, would you?" Rosie handed me her canvas shopping bag so she could focus on undoing the metal clasp on her purse, then started digging through it. She drew out a card and handed it to me. "20% off for friends and family!"

I thanked her for the discount card and tried to hand back the shopping bag, but Rosie seemed to be distracted. She was eyeballing someone crossing the street in front of us. I glanced up, my heart stopped, then went into overdrive.

Lila was an absolute goddess. Gone were the 'Nest scrubs and fun socks with mermaids and frogs. In their place was a pair of paper white converse and slim jeans that ended above the ankle.

She wore an oversized sweater and a stack of silver bracelets that reflected light as she walked. I could tell the moment she recognized us because for once a look of surprise crossed her face.

I smiled weakly and waved, still trying to hand Rosie her shopping bag. "Here you go, Rosie. Good night," I stammered.

At last Rosie took the bag, her eyes once again barely visible in the folds of her happy cheeks. She elbowed me in the ribs. "Remember to smile," she whispered and rushed into the costume shop.

Chaos was dark. The corners of the pub were shadowed in darkness, the only light came from the candles resting on tables and the illuminated beer signs from behind the bar. We chose a table near the mirrored front windows because it was furthest away from the speakers. A Duran Duran classic was belting out the sound system. Why had she chosen this place?

As soon as we sat a woman came by to take our order. She shouted out the specials and I ordered a pint of the first draft she listed. Lila requested a gin and tonic. In record time she was back with our order and then, officially, we were alone. No kid. No senior. No one to run interference but 80s bands on the sound system.

"So," said Lila. "I didn't realize you hung out with seniors outside the 'Nest too."

I laughed weakly. "That was a total fluke. Total." My throat was dry. I took a sip of my beer. It hit the back of my throat with a bitter flatness and I swallowed hard, reminding myself to blink. "Did you know Rosie worked at that costume shop? I didn't realize anyone from the 'Nest still worked."

"Not everyone is rich."

"Right. Of course. I just. I know that." My mind raced for something to say and I blurted the first thing that came to mind. "I volunteer with underprivileged youth. I do that. Starting to do that right away here. Basketball program? Very important. Skills and such. Teamwork."

"Wow. You're busy."

Lonely nights at home flashed through my brain. "Not as busy as you, I'm sure. You've got school. Quinn. Work. I'm just, sort of..." My voice trailed off and I finished the sentence in my head.

Filling time.

Lila gave me a curious look I couldn't interpret. Why had I never mastered small talk? And why was I suddenly sweating like a marathon runner? Damnit, I was lost and we'd just got here. What would Imran say on a date? Or Martin? I took a hesitant sip of my flat beer.

"I was wondering what you did for work?" Lila asked. "You didn't say when we were at the park."

Okay. She wants to know something about me. That has to be a good sign. "I work for a telecommunications company."

"Cool. Doing…?"

"Er. The complaints department. So…ya. Not a lot of happy campers."

"Complaints? Wow. I'd take silent bodies any day over that. You don't find it tiring?"

"I do. I mean, it can be exhausting listening to unhappy people all day. But you know management. They aren't interested in moving me to another department; say I've a calming presence. And it's a job. Pays the bills. I guess I've not been motivated to find something more, well, upbeat."

"Upbeat?"

"Ya, which would be just about anything else." I smiled. "Except maybe, well… deceased bodies." Lila chuckled. Okay, not a full out laugh, but still. My spirits soared. "What do you do for fun?"

"We like board games. That's kind of mine and Quinn's thing."

Gaming? Could this get more perfect? I was just about to launch into a question about their favourites when the cell phone she'd placed on the table rang. I couldn't hear it over the music but felt the vibrations through my elbow which was resting on the table. "Sorry," she said, "I think it's my father." With one hand she held the phone to her right ear and with the other covered her left ear in an attempt to block noise from the bar.

"Hello? Ba ba?" I took a sip of my beer and looked out the darkened window, pretending I wasn't listening to her conversation. "You're sick? What's wrong?" Lila hadn't mentioned her father before. Maybe she did a lot of juggling elderly people in her spare time too? Or maybe it was a friend on the line and this was a pre-planned escape. I couldn't help but be insecure. I checked the time on my own phone as nonchalantly as possible. We'd only just gotten here. "Where does it hurt?" Lila was saying. She paused and looked up at me before asking into the phone "Have you tried using the toilet?"

What? No way. I couldn't see anyone asking their dad a question like that. My heart folded in on itself, but I tried to look like I didn't care.

Lila hung up the phone and bit her lip. "I've got to go. It seems--"

I pasted a plastic smile on my face and cut her off. I would make this easier on her and save us both some embarrassment. "Oh. No worries. Do what you've got to do. See you around--"

She pulled out her wallet. "I'll get this."

"No worries, it's on me." I was nauseous with failure. I'd spent more time with Rosie than Lila. "I'll go pay at the bar." As I stood up my knee banged on the edge of the table-top and sent my half-finished beer sloshing around in its pint glass.

"Are you sure? Thanks." For once Lila seemed a bit uncertain what to do. She put her wallet and phone back in her coat pocket and carefully stood up, managing not to spill her own half-finished gin and tonic. "You know, I—"

"It's fine. Honestly. It sounds like you need to be somewhere else." We stood across the table from each other, immobilized and unsure what to say.

Who had ever heard of someone leaving a date this early? I could feel myself floating in a sea of embarrassment. I really had to get out of there. "Okay. So long." I backed out from the table.

"I'll text you." Her words came in a rush over the music. She was too polite not to feel guilty. "Maybe we can reschedule?"

"Sure. But no pressure. I know you're busy. With your studies. And Quinn. No worries if you are just, well. And your dad. Not to worry." I waved and rushed to the end of the bar ready to settle our tab and get out of there.

***

The night was young. Incredibly, depressingly young. Without thinking much about it I stopped at the costume shop on my walk back to the bus stop. It was the kind of place I was comfortable in.

It catered to my kind of people: geeks and nerds and there would be absolutely no one I would need to impress.

I pushed open the glass door and a jingle of bells announced my presence. At my feet, a Trekkie rug. Live Long and Prosper. Nice.

"Hello?" Rosie's voice called out from behind a tall stack of boxes to my left.

"Hey, Rosie. It's me, Chad. From the bus? Martin's nephew?"

Rosie's head popped up from behind the boxes. "Oh my! Come in, dear. Come in." She scurried around the unpacked merchandise and was standing in front of me before I knew it. "Is that coupon burning a hole in your pocket already?"

I smiled. If only that were it. I'd put it all on the line and the line had been cut. Fast and sharp. My stomach clenched, and I put it out of my mind as best I could. "I was thinking you might help me find some ideas for the next comic con. What do you say, Rosie?"

"Oh, my land! I've just the thing. What do you say to a *couples* costume?" She wrinkled her forehead in a way that made her eyebrows float up and down in a suggestive manner.

My face must have said it all. Rosie's mouth opened into a round little 'O,' and I tried hard to redeem the situation. "I was thinking more of a solo situation."

"Solo. Right. I've just the thing." She led me to the Star Wars section. "You'll be perfect as Hans. So handsome!" *Me?* I wasn't so sure. Martin was the perfect Harrison Ford. Still, my trampled pride would take what it could get. I let Rosie wrap her small hand around my elbow and show me the options.

As I walked back to the bus stop carrying a shopping bag full of Rosie's selections, I heard my phone beep. It was probably Martin. Reminding me of his latest shopping needs. I didn't bother checking until I was back on the bus heading home.

But it wasn't Martin with a laundry list of men's products. It was a text from Lila.

Do you want to catch a movie next week?

My heart stopped. I had that feeling you get on an amusement park rollercoaster. With trembling fingers, I sent her a text back.

Absolutely.

Martin: Power of the Herd

Martin had done the gentlemanly thing and removed his hat. Cleared his throat. Twice. It did no good. The place was jam-packed with people, headsets wrapped around their ears, and not even one bothered to look up.

Martin knew a thing or two about working for 'the man,' but this wasn't something he'd seen outside of a National Geographic special. There was no sign of individuality at all; like a damn herd of bison.

No matter. He knew what to do. Break into the pack by singling one out. Appeal to him or her on an individual level.

Leaning over the nearest half-wall, Martin waited until—bingo!—he achieved eye contact with a bewildered young buck. The buck gave Martin a faint smile then looked over at the woman in the next human parking stall for support. No luck. It was clear from her turned back and hunched shoulders she'd not be leaving the safety of the pack on his account.

Martin didn't rush his target. Instead he plastered a smile on his face and waited as the young buck—ever so slowly—drew away from the hive-mind and removed his headset.

Martin pointed at the man's shirt and nodded his approval. "That's a fine paisley you've got on."

"Uh..." The younger man looked down at his dress shirt then back up at Martin. "Thanks? Is there something I could help you with?"

"Certainly. Could you tell me which department I've landed in?"

"Well sir, we are what's called the Complaints Department. Do you have a complaint with your phone bill? We usually handle it, you know, over the phone, but I could…um."

"Complaints, you say? Perfect." Martin rubbed his hands together then edged over to the low filing cabinet in the young man's workspace. "Mind if I sit?" Martin didn't wait for an answer and gingerly lowered himself onto the two-drawer cabinet, shifted his weight and stretched his sore leg out. "I think I've come to the right spot. I'm looking for a Chad MacEwan. Know him by chance?"

The man jumped up like a damn jack in the box, "Sure do! I'll grab him for you, sir." Martin chuckled; he'd selected his target well. Now all he had to do was sit and wait until the buck had done his bidding. Wait and look around.

The low ceiling, fluorescent lights and puzzle of partitions reminded him of a rat maze. Martin couldn't understand why his nephew would willingly waste his life in a bloody labyrinth when he could be outdoors. Pushing dirt. Building roads, or even better, delivering the post.

It hadn't done Martin any harm. But no, the kid insisted on sitting in a maze all day, wearing a set of wires on his head like a damn robot. Most of these people looked like they wouldn't know how to crawl their way out of an Easter basket on Sunday morning if they weren't told how to do it.

It took less than two minutes for the buck to weave his way back through the maze, Martin's nephew in tow. Chad's eyes were popping out of his head, clearly surprised to see Martin at his place of work.

"Uncle Martin! Is everything alright?"

"Absolutely." Martin lowered his voice. "What do they call this?" He moved his arm in a vague circle, trying to encompass the various workstations. "Open space or something?"

"They're cubicles. Individual workstations." Chad turned toward the young man whose filing cabinet Martin still sat on. "Thanks, Imran."

"Any time, my friend." He gave a last nod in Martin's direction, jammed his headset thingy back on, then got busy talking into thin air like the rest of the herd.

"Here, help me up." Martin lifted his arm and Chad got a firm grasp around his elbow, pulling Martin up in one smooth motion. "Thanks. Got time for a quick beer?"

A look of panic crossed Chad's face and he glanced at the woman in the cubicle across from Imran's. Her eyes were narrowed into little slits of disapproval.

"Perhaps a coffee might be more appropriate?"

"Alright, alright. It's not the bloody prohibition you know."

"It's not quite noon, either. I'll just finish up what I'm working on."

"Perfect. I'll meet you at that doughnut shop on the main floor." Martin tipped his hat at the young man named Imran. Then, just for fun, he gave a slow wink to the prickly woman. She flushed and turned back to her computer screen with a quick swivel of her chair.

Shake things up. That was how it was done. Now Martin had eighteen minutes to figure out how much to tell his nephew. Chad didn't, perhaps, need the full dang story. Not yet, anyhow.

***

"Damn 1984 machine the boss-class is running up there. You're like cogs in a wheel. Cogs are replaceable, you know." Chad shrugged but didn't comment. "Besides, don't you feel a little dead spending your days in that human warehouse answering the phone all day?"

"Dead? I don't know about that. Maybe a little unfulfilled, but that's work. Sometimes a job is just a job."

Martin's lips pursed in thought. "I've still got some contacts at the Post, you know. Can't feel unfulfilled when you've got pavement to pound and sweat to wipe off your brow. Mind you, winter comes and it's not always fun to freeze your ball-hairs off. Even that's got its perks though…" he looked left then right before continuing. "There's at least one lonely woman on every route, I kid you not. Back in my day—"

"Whoa, Uncle Martin, I'm sorry to cut you off." Chad also looked left then right, his face a ripe tomato. He was a fun one; easy to get riled up and sometimes Martin just couldn't help himself from doing it. "Was there a reason you came to my work? I thought maybe something was wrong. Or that you needed help?"

Martin fidgeted with his coffee cup before setting it down on the tabletop and sighing. Cutting to the chase, he was. These young millennials had no time for chit-chat. "I need a little help." He withdrew a folded piece of paper and his reading glasses from the breast pocket of his sports coat. After putting them on, Martin unfolded the paper. There were several points he needed to discuss, and he didn't want to miss anything important. "It's the Internet."

"The Internet?"

"I need to know how to do a few things." Martin looked down, referencing his list. "Like open this Facebook thing. And 'surfing' sounds like something I should know how to do. Do you know what the Wikipedia is?"

"I do. But I thought there were introductory computer classes being offered at the Eldernest. Remember? We saw a poster about it on the bulletin board. Facebook, email..."

"Right, right. It's just I can't go." Martin shifted in his seat and lowered his voice. "Clara's the instructor."

"Perfect. You like Clara, you've said so yourself."

"I can't show up knowing *nothing*. She'll figure it out in a jiffy. Then what am I going to tell her?"

Chad scrunched up his eyebrows and took a bite of his bagel. He looked like he was grinding it down to a fine pulp as he thought about his uncle's predicament.

"See?" said Martin. "Not easy, is it?"

"I don't know, you always seem to know how to charm the ladies. What's so hard about this?"

Martin rubbed his swollen knuckles and tried not to make eye contact with his nephew. Back in his day a man would never have admitted to not knowing how to use machines. Unless it was the clothes dryer. Or maybe the kitchen mixer. And that had been a point of pride! Truth was, all these computerized gadgets made him feel vulnerable. He could feel his shoulders rounding, his chest caving in. He wasn't ready to be obsolete.

"Damnit Chad, it makes me feel weak. Damn exposed, you know?"

Chad blinked, his eyes round as saucers. "Exposed? I just. Well. I don't think of you that way. You just seem so...well, confident all the time." He took a sip of his coffee before continuing. "Why don't you be open with Clara? She seems like a nice enough lady. Tell her you're feeling vulnerable and explain what you'd like to learn about the internet. Who knows, maybe it will be fun having Clara show you the ropes for a change."

"*Tell her?*" A bark of laughter escaped Martin. It wasn't a move he'd considered. Yet…sometimes the unexpected move was the one that yielded the best results, wasn't that just the truth. His nephew might be on to something. He'd grown up with a lot of womanly influence; no man in the house to guide him along the way. Martin had always considered that a detriment, but maybe it had given the lad an unexpected advantage; an understanding of how the fairer sex were mentally wired.

After a few moments of quiet contemplation Martin nodded and a pleased look blossomed on his face.

"I see where you're angling on this. Smarter than you look, my man. Smarter than you look."

Both men glanced down at the younger man's Vans, his tight jeans and pullover sweater. Martin's casualwear appeared sharper than what his nephew wore to his office. Back in Martin's day you couldn't underestimate the power of a tidy postal uniform. But what did it matter? He'd seen Chad's office. It was clear none of his customers would be able to tell what he was wearing through that wire headset contraption.

"So let me get this straight, Uncle Martin. You took a taxi all the way over here to ask how to use the Internet?"

Martin looked down at his list. "There's another thing. Herbert and Grant want to do some online dating and need your help cause they're *definitely* not going to ask Clara 'bout that."

"Ah. I see." Chad's face contorted and scrunched; a smile lurked at the corners of his mouth. "But not you? Surely you're in on this too?"

Martin flapped his hand in dismissal. "Nah. I've got enough action at the 'Nest. No point looking for more than I can handle."

"Right. There's Clara, of course. But I haven't heard you mention Felicity in a while. What's going on there?"

"That's all wrapped up."

"Wrapped up? A man of your prodigious talents…" for a

second time Chad's face contorted as if he were trying to hold in his laughter. Martin chose to ignore him.

"There's one more thing." He fumbled with the paper in his hand, folding then unfolding the note. "Have you heard of something called Go Fund Me?" Chad nodded. "We've got to set one up for Harold."

"Isn't he the night nurse?"

"You got it."

"The one who kind of helps with the night…liaisons, right?"

Martin rolled his eyes. "He's not unrolling the damn condom!"

"Shhhh!"

"He just sort'a turns a blind eye. Besides, we're adults. Not under-aged teenagers. The point is this Go Fund Me thingamajig. Can you set one up?"

"Shouldn't be too hard." Martin relaxed into the metal donut shop chair as though a weight had lifted off him. "I'll bring my laptop when I come for coffee on Saturday."

Martin jumped back up in his seat. "No, no, no, no. You can't be doing that. The whole point is this must be kept secret. The lads and I, we will travel to your house. How about Thursday night?"

"Whoa. I have plans Thursday night."

"Plans with *us*. We've already booked the Access van and it's not the kind of service you can just reschedule. Is your elevator working? Herbert'll need that, what with the walker."

"I really can't. I've got to be somewhere at 8:00. It involves, well you know, a woman."

Martin's eyebrows shot up. He wondered if the woman was the same sharp-eyed lady from the cafeteria Chad had been stumbling over himself trying to impress for weeks.

"Why do you look so surprised?"

"I'm not surprised." Martin picked up his coffee and took a sip in an effort to hide his surprise. "It's just that changes things. We can't come between a man and his woman, can we? Of course not." Martin rubbed his knuckles while working out an option. "We'll arrive at 6:00 and we'll be hungry. Have some pizza. Meat Lovers and maybe some forks and knives because you know about Grant's teeth. We'll get straight to work and be out of your hair in time for you to get to your date."

With business settled Martin polished off his coffee and had his nephew order him a cab. He buttoned up his coat and put his hat on and then they walked outside to watch for the yellow-top.

They hadn't called it vulnerability back in his postie days, but what was true then was still true now. Sometimes an old buck needed to know when to call on a young buck for help, cause sometimes you just had to rely on the herd. As the taxi pulled up Martin shook his nephew's hand. "The two of us together…we're a good team."

Chad rubbed his chin and gave his uncle a half-smile. "Are you okay? I'm still a little unclear what this whole thing was about."

"I'm fine, just fine. Getting comfortable with my vulnerable side, you know?" Martin chuckled, carefully climbed into the taxi and waved goodbye.

Chad: Time of Plenty

The pizza had just been delivered when I heard a commotion in the hallway. It sounded as though a shopping cart had smashed the corridor outside my apartment. It was quickly followed by a "Jeez Louise," then a "watch where you push that thing, Herb!"

I opened my door and was not at all surprised to find my uncle and his comrades from the Eldernest. They filed in one at a time. First Herbert and his walker, then Grant, and in the rear, Uncle Martin.

"Two outings in one week," Martin said by way of greeting. He hobbled into the dining area and lowered himself into one of the sturdy chairs my ex had insisted we buy. "My damn knee is acting up."

"Maybe you should have it checked out."

"Nah. It's just age."

It gave me a jolt to see Martin looking frail. I thought of him as nimble for an elderly man, but then I rarely saw him outside the safe confines of the Eldernest. "I'm sure we could've managed to do this at the 'Nest."

"Are you kidding?" butted in Herbert. "We could've been overheard." He maneuvered himself over to the table, and I jostled chairs out of the way so he and his walker could get by. "Besides, they're always trying to supervise our meals. Can't even order a box of pizza in peace." His face was sweaty and flushed.

Grant pulled a chair out from the table for Herbert, and then one for himself. "Pizza's high in sodium, they say. Could be bad for the heart. Might you have any lager on hand, Chad?"

"Beer? Er...ya. I've got some beer." Did any of these guys have heart conditions? Or diabetes? It was too late to worry now; Herbert was already chowing down on a slice of meat lovers. I pulled a six-pack out of the fridge, snagged one for myself, and placed the rest on the table.

My uncle picked up a can and held it away from his face so he could read the label. "Bud-lite-lime." It wasn't a question exactly, more a statement, and I had the impression I'd failed some kind of test.

Herbert's eyebrows arched halfway to his hairline as he too picked up a can and examined the label. It didn't stop him pulling the tab and taking a sip. His eyes bugged out before he swallowed. He took a second look at the label then another drink. It couldn't be too bad.

Now that everyone was eating, I managed a quick look at my phone. My heart fluttered in a way that was becoming increasingly familiar. A text from Lila:

Meet U @ Sentry? 8pm?

4 sure. Xx. I deleted the X's and added a smiley face. Then deleted the smiley face. Could men use emoji's? I didn't know.

Lila responded right away with a yellow thumbs up. What did that mean? 'Cool' or 'excellent' or just 'alright'? I put my phone in my pocket, looking forward to the evening. We'd been on a handful of dates, if you counted our first failed attempt at the pub and a kid's movie with her daughter. A few weeks ago I'd told her about the Thursday gaming group at Sentry and was on cloud nine when she said she'd like to check it out together. We'd met at Sentry twice now, each time more relaxed and more comfortable than the time before. I could be myself while surrounded by board games and gamers and show my best, most confident side to Lila.

I cleared my throat to get the men's attention. "You mentioned Go Fund Me. Should we start there?"

"As long as you don't forget the Plenty of Fish," said Herbert, nudging Grant with his elbow. "We'll need to take photos for our dating profiles." He turned around and assessed the look of my well-used couch and cluttered coffee table before grimacing at the manga poster. "At least there won't be call buttons and hand washing signs in the background."

Grant looked up from his pizza. "In an effort to use our time wisely perhaps we should start on the Harold situation?"

A hush settled over the room. The three men's foreheads seemed to furrow in unison, and I sensed a fair amount of guilt waft between them.

I was trying my best to be patient, but I had less than an hour to get these guys sorted and out of my apartment if I were going to meet Lila on time. "Why does Harold need a Go Fund Me campaign anyway? Has he invented something? Or maybe... damn. He's not sick, is he?"

My uncle was the first to crack. "Alright, alright." He held up his hands as though to stop oncoming traffic. "No need to push. He's lost his job, is all."

"Harold lost his job? At the 'Nest?"

"Of course at the 'Nest. And it's a crying shame; he's a great guy."

I kneaded the base of my neck and looked from one to the other. "Can I ask what happened?"

Grant picked up a napkin and wiped his hands before answering. "It was the late-night poker ring. Wouldn't have been a problem if it weren't for Edgar. Do you know him? His suite is across the hall from your uncle's. Edgar's a sore loser, if you ask me."

Herbert slammed his palm down on the table. "Edgar's an ass. Harold won fair and square."

Wow. Did they not have enough to do with their social committees and clubs during the daytime hours? And that was apart from their rampant dating. Life at the 'Nest reminded me more and more of college without the classes or homework.

Grant took a sip of his beer and looked at my uncle. "The conjugal visits didn't help." Martin's chin dipped toward his chest. He didn't bother denying the accusation.

Herbert shrugged. "That's true, but it could've been any one of us. Just bad luck it was you, Martin."

"Come off it, Herbert," Grant pressed his lips together as if trying to hold back laughter. "You know you weren't in the running. Can't remember the last time you've even sat at the same dining table as Maggie."

I could see Herbert's face tinging purple and I doubted it was because of the sodium. I stepped in before I had a mature MMA fight on my hands. "Okay, so Harold's out of work. Have you asked his permission to create a Go Fund Me campaign?"

"Haven't asked," said Grant.

"But of course he'd want us to do it." Martin added.

"Needs the money, and money's money, right?" Herbert had recovered himself enough to join the conversation. "He's got two kids and another on the way."

"Okay, that could help with the sympathy vote." I grabbed a pizza napkin and a pen from the counter and started writing. Kids. Baby on the way. "Any skills that you know of?"

"He's pretty gentle from what I've seen," Martin said. "With the lifting and such."

"Okay, gentle. And he's also strong if he's doing lifting. Maybe we could do a LinkedIn too."

"LinkedIn," began Herbert, "Is that for dating?"

"Nah," I said, "It's just for career networking, Herbert."

"Are you sure?"

"Very."

No one seemed to know if Harold was a registered nurse, had a practical nursing license or some other designation. To them he was simply 'Harold the Night Nurse. Easy going and helpful.'

Martin pulled out a photograph that could be used: Harold in his white Eldernest uniform surrounded by several men from the 'Nest. Each had a party hat on, several strands of Mardi Gras beads around their neck, and a cigar between their smiling lips.

"They let you smoke those in the 'Nest?" I was surprised given the staff concern over pizza, never mind the large quantity of air tanks rolling around the place.

"Not officially," said Martin.

I cleared my throat and didn't bother asking anymore questions. "Okay, I'll scan this photo and get it back to you." I looked at the clock. We were running out of time. "I think this'll be enough information for me to scrap something together." There was no point putting it off any longer. "On to Plenty of Fish."

It was a relief to see the back of my uncle and his posse. Explaining how to navigate the dating site and check for messages had taken both patience and time, but it was the photo shoot that had been truly painful. It was dominated by a few rather uncomfortable poses by Herbert.

I recommended he drop down to 'Herb' for his profile and that was about all the advice he was willing to take. Martin strongly opposed the bit about him seeking a mate who enjoyed watching American football, but Herb could not be shaken. I suppose it was good to know what it was you wanted in a companion.

***

I arrived at The Sentry perspiring and slightly out of breath. It was sweet relief when I spotted Lila, her arm raised high in the air waving to me, and an empty chair beside her.

The Thursday night gamers group was heavily skewed toward males, and Lila had been an instant hit with the other players. I didn't let it shake me, not even for a minute. I had the upper hand: I'd invited Lila along in the first place. I also had a job. A haircut. And she laughed when she thought I was trying to be funny.

I weaved my way through the tables nodding at the people I knew, saying hello to the ones I liked. These were my people. Besides, the smartest, most gorgeous, most interesting woman that had ever graced this room was holding an empty chair for me.

When I made it to the table I grinned at Lila and slid down into the chair beside her. The night turned out glorious. Maybe not fireworks glorious, or the kind of evening Martin would gloat over for a week. From the outside it looked no different than two friends gaming at the same table. Still, I left feeling like something incredible had happened.

I set up the Plenty of Fish accounts the next day, answering the profile questions with the information Herb and Grant had given me the night before. Hobbies and pastimes, general demographics and dating range: women aged fifty and older. *Fifty?* I shook my head. *In their dreams.*

Uploading the profile pictures onto the Plenty of Fish site was easy but trying to make them look decent was another matter; filters could only do so much. *Good luck, lads.* At least it was done.

The Go Fund Me campaign wasn't nearly as straightforward. I suffered through several attempts before pushing the laptop away and vigorously scratching my nails across my scalp. The platform wasn't complicated; the problem was my writing skills. They were crap. Janice, my crank-ass colleague, had assured me of that several times.

It didn't help that I couldn't ask Harold any questions. I had never met the man and only knew what my uncle and his friends shared with me.

But maybe this was the perfect excuse. The perfect excuse to ask Lila for help. I could take a page off the old guys and take things one step past friendship. It was risky; she could say no. But what if she didn't? I dialed her number before I could second-guess myself.

***

It was the first time Lila came over to my apartment. I pulled out all the stops: vacuumed the carpet, threw out the trash and put a new roll of toilet paper on the dispenser. In the twenty minutes before she arrived I checked my hair in the bathroom mirror four times; changed my shirt twice.

The buzzer had my heart hammering and it was all I could do to try and breathe calmly while I waited for her to make her way upstairs and down the hall to my apartment. I gave her the quick tour, then powered up my laptop where it sat on the table.

"Who's this?" Lila asked. I turned to see her by the bookshelf, a framed picture cradled in her hands. The photo was taken on a camping trip when I was twelve. Two sets of knobby knees and over-sized 80s glasses on the pair of us. "Well, me…and my mom."

I didn't explain more than that. Not that mom had died nearly two years ago from lung cancer, or that the photo was taken on our first summer after dad left. I knew Lila wanted to be a funeral director and seemed to love talking about death, but I couldn't do it. I sucked at talking about Mom without a weird quaver sabotaging my voice.

"Do you want a drink?" I asked. She nodded and I got up and grabbed two beers from the fridge—*was there something wrong with Bud lite lime?*—then we both sat down at the kitchen table. My laptop was open to the Go Fund Me website and the happy faces of successful fundraisers starred back at us.

Lila pulled the computer toward herself and took over. "We need a unique title. Something catchy."

"Good idea. Their tip-sheet says we also need something like a 'call to action.'"

"That's easy: 'Donate money to a bloke that supports sex across the ages,' right?"

"Uhhh...right." I'd filled Lila in on the details over text. She didn't seem surprised at all, and I wondered how much the Eldernest staff talked about what was going on with the 'Nest inhabitants. "I suppose that's accurate. I don't know if he'd want us to say that though?"

"How about...Support Harold; he supported your lonely grandparent."

"Ya, maybe. Or: Help Harold who helped the Elderly?"

"That's pretty good." Lila started typing. I looked over her shoulder. *'Harold worked for several years at a senior's lodge. He recently lost his employment because he supported the rights of older adults to enjoy intimate time together. He'd—'*

I bit my lip. "I really don't know if we should say that, Lila. We didn't get Harold's permission. What if it...I don't know, causes him trouble getting another job?"

"Oh, right. How about this: Harold was known for respecting the rights of older adults to live socially complete lives."

"Wow! That's great. Powerful but not specific. I think that might be the way to go." I watched Lila tap away at the keyboard. I was trying to stay focused on Harold, but all I kept thinking about was how to know if Lila was interested in more than friendship.

Maybe if I leaned in and placed my hand on the space between her shoulder blades? If she moved away, fine. She wasn't interested. Nothing too alarming would have happened. I could apologize and never. Touch. Her. Again.

But if she didn't pull away. If she pressed her back into my hand. Maybe that would mean something?

"Then what about something like: Harold finds himself out of work at the worst time. He has two children and another on the way."

"Pardon? Oh. Ya, I think that sounds excellent." I looked down at the tip-sheet, trying to get refocused. "Should we tell people what their donations will be used for?"

"Why don't we just say, 'family living expenses until Harold can find more work in the field he loves, supporting older adults to live with dignity.'"

"Wow. You're really good at this. We won't even need to edit it."

"Thanks. After that we can just add: 'Harold was good to us. Now we want to be good to Harold.' What do you think? It'll sound like it came from your uncle and his friends."

"Sounds great!" I gently placed my hand on Lila's back. And she twisted. Shit. I snatched my hand back as though it were on fire and scratched the stubble along my jaw. What did a twist mean?

I was pretty damn sure it meant 'keep your hands to yourself.' My face burned. What else could a twist mean?

Lila didn't look up from the computer screen. "That was easy. Look, the campaign is already live. Now we'll see what happens. I should do one for my embalming license."

"Definitely. I'd donate."

"You would? Thanks, Chad." Lila smiled, leaned over and pecked me on the cheek.

Her fingers were still on the keyboard, her mind still on dead body school, and I turned my face toward hers and kissed her on the lips. Sweet Jesus, her hands left the keyboard and moved to my shoulders and *she kissed me back!*

I was too shocked to close my eyes, and instead met her gaze smack on. The corners of her eyes crinkled in happiness and mine followed.

Harold was obviously a magical talisman. He'd been lucky for Martin and his friends and now he seemed to be helping me live a socially complete life too. I would definitely be making a donation to his campaign.

Rosie: Trap

Kathleen sat on the picnic bench with her legs crossed, one over the other, her top leg kicking and jumping like a Jack Russell on drugs. It was a dead giveaway Kathleen was irritated. In fact, Kathleen spent so much time being irritated, Rosie was secretly amazed her daughter didn't suffer from repetitive strain injury of the knee.

Her daughter cleared her throat. "Mr. Terrance has been dead for nearly two decades, Mom."

"Right. That's true. And what a good cat. Do you remember the way he used to stretch up on the armrest of Dad's chair and scratch the fabric? That used to make your dad so mad!"

"I don't remember that. I do remember Mr. Terrance is dead."

Rosie pulled her cardigan together at the neckline. "Of course, of course. No one's arguing that." She should've worn something warmer. It had looked so sunny outside that Rosie had wanted to sit in the garden. She hadn't counted on the wind. She hadn't counted on Kathleen's sharp P.I. skills either.

"Here's the thing, Mom. When we were speaking on the phone Thursday, you told me Terrance was eating more than he used to. Now how could a cat who's dead," she paused and placed a hand on her mother's knee and squeezed it before letting go. "A lovely cat, I remember that—be eating *more* than he used to?"

Damn. She shouldn't have let that slip. Kathleen wasn't the type to understand. She'd never been what you'd call 'a rule breaker.' "It was just my imagination, Kathy—"

"Kathleen."

"Fine. Kathleen. I was just *imagining* Terry was still with us and who wouldn't be hungry after so many years not eating?" A sick feeling crept over Rosie. She knew where this was going. Straight back to that damn head doctor of Kathleen's.

A mother should be able to trust her daughter, but had Rosie been able to do that? Nooo. Had Kathleen kicked up a stink about Rosie's part-time job at the costume shop? Yeeess. And did Rosie believe Kathleen would help her if she knew the truth about the new Mr. Terrance? Ha! Kathleen never wanted her mother to do anything that might jeopardize her spot at the Eldernest.

"Let me get this straight, Mom. You *imagined* our dead cat was eating?" Kathleen rubbing her temples with her fingertips. "I've made a doctor's appointment for you."

"What! I'm fit as a fiddle."

"I'm not worried about your body, Mom." Kathleen stretched over her crossed and jumping leg, this time picking up her mother's cold hand in hers. "Thomas called me this week."

"Thomas?"

"Director Knightly, Mom. Thomas Knightly. He says you've been agitated. Not only that, you've been agitating the other residents."

"Agitating! You better believe I'm agitating. Director Knightly won't consider the facts. All he wants is to keep us older adults isolated. He doesn't care two shakes of a donkey's butt about our mental health—"

"That's not true, Mom. He's *concerned* about your mental health. That's exactly why he called me."

It was small relief they wouldn't be overheard. While the sun had drawn a few others out into the garden, the wind had made most of the other residents quickly change their minds and head back indoors. "Listen to me, Kathleen: I'm right about a companion animal being a good thing for the people here at the Eldernest." Rosie's voice burned with certainty. "I've research to back me up! It's just Director Knightly doesn't want to admit it. He's just scared because he doesn't want me to go the board of directors with my PET-ition. *That's* why he called. He's using *you*, Kathleen, to get to *me*."

"Oh Mom!" Kathleen's voice cut the air with all the frustration stored in her jittery, jumpy leg. "That's just not true. Other seniors could have allergies. Thomas has to consider the needs—"

"You can't trust him, Kathleen. He's a slippery no-good fish, that one." Rosie felt a shiver run up and down her spin. Why couldn't her daughter just trust her?

"After everything he's done for you. Can you not just follow the rules, Mom?"

Rosie's face flushed. Everything he's done. That damn government subsidy. Always being held against her. No one would let her forget she wasn't an equal here. Not even her daughter.

Rosie dropped her daughter's hand and tucked her own hands between the bench and her knees. Closing her eyes, she took three calming breaths before speaking again. "I'm sorry to have worried you, dear. I was just imagining about Mr. Terrance and got my words confused. I don't need to see the doctor, and I'd ask you kindly not to discuss me with Director Knightly. He should be talking to me, not you. I'm an adult."

"He's worried about you, Mom. And I'm your daughter. No one's here to hurt you."

Kathleen's words, although intended to calm her down, did nothing to appease Rosie. Instead they made her chest tighten, her legs stiffen. "You aren't my guardian, Kathleen. Not yet, anyway. You can surely care for me when I can't care for myself, but until then I've got a right to make my own choices."

Kathleen shifted on the bench. "And what if you're not…able to judge when that time comes? Mom, I love you, but look—I'm worried you're not able to take proper care of yourself anymore."

"Heavens! I'm the fastest in the walking club, faster than anyone else by a mile. And I even manage my part-time job without any trouble."

"What about your shirt then? It's the same one you were wearing last time I visited. With the same brown stain." Kathleen's voice faltered. "It's not like you to wear dirty clothing, Mom."

Rosie looked down and sure shooting, there was an ugly stain on the sleeve of her white sweater. Why hadn't she noticed it? She'd even worn it for her evening shift at the costume shop the other night. Had it been dirty then? Shame warmed her face.

The sweater had been purchased at the mall on one of the

Eldernest shopping trips. Fifty percent off the ticket price and not a darn thing wrong with it. It was a sweater only an old lady could get away wearing, a print of a sweet gray kitten with round, oversized green eyes, and Rosie had earned that right. But she'd have to do better if she were to convince everyone she still had her marbles about her. Was still able to make good choices. It wasn't just her freedom at risk. There was Terry to consider too. Who would put out his food if Rosie wasn't there?

"Kathleen, honey. I'm fine. I promise you." Rosie bit her lip. Her daughter wasn't buying it. She was rubbing her temples again, looking as bothered as a fish out of water. "I'm sorry I've worried you, I really am."

"This petition thing, Mom? You need to stop with that. It's a concern to Thomas. To Director Knightly."

Rosie felt her fingers trembling where they lay squished between the bench and her knees. She crossed them tightly, keeping her hands hidden where her daughter wouldn't see. She smiled at her daughter, lips trembling, and nodded. "Okay, honey. I understand."

Lila: Precautionary Measures

Rumors poured into the lunchroom. The staff were divided. Some, including Lila, were pragmatic—it was a medical fact Linus would not recover. Besides, they'd seen it before, hadn't they? While it was true most of the staff were not excessively bothered by the morally questionable romance a few burned with outrage. And it was those few, it seemed to Lila, who always dominated the lunchroom discussion.

"The poor man." Martha rubbed the crucifix she wore on a chain around her neck as she rocked back and forth on the floral-patterned sofa. "And under his own roof!" Lila knew that Martha was one of Linus's regular caregivers. She could understand a certain loyalty to the man who was her patient, yet the intensity of Martha's feelings confused Lila. It was as though Martha were personally affronted on her patient's behalf.

"I don't know," said Cook, glancing up from her magazine. "Is he even aware?"

"Aware? Of course he's *aware*—aware his wife has abandoned him."

"Abandoned? She still visits, doesn't she? I'm sure I've seen her reading to him."

"Sure, occasionally. But she's not making time for him the way she used to. He's lonely."

"Lonely?" Cook repeated. "How can you tell?"

Martha gazed into the distance and said in a fervent whisper, "I can see it in his eyes."

A murmur of agreement shimmered through the room and Lila

bent her head over her textbook so no one would see her scornful expression. *In his eyes?* What would Linus say if he were capable of doing so, that's what mattered. Maybe he'd want his wife to be happy. To move on. Anyway, the way Lila saw it, this was Clara's business and certainly not the staffers.

"It's wrong; an extra-marital affair." Martha's words were picking up speed; falling faster and faster out of her mouth. She looked around the room searching for agreement. "There's right and then there's plain wrong."

"Is there?" The words popped out of Lila's mouth without her thinking. Damn. It never paid to weigh in on these discussions. Normally she avoided doing so by spending her breaks trawling through social media or studying for school. Today Lila was trying to finish up an assignment on infection control procedures, but she'd done it. Got distracted, poked the bear and now all eyes were on her. "It's just…shouldn't Clara have a chance at being happy?" Lila's voice trailed off into the electrified silence.

Her eyes swept the room in a desperate attempt to make eye contact with anyone who would agree with her. Perhaps Phil from laundry? He didn't look up from his newspaper. Maybe he didn't care or maybe he was just smarter than her; unwilling to invite the wrath of Martha and her God.

Martha's mouth gaped open before she snapped it shut. "Happy? You've got to be kidding. Guilt-ridden, I'd say." Again she picked up the crucifix from around her neck and rubbed it between her thumb and forefinger. Lila wondered if the crucifix provided Martha comfort or assurance of her personal virtue.

"Let's be serious," edged in Bernadette. As all eyes moved to her, Bernadette leaned forward, the better for everyone to see her nurse's uniform. It was a powerful reminder of the position professionals held in the staff pecking order. "I'm fairly new here, but we're talking about *Martin*, aren't we? Clara might be happy now, but it's obvious she won't be for long. Martin's left a string of broken hearts from the Garden wing to the Atrium. It's a complete fiasco."

Martha nodded. "Director Knightly needs to take a stand against immorality." Her followers murmured agreement and this time Lila swallowed her dissent. It would do no good arguing.

Martha had been chosen as the official measuring tape on morality.

It was true that Chad's uncle was a total player and he very well might break Clara's heart. Still, it was Clara's choice to get involved with him. Anyway, it wasn't just that getting under Lila's skin. What irritated the *absolute* shit out of her was the way her middle-aged working-class colleagues were such obedient rule followers.

Like, come on! When had the rules ever worked for any of them? The lot of them—excluding the registered nurses and perhaps Cook—were lucky to clear minimum wage, and yet the whole lot of them seemed to believe getting ahead depended on hard work, never questioning authority, and following the rules.

Lila disagreed. On all counts. Head down, ass up might guarantee you a job. It didn't guarantee getting ahead. It certainly hadn't gotten her to the point she could sleep through the night and not worry about squeezing her budget. Besides, rule followers and rule breakers met the same end—the stainless-steel table in the embalmers room. Or maybe, as was often the case these days, the cremation chamber.

Phil folded his newspaper and set it down on the coffee table. "I don't know," he drawled. "I kind of admire old Martin. He's a regular Don Juan."

"You would!" laughed Cook and slapped Phil on the back. It was Cook who always had the final say. The lunchroom bubbled with laughter and the conversation shifted to less controversial topics. Everyone appeared happy to drop the subject except Martha. In her peripheral vision Lila watched Martha clench and unclench her jaw, her fingers continuing to worry the crucifix around her neck.

Sometimes Lila wondered if Chad knew about Linus. She guessed he didn't, although he'd told her about Clara and Martin. Said his uncle was smitten with Clara. That's the word he'd used. *Smitten.* The old-fashion term had made Lila smile. Made her ask Chad if he was smitten with anyone himself. He'd blushed and stammered in that very Mr. Darcy way of his, "You know I am, Lila." Yes, she knew he was.

She liked Chad too...more than she'd anticipated. He was different than many of the men she knew. He was certainly different than Quinn's father; not that she stayed in contact with the mansplaining fool. It was easier to describe Chad by all the things he wasn't than pinning down exactly what it was that drew her to him.

Maybe it was the very proper, full sentence texts he sent. Or the way he was so nervous to impress and never seemed sure he was saying the right thing.

She shook her head, trying to block out both her thoughts and the chatter around her. What she needed to do was focus on her assignment if she wanted her night free.

She'd finished the section on precautionary measures for infectious disease control: Proper hand hygiene. Protective clothing. Care when using sharp instruments. She still had the section on increased risk when embalming, but it was difficult to concentrate with the animated conversation around her. She reached into her backpack, searching for her headphones. No luck. She'd forgotten to pack them.

She went on studying as best she could. Embalmers needed to be trained to a high standard before practicing in the field. That made sense, although her instructor always stressed infectious diseases in the living were almost always a greater hazard than those in the dead.

How ironic. Better training was provided for working with the dead than with living people. Take the Eldernest, for instance. It was probably easier for Lila to catch something here than it was during her embalming practicum.

It was no use. Her mind was wandering again, and the room was too loud. She closed her textbook and balanced it on her lap.

All around Lila multiple languages competed against each other, English flowing in and out and tying all the conversations together. She liked the way it sounded, reminding her of the Friday night parties she attended with her parents growing up.

In the safety of the staffroom people spoke whatever languages came most natural to them, but everyone switched to English as they exited. It would be as abrupt as flipping a light switch. And those with accents? They would speak softer, more conscious of making a mistake.

The residents complained about the accents. She'd heard

plenty of grumbling during her time working there. They wanted more 'native English speakers' on staff. Right. Like people who had a choice would work for the crappy wages doled out at the Eldernest?

Lila didn't think so. At least she escaped the accent complaints, but it wasn't so easy avoiding questions. "Where are you from, dear?" and her favourite, "My, your English is very good. How long have you been practicing?"

She'd voiced her frustration in the staff room when she was still new on the job. "I'm from right damn here," she'd said, arms raised in frustration. "I'm just as Canadian as any of them. Besides, I've been speaking English my whole damn life."

Cook had shared a knowing look with several other staff before switching her gaze to Lila. "That make you special, does it?"

Lila's face had burned. Her anger deflated faster than a burst balloon and was replaced by embarrassed shame. Nothing more needed to be said.

After that she let the old people think what they wanted and didn't bother to correct them. Let them see who they wanted to see. She got in the habit of giving one-word answers and simple gestures in the cafeteria; minding her own business in the staff room. It was only a job. She wasn't here to make friends.

She felt a nudge on her shoulder and looked up to see Cook standing over here. "Break time's over. Time to get your nose outta those books. You're on coffee."

Coffee. *What a surprise.* It took effort not to roll her eyes.

***

Few 'Nest residents got past Lila's mask. Those who did, like Rosie the old lady who worked at the costume shop in Lila's neighbourhood, were her favourites. Carrying a pot of coffee in each hand, Lila edged over to where Rosie sat alone amid a sea of visiting families. She filled the woman's coffee cup, leaving lots of room for cream. "How are you today, Mrs. Dylan?"

Rosie looked up and gave Lila a watery smile from behind her round glasses. "Oh I'm fine, dear. As right as rain, I'd say. A bit tired but nothing a little sleep won't fix."

"Late night at the shop?"

"My land, yes! And guess what my nephew said during

inventory last night? He owns the shop you remember, and he said, 'There's no one quite like Rosie.'" Rosie beamed and Lila smiled back, hoping the comment had been meant in a good way. Rosie needed fans in her corner. She deserved them.

Putting down one of the coffee carafes on the table, Lila touched the cuff of Rosie's sweater where a splash of juice had left an orange stain. "I've brought my own detergent from home today. I'm going to run all my cleaning rags through in a separate load—you know how my eczema flares up with that institution stuff they use around here." Lila rubbed her fingertips together so Rosie could see how dry they were.

It was tough on many of the residents, not having control over the simplest things. Not even the kind of laundry soap they liked or being able to raid the kitchen for a late-night snack the way they'd done their whole adult life without thinking twice about it. "Would you like me to run some of your clothes through with my stuff?"

Rosie fumbled with her sleeve. Her cheeks were pinkening and Lila continued, trying to prevent her from getting embarrassed.

"It's no trouble, Rosie. I've got just the washing-up rags...and it's better for the environment to do a full load, don't you think?" Lila winked at the older woman. "My treat?" Rosie bit her lip, indecision still on her face. "You know Rosie, maybe you can do me a favour in exchange? I'm looking for..." Lila paused, trying to come up with something fast. What could she ask for? "Do you have any Zelda costumes at the shop? You know, Link? That's the guy with the hat and the pointy ears."

Rosie lit up. "Do I have Zelda merchandise? That's like asking if you have coffee in those pots!"

"Great! Put some ears aside for me, won't you? I'll swing by for them next week."

Lila had always loved the Legend of Zelda, and it was cool to see the classic games making a comeback in popularity. Her parents hadn't been onboard with getting a gaming system when she was young, but she'd persevered.

"A Nintendo is a computer," she'd told them. "It'll train my brain to think quickly."

Her parents hadn't been swayed. "Video games, bah! They

won't help with homework. Besides, too expensive."

Lila knew better than to push when her parents said no. But she kept quietly dreaming. Imagining herself blowing on her very own game cartridges, back and forth, zip, zip before inserting them into the system. She dreamt of being player one and not having to sit back and wait for a turn on the player two controller.

And then, without even trying, her parents changed their minds. First one, then two, then a handful of the Friday night families bought Nintendos or the rival Saga System. The video games entertained the kids as the parents gathered and talked about business, bad landlords, and the best schools in the area for their children's education. After that it hadn't taken long. Lila's parents found a gaming system on sale and brought it home for her brother.

It was bittersweet. Uncomplaining, Lila would wait her turn. When the controller was finally handed over, she took a secret pleasure in destroying her brother's score on The Legend of Zelda.

"Yes Rosie, I would love if you could get me some ears. I've got a gift to send someone." Her brother's birthday was next month. She would mail the ears to him where he lived on the coast.

After the lunch rush Lila gathered a small pile of clothes from Rosie's room and took them to the laundry room.

Phil was already there, working away in the humid conditions.

"Hey Phil, can you throw these in for me?" She held up the small pile of Rosie's clothing, a few of her cleaning rags on top. Her container of fragrance-free soap was tucked under her arm.

"You doing that lady's laundry again? She's a wingbat."

"She's harmless. Unlike some of them."

Phil laughed. "You tellin' me. Why'd you think I hide in Laundry?" He took the clothes from Lila's arms. "I'll have them ready by 4:00."

Phil dropped the clothes in a wheeled laundry cart, the soap on top then grabbed a stack of folded sheets and held them out to Lila. "Here's her highnesses bedding. Have fun."

"Ugh. Right. Can't wait." She took the 600 thread-count Egyptian cotton sheets and went back upstairs. Housekeeping was next on her schedule.

Tidying up the bedrooms of rich Eldernesters who could afford the add-on service was the absolute worst. As usual she would start with Felicity and get her out of the way. The rest would be a breeze in comparison.

Pushing her cleaning-cart up against the hall wall, Lila rapped on Felicity's door. "Housekeeping."

She was about to thank her lucky stars when she heard Felicity respond. "Come in." Figures. Most residents stayed in the social room when the housekeepers were in their room, but not Felicity.

Bracing herself, Lila pushed open the door. Felicity sat waiting on one of her plush armchairs, a magazine unfolded on her lap. It was the perfect perch to sit and supervise.

Only the worst Eldernesters stayed and watched the housekeeping staff, waiting for a slip-up or a chance to point out what they were doing wrong. Felicity was Queen among them.

Did the old bat really think someone would pinch her stuff? Pocket a tin of face powder off the dresser, or a china figurine off the bookshelf? No thank you. If Lila wanted some tacky old person's stuff, she could find it down at the thrift store where her mother worked.

"Don't forget to move the items before dusting. *Some people don't move the items first.*"

Some people have a hell of a lot of knickknacks. Forget infectious disease precautionary measures for the deceased. What Lila needed was precautionary measures for working with people like Felicity. First on the list: move fast so you can get outta there.

"Will you be vacuuming into the corners today?" Felicity looked over the top of her magazine at Lila.

Lila grit her teeth, her irritation bubbling up. "Pardon? You want tea?"

Felicity rolled her eyes.

"You like tea, right? I get you tea."

"I don't want any tea." Felicity pointed to the vacuum. "Vacuum! Right up to the corners. I don't want to see any crud in the corners."

"Crud? What's this crud?" Lila bent over, taking a closer look at the carpet.

"Oh, for the love of…"

Lila bit her lip to keep from smiling. If Felicity knew it was an act there would be hell to pay.

Felicity got out of her chair intent on providing instruction, but Lila didn't wait. She turned on the vacuum, the roar of the machine making it impossible to hear what Felicity was saying. "I vacuum crud, Ms. Felicity. You sit down." Lila turned her back on her and got vacuuming. The sooner she was done, the sooner she could finish the Garden Wing and get back to gather Rosie's clothes from the laundry. And then she'd be out of there. Home in time to hang out with Quinn and Chad.

***

When her shift was nearly over, Lila returned her cleaning supply kit to the storage room. She only had to pick up the laundry, take Rosie's to her room, placed the laundered cleaning rags in their storage cupboard and then she'd be free to go. She hustled down to the laundry and found Rosie's clothes stacked and neatly folded on a side table.

"Nice. Thanks Philip," she called over the thrum of the machines.

"Any time, my friend." He glanced over at her. "Plans tonight? You seem eager to get the hell outta here."

"And you're not?" Lila smiled. "Yes. I have plans. With a boy." It was the first time she'd told anyone at the Eldernest. She couldn't help the grin that spread across her face.

"Nice! This a new development?" Philip paused, waiting for details but Lila wasn't giving away much.

"Fairly," she winked, picked up the clothes and yelled "thanks again," over her shoulder. Gawd, she was happy to get out of there. She'd try and complete her homework on the bus and then she'd have a full night and day off both work and school. She was desperate for a break.

When she got to Rosie's room, she switched the stack of laundry into one arm and used her free hand to knock on Rosie's door. "Laundry's done," she called.

She heard a shuffling from inside the room. "Oh dear," she heard Rosie say.

"Don't trouble yourself, Rosie. It's just Lila; I'll let myself in." Lila twisted the doorknob and pulled the door open.

A streak of orange shot past Lila's knees, nearly making her drop Rosie's clothes. "Jeez!"

"Mr. Terrance!" Rosie scrambled toward the door, a look of horror on her face. "My land!" Down the hall an orange tail zipped around the corner. This was not good.

"What was that, Rosie?"

Rosie didn't stop to answer. She sidestepped Lila and raced after the animal. Setting the stack of clothes on the bed, Lila chased after Rosie, after whatever it was Rosie had been hiding in her room. Good lord. Had it been a cat? A ferret?

It was a cat. And it hadn't gotten far. Hissing, back arched, claws dug into the back of one of the hall couches was how Lila and Rosie found it. It was mangy and it wasn't alone. Mr. Knightly stood with what looked to be a perspective family on a tour of the facility. Knightly's jaw hung open, his eyes darting back and forth between the cat and a hyperventilating Rosie.

With everyone else immobile in shock, Lila jumped into action. She grabbed the cat by the scruff of its neck. There was no time to bother with protective clothing or proper hand hygiene, but she did manage to keep its sharp claws turned away from her. She caught one glimpse of Knightly as she scooted to the nearest exit, the cat in her outstretched arms. A vein across his temple pulsed, his teeth clenched in anger.

Her instructor was right. Hands down the living were more hazardous than the dead.

***

The staff were divided. "That thing's feral. Dangerous even."

"Shucks, cats are harmless," said Phil. "Plus they take care of mice before they're a problem."

"But it's against the rules!" Martha was adamant. "And it won't be *you* cleaning up after them. Just imagine the overflowing litter boxes. It would be a disaster."

Lila felt awful. It was her fault. She'd apologised profusely to Rosie. The poor woman had wrung her hands, her shoulders slumping forward as she'd told Lila not to worry. Then Lila had gone to Knightly and told him she'd seen the cat by the front door; had suggested it probably got in all on its own and had nothing to do with Rosie.

Knightly had clearly been sceptical, but without proof he

couldn't do anything to Rosie. That hadn't stopped him making threats.

"If word gets out the Eldernest isn't a safe facility there will be implications. That family? The one on the tour? They were practically signing the papers before we encountered that pest. Well, not anymore. They've signed with St. Phil's."

Lila tried her best to look concerned, but her shoulder kind of lifted on its own. It was just a cat for f sakes. And there was lots of old people out there who needed a place to live. Always would be.

"You think this isn't serious?" Knightly said, shaking his head. "Cause here's the thing, if we don't have a full house there'll be staffing consequences. You understand what I'm saying?"

She understood. The man was a douche. A powerful douche.

Now looking around the staffroom her opinion was confirmed. People weren't blaming Knightly for mishandling the situation. Instead they continued on with their little minds and narrow thinking.

"The point is," Martha continued to ruminate. "It's wrong to sneak in animals. It's possibly even dangerous. And we all know that woman has been stirring up trouble, trying to get the Eldernest to bring in pets." Martha looked around piously at the other staff on break. "There are rules here. Pets are against the rules. I think she broke the rules and let that animal in on purpose."

Lila could feel her blood pulsing in her chest like a hammer. "Just because it's a rule doesn't mean it shouldn't be changed. Like, who makes these dumb rules anyway? I've heard of bookstores with a resident cat before. Why not here? Maybe some of these rules are just bullshit."

The other staff looked at Lila and then back at each other. It was Cook who cleared her throat and spoke first. "Director Knightly makes the rules. The board makes the rules."

"Look, I wouldn't follow Knightly down a dark alley if I were being chased by criminals. He cuts staff hours to increase profit margins any chance he gets. You know he does."

"He's given you a job, Lila." Cook narrowed her eyes. "It's your responsibility to abide by the rules. You aren't here to question things."

"So…we should just accept shitty rules?"

Cook didn't have a chance to answer before the nurse named Bernadette chuckled. "What makes you think you know how to run a large facility like this better than Director Knightly?" She crossed her arms over her ample chest, a condescending smile stretched across her face. "You pick up the dishes for goodness sake."

Silence descended like a blanket. That's what most of them did. Picked up the dishes, cleaned floors, washed bodies and did the laundry.

It was Phil, as usual, who broke the tension. "You're a shit disturber, Lila, and so is that Rosie. A regular old Thelma and Louise, the pair of you." He winked at Lila to take the edge off. Everyone else laughed, happy to shift the conversation.

Chad: Turning Tables

When I arrived at the Eldernest for my regular Sunday coffee with Martin, I expected to find him in the cafeteria at our regular table. Instead he was waiting for me in the lobby, pacing the well-used carpet with his hands tightly knotted behind his back. His shoulders were hunched around his ears in a way I wasn't used to seeing.

"Hey there, Uncle Martin. Aren't we having coffee?" I tried handing him the bag of requested supplies – this week it had been vanilla flavoured protein powder and sandalwood massage oil – but he ignored it and I let my hand drop back to my side.

"Mind if we took a pass today?" He glanced over his shoulder to make sure we weren't being overheard. "I thought about what you said." He took a deep breath, letting it out in a weary sounding exhale. "I've signed up for the Facebook 101 session. *The one Clara teaches.*"

I gave him a light punch on the shoulder, "Nicely done."

He gave me a lopsided grin. "I'm damn nervous. Feel like a kid on the first day of kindy-garten."

"But you look great." He was wearing a tie I didn't recognize. *Had he bought a new tie for a computer class? The old man was nervous!*

"You know what I always say: Dress the part—"

"Act the part." I finished his mantra for him. "You've got this, Romeo."

I was touched by how nervous my uncle appeared. Could Martin finally have found someone worth being nervous about?

I wanted to tell him my own good news about Lila, but how

could I explain it? Yes, there had been that first kiss. In the few weeks that had passed there had been several more, plus hundreds of texts and hours of talking about anything and everything that mattered. But more crucial than all of that was knowing the person I liked, *liked me back*.

A man like my uncle...I wasn't sure he'd understand. Charm and magnetism were his middle names. Even if he were nervous today, I'd bet money he'd never experienced a true dry spell. Growing up I'd only known Martin with a woman hanging off his arm or a female name floating through his conversations. Not always the same woman, but a woman nonetheless. Where my mother's relationship status had been static—forever single—her brother's had been remarkable dynamic; jumping and bouncing and never solitary.

"Your mom would tease me, no doubt. Trying to surf the 'net at my age. Nervous Nellie, I am. And I'll probably screw it right up too."

I gripped Martin's shoulder, trying to express everything I felt in as manly a fashion possible. "No way. You'll be great at Facebook. It's a very sociable online space." I cleared my throat, trying to get rid of the bubble of emotion that had suddenly dropped over me. "Besides, I've got a job for you. Why don't you try and find Harold? Send him something called 'a friend request.' I've got some news about the Go Fund Me page."

As Martin huffed on about "men his age not asking other men to be their friends," I pulled out my phone and opened our 'Help Harold who Helped the Elderly' campaign page. Martin put on his reading glasses and peered at the screen. "Not sure what it means, lad."

"The campaign is live. That means people can make donations. We've got $612 for Harold so far." I was, frankly, baffled.

"Well, I'll be." Martin's eyes misted over as he stared at the smart phone screen. This was turning out to be quite the emotional day for him. "Not bad at all. I wonder who these people are?"

"I don't have a clue. I'll leave the campaign active for another week or so, but then we should get this cash to Harold."

I hoped Harold would be pleased the 'Nest gentleman had wanted to do something nice for him. He must have meant a lot to them. Or, at the least, they felt guilty about his situation.

Before saying goodbye, I walked Martin to the computer room. "You know Harold's last name, right?"

"Certainly. Brown. Harold Brown. Nice, common name. Shouldn't be too hard to find."

I bit my lip, choking off a laugh. It might take a while.

Sunshine streamed into the computer room through a bank of windows. They offered a view onto the garden and walking paths behind the 'Nest and the view gave the room a calm and peaceful energy. Clara stood, her back to us, helping a woman I didn't recognize get set-up on one of the four desktops in the room.

The computers were archaic by my standards; the bulky monitors took up half the desk space, but what did it matter? Neither my uncle nor any of the other students would be picky.

Beside me Martin took a deep, raspy breath. "Here goes nothing. Wish me luck, lad," then marched into the room. I watched as he quietly took a seat in front of a computer, ran a hand over his carefully styled hair then looked back at me. I gave him the thumbs up before turning away.

I decided I'd leave Martin's bag of supplies in his room so I wouldn't have to bring them back on another day. Detouring down his hall, I hung the shopping bag on his bedroom door handle and headed toward the exit. That's when I spotted Grant.

He was sitting on a sofa by a large picture window in the hallway reading a newspaper. It was one of the things the Eldernest seemed to do well: strategically placed resting spots throughout the building that looked more like mini living rooms than tired medical waiting rooms. They all had at least one potted plant, a floor lamp and a sturdy looking couch upholstered in a dated floral fabric. Accessible, tucked into alcoves at regular intervals, but out of the way to prevent seniors from tripping on the furniture.

Grant looked up from his newspaper and smiled at me. "Hello there, Chad."

"Hey!" Of all my uncle's Eldernest friends, Grant was the one I liked best. He was easy to be around. Polite and undemanding. I sat down beside him. "I've got some news about the Go Fund Me."

I showed him the donation page and told him how much we'd raised so far. "It's really coming along."

"Sure seems to be," he nodded in agreement, "thanks to your hard work and know-how. It was good of you to help some old geezers out of a sticky situation."

"Oh heck, anytime." I cleared my throat, curious about the other project we'd worked on. "Any luck with the online dating?"

Grant chuckled. "Have you heard about Herb's new love interest?" Glee passed over his face. "She's in New Zealand. Can you believe that? He's got himself in one of those new-fangled virtual connections."

"New Zealand! I thought we set his search radius to the city limits?"

"Wasn't getting any action. He got impatient and asked me to help him adjust his profile. Took an afternoon, but I managed it. Set his limit a bit further afield." Grant was rocking with barely suppressed laughter.

"You don't say." I left laughing. It didn't hit me until much later that he hadn't offered an update on his own online dating situation. Alas, there had probably been nothing to tell. Too bad.

***

Harold's campaign drew in a few thousand dollars before the finish date. I wasn't sure how much had been donated by strangers, and how much from the guilt-ridden members of the Eldernest late night poker ring. Unfortunately, Martin had no luck locating the correct Harold Brown. Instead he'd sent a friend request to me, (which I accepted without reminding him what he'd said about men his age not requesting friendship with other men), but I refused several follow-up invitations to play online poker.

The number of virtual poker invites got so frequent I almost blocked him. It also made me nervous. What other trouble could my uncle get into online? He might be savvy with the ladies, but the internet was a whole new ball game. "You know not to give out your credit card information, right?"

"I'm not a youngster, Chad. Besides, this Facebook stuff is easy, peasy. Honestly, with the number of women on the thing I'm not sure why you had trouble finding someone." I rolled my eyes and didn't bother to respond. "You know, if things don't go the way you want with your lady friend, just let me know. I'll fix you up with one of my new women friends on the Facebook." That was not the kind of help I wanted. And besides, things were going great with Lila.

It seemed we always had something to talk about; something to agree on. Lila was particularly interested in what it was like for me being raised by a single parent. Had it affected me in any negative ways? Was there anything I wish my mom had done differently?

I told her about the good times; memories I didn't have anyone else to share with. And I told her she had nothing to worry about. "You're doing a good job. Your kid is happy, right? That's what matters."

For a woman who always appeared certain, she seemed very much in need of reassurance.

"Do you think?"

"Sure. Definitely," Besides, a person could only do what they could. There were lots of things outside a parent's control: peers, health, the price of 'cool' clothes. I bit my tongue and didn't mention those things. What good did worrying do?

***

It was Lila who ended up putting us in touch with Harold. She asked Esther in personal care who suggested she check with Phil in laundry. Phil had been only too happy to jot Harold's number down on a small square of paper. It was wrinkled and folded but still perfectly legible by the time it made its way back to me.

"Give him a call now." Lila said, radiating excitement. "I want to hear what he says." We were hanging out in a coffee shop near the One Spirit Dojo while Quinn was in class. It was the way we'd found to spend time together: squeezing it into the cracks and crannies in their already busy schedule. It didn't matter that Lila's homework was spread over the table; her focus more on it than me. I was happy enough to drink my coffee while she studied. It was heaven.

"Nah. I hate making public phone calls."

"Oh come on. No one's here." She was right. The place was deserted except us and the man behind the counter. "Besides, it's kind of fun; like telling someone they've won the lottery."

Her face was lit up with a carefree energy seldom seen, and it easily overpowered my self-consciousness. "Alright. Let's do it." I punched Harold's number into my phone. Half expecting to get voicemail, I was thinking of what message to leave when he picked up.

I launched into our story, fast and rambling. I was disjointed in the telling, but still assuming his reaction would be positive. How couldn't it be? Instead the conversation quickly descended into something like what I was used to receiving on the complaints line. Guarded at first, accusatory before long.

"How'd you get my number?"

"Er…Phil. In laundry?"

"And what's this about again?"

I carefully explained what Go Fund Me was, this time slower. "Essentially it's a fundraiser. Sometimes it's called crowdfunding? It was organized by a certain group of gentlemen from the Eldernest. Maybe you remember them. Martin MacEwan—that's my uncle—and his friends, Herbert and Grant. From the poker—"

Harold groaned. "Let's not talk about that poker thing. Let me get this straight: you've got money. To give to me?"

"That's right."

I nodded even though he couldn't see me. Lila smiled encouragingly but all I could hear through the phone was silence punctuated by muttering sighs of indecision and frustration. Finally, Harold spoke. "I'm not some charity case. I don't take handouts."

"Right, I get that. I think they just wanted to help out." I looked at Lila for help and she mouthed the words 'the baby.' Sheer genius. "It's for the baby. The money is for the baby. I understand your wife's expecting?"

That seemed to do it. He agreed to meet me on the weekend so I could pass him the money raised.

I ended the call and put my phone back in my pocket before saying anything to Lila. "That didn't go the way I thought it would. What do you think happened at that poker game anyway?"

"Phil says Harold was accused of cheating by one of the residents. That guy Edgar? He apparently went to flipping Knightly. Knightly said staff are hired to do a job, not 'swindle' seniors." She used air quotes around the word swindle. "Fired Harold on the spot."

I picked up one of Lila's forgotten highlighters and spun it absently through my fingers. "Do you think he did?"

"Did what? Swindle seniors?" Lila shrugged. "Sounds like your uncle doesn't think so or why would he have gone to all this trouble?"

She had a good point. There was also Grant and Herb who felt some responsibility to make amends, or why else would they have wanted to set up a Go Fund Me for him?

"I think you've done a good thing here." Lila squeezed my forearm and I easily forgot about Harold and his problems. Happiness radiated through my chest and down my limbs. I knew I was blushing, and I didn't care. I was on top of the world.

***

When I arrived at the tired looking pub where I'd agreed to meet Harold, I recognized him immediately from the snapshot Martin had brought to my apartment. I met his uncertain gaze and gave a sort of 'hey there' wave.

"Are you Chad?"

"That's me." I pulled out the chair across from him and sat down. Gone was the smile that had splashed across his face in the Mardi Gras picture. In its place was a pinched expression and all the frustration I'd heard on the phone. "I've got your money."

Harold's lip curled as he gave me the once over. Wow, this guy was pretty aggressive for someone about to receive free money; did it threaten his ego that much? I should have insisted on Martin doing the money transfer; he was the one who knew the guy in the first place. "I'm sorry about everything. The 'Nest guys just wanted to help out."

"You explained that on the phone. What you didn't bother explaining was why you're making me look like an old man pimp."

I halted, unsure what he was talking about. "Pardon?"

Harold's face was becoming blotchy and mottled with barely suppressed anger, and as he cracked his knuckles, I remembered the men saying he was strong. *But was he stable?* Maybe there was more to him losing his job than they realized?

"What about this: Hugh Hefner and his geriatric male bunnies? My brother-in-law loved that one." Harold let out a bark of laughter, but it wasn't very funny sounding. Hadn't Grant said he was gentle? A good guy? I shifted in my seat.

"Never...never heard of that either."

Harold took a deep breath and ran his fingers through his curly, thick hair. I guessed him to be nearly a foot taller than me, with a much longer arm span. I wanted to put some space between us but how without looking like I was terrified?

"I've got an angry mother-in-law and I'd like to know what kind of ass-wipe sets someone up like this. I'm unemployed, my wife is nearly nine months pregnant, and now some jackass makes a social media fiasco out of me? I thought it was Edgar. Trying to get back at me. Damn rat. But no. It seems it's just some computer geek." He pointed accusingly at me. "I've never even met you before, have I?"

"I...no. I don't think so." I had been right in the first place. We should have asked his permission before setting up the Go Fund Me campaign. "Look, I'm really sorry—"

Harold didn't let me finish. "Are you mad I helped your uncle have a life? Is that it? He's old, sure, but he's still a human being. There was never anything that wasn't consensual, cause believe me I would've put a stop to that." Harold ground one meaty fist into the palm of his other hand.

"Can we slow this down for a second?" I took a deep breath. "I'm sorry we didn't ask your permission about the Go Fund Me—"

"I'm not talking about the Go Fund Me. It's the dating sites that are screwing me over!"

Dating sites? "The...Plenty of Fish accounts?"

"They've a right to date. But why would you implicate me?" Harold again jabbed a finger at me. His arms looked like he picked up weights on a regular basis. Picked them up and threw them as though they were paper airplanes.

"Sorry. Implicate you?"

"My picture is all over their damn dating profiles!"

He pulled out his phone, punched some buttons then shoved it in my face. Not that he needed to. It was all coming back to me like a tractor trailer speeding down the highway. First he showed me the photo of Herbert lounging on my couch, a stern but what he called 'masculine' look on his face. Harold swiped the screen and a second image popped up. This the one of Harold and the gentlemen in Mardi Gras beads.

The picture had initially been intended for the Go Fund Me campaign, but I'd decided to use it on Herb and Grant's dating profiles too. They all seemed so happy and relaxed in the photo, a group of friends having a good time. It was a lot better photo than some of the posed shots we'd taken in my apartment. I'd made a split-second decision, never realizing there could be far-reaching implications.

"My mother-in-law is NOT happy. She's a very conservative woman."

I licked my lips and tried to swallow. The air was dry, as though every last drop of moisture had been sucked out of the pub. I could tell by the way Harold kept mashing one fist into his other hand he wanted to pound my face in, but it seemed a bit unfair. "I wonder why your mother-in-law is on Plenty of Fish?" Harold jerked forward, and just as quickly I lurched back.

"Remove the picture. Got it?"

"Sure. Right. No problem. I'll take it down." How had I gotten into this fiasco? I passed over the envelope of unmarked bills. As Harold reached out to grab it, I noticed something I hadn't expected. Something I would have missed if I'd been confident enough to look him in the eye. His hand was trembling. Under his anger was something else. Something I was familiar enough with to recognize in a split second. I knew what it was to be knocked down. Discouraged.

I quickly wished Harold well with the job search and got the hell out of there while I was still in one piece.

Back in my apartment I wasted no time loading up the Plenty of Fish site.

I started with Herb's. It was easy to crop Harold out of the photo. Why hadn't I just done that in the first place? I logged off Herb and pulled up Grant's profile next. With a click of the mouse I'd cropped his photo and I pressed the button to save the changes.

As the circle flipped around and around saving the update, my gaze caught on something else. Sexual preference: male. What the hell. How had I messed up that too?

I'd correct it now, before any harm was done. I didn't need anyone else angry with me. I moved the mouse over the edit button but then stilled my hand.

Was it an error?

I could clearly remember the gentlemen taking it in turns to sit beside me at the laptop as I rushed through the questions in eagerness to see Lila at the Sentry. I could recall Herb, then Grant telling me their age and the ridiculously younger age-range they were hoping to attract. I could easily recall the debate over which hobbies and interests would make them sound the most appealing. I even remembered the quick run-down I'd given them on how to respond if anyone was interested ('*When,*' Herb had corrected. '*When.*') What I couldn't recall was either of them explicitly telling me their orientation.

Because I hadn't asked. I hadn't thought twice about asking. That meant someone else had gone into Grant's account and initiated the update. There were only two people who knew his password. There was me; there was Grant. If I hadn't changed it, then it meant he had. If he could figure out how to change Harold's search radius, Grant could surely make changes to his own profile.

Why hadn't he just said so? He could've just said.

I rubbed the back of my neck. *Could he have?*

And what unintended consequences may have happened if he'd been overheard by the other 'Nest men? My stomach felt queasy, and it wasn't just that I'd pissed off a big guy like Harold.

I moved the mouse off the edit button and closed the Plenty of Fish account, leaving Grant's status the way it was.

PART TWO

Chad: Postie One-Two

I stopped by the pharmacy to pick up Martin's regular selections. He'd added the new Axe body wash to his list of 'must haves,' so I suspected my septuagenarian uncle would soon smell rather pubescent. It might be a nice change from the Jovan Musk. While the soap aisle was rather uneventful, the same couldn't be said for the small section of magazines and paperbacks.

Janice, my arch-nemesis from the office, stood between me and the latest GQ which Martin had requested. She was voraciously reading the back cover of a thick paperback and had yet to see me. My first instinct was to quickly sneak back out the aisle, but it was too late. Janice had somehow sensed my presence. She glanced up from the paperback and locked her hunter eyes on me. A look of shock and dislike passed between us but unlike at the office there was no cubicle half-wall to hide behind. Like a deer, I froze.

It was just me, a bottle of youthful body wash, and Janice. She clutched the paperback to her chest. It did little good trying to hide it as I could clearly see the steamy cover. It boasted a highland warrior in a rather topless state.

"Good read?" I attempted a straight face, but the corners of my mouth twitched.

Janice flushed then gave me a cold smile. "I was sorry to see that memo about the layoffs."

"Sure." My smirk disappeared. "I think everyone was." The memo hadn't said layoffs. It had said restructure, yet everyone knew that it amounted to the same damn thing.

"Oh, I wouldn't say everyone. Seniority has its perks." Ah.

Janice's favourite subject. She enjoyed slipping her numerous years of service into any conversation she could. This was especially the case in summer, when she took five weeks paid leave and the rest of us carefully budgeted out our two- and three-week allotment of freedom. We told each other five weeks without Janice was practically a holiday in and of itself.

"I worry about you younger ones. It's tough finding work right now." A look of false sympathy spread across her doughy face. She turned on her squat heel and marched away.

I didn't mean to say it. I really didn't. It just kind of bubbled up.

"Freeeeedommmmm!"

Mel Gibson would've been proud. I grabbed Martin's GQ and made a beeline for the cashier. Resentment curdled in my gut. Janice was right. It would be the bottom of the seniority heap cut first. And that, unfortunately, didn't mean her.

That night Janice seeped through my skull and somehow wrapped herself insidiously around my amygdala. The amygdala is responsible for managing anxiety, something I learned while self-diagnosing my condition at 3:00 in the morning, lying in bed, my face illuminated by my cell phone. What I was less successful discovering were help-centre desk jobs that paid a reasonable wage to live on.

Did I love my job? Well, no. I did not feel enthusiastic about answering phones with anywhere near the same kind of passion Lila used to describe the challenges of embalming a decendent after a traumatic accident. Not many people I knew had that kind of enthusiasm about their studies or their work.

If I didn't want to lose my complaint line job, it was only because it made my life comfortable. I liked not having to job-search. Or interview. Or think. It was the type of job you didn't worry about on the weekend. I arrived Monday to Friday at eight in the morning and at 4:30 sharp I took my headset off and left everything behind. Twice a month money was magically deposited in my bank account and although it wasn't a huge amount, it met my needs. It was a mediocre job, and mediocre was incredibly comfortable.

The next morning I arrived at the office sleep-deprived but determined. The job was too comfortable to lose without a fight.

My weapons of choice included a large double-double coffee, a somewhat wrinkle-free dress shirt, and a commitment to impress management with my complaint-resolution skills. It took only a few steps into the Complaints Department to understand I wasn't the only one employing the same strategy.

"Morning, Imran." I set my coffee down on my desk, eyeing my colleague's tailored paisley shirt. He'd followed me down to my cubicle, a wild look in his eyes. "Nice shirt."

"Same to you."

Imran was the kind of guy known for getting dates while working the complaint line. He was the first to crack a joke at the staff Christmas party, the first to be served at the bar when we went for drinks after work.

He ran his hand through his freshly cut hair. "Have you seen my numbers? I've racked up an 86% success rate this month; I'm well above quota but I wonder if it'll be enough?" An uncharacteristic look of stress scrunched his eyebrows together. "Where are you sitting?"

"Not sure. Maybe 75% or so?"

Imran grimaced and sucked in air between his teeth. "Buddy, you've gotta wake-up. That's barely average on the bell curve. Might not be good enough."

I could actually feel my heartrate rev up all the way to my fingertips. "I'm not worried. Why would I be worried?" I casually placed my headset on, then swiveled in my chair toward my computer screen. I wasted no time in hitting the 'Ready to Receive Caller' button and was saying hello before Imran had even turned back to his desk.

"Good morning, this is Chad. How may I help you?"

***

The pace at the office was harried and it stayed that way for two weeks. Management had given few details; only notifying employees that staff reductions would occur within the month. Anyone experiencing stress was encouraged to call the employee assistance counselling service. I broke down and called during the second week only to hear an automated recording.

"We are experiencing heavy call delays. Our wait time for a one-on-one session is currently four weeks. If you're thinking of harming yourself, please visit the nearest emergency department."

Gone were long coffees in the breakroom, and chatter between the cubicles. Everyone was trying to look like an ace employee at all times. I tried to look productive at my desk, but there was only so much cleaning out of an email inbox I could stand.

The only employees not concerned appeared to be Janice and a few of the other old-timers. Janice plodded along, answering her phone on the third or fourth ring, taking several trips to the coffee machine every day and generally keeping a gleeful eye on the rest of us. "Tsk. So much stress on the young ones."

Imran was experiencing a particularly good run on the phone lines, even for him. He'd managed to turn a rather livid customer into an up sale that morning. I, on the other hand, was more despondent than ever.

I continued to solve people's problems. That was the job. What I wasn't good at was leaving a lasting impression. I could have been Bob, Joe or in one case, Sally. In the past I hadn't cared. Now, I did.

When customer service reports could be the difference between keeping my job and being unemployed, I realized the danger of being a nameless voice on the phone.

"Of course you're memorable," Lila said, trying to reassure me. "Those sweet puppy dog eyes are hard to forget." She patted me on the cheek. Kissed my brow.

"I don't think the callers can see my eyes."

"Right. Of course." She bit her lip. "I'm sure it'll work out."

I felt like an imposter—Lila believed I was more competent than I knew myself to be. School yard picks had never worked in my favour. They worked for other guys; guys like Imran. He even had a system for dropping his name into a customer's memory bank.

"Imran, sir. That's right. Like 'Him Ran,' just drop the H."

I'd tried it myself a few times. "Chad, like the country."

"Is that a real country?"

"Yes, I believe so."

"Where is it?"

"Er...horn of...Africa?" I didn't know anything about Chad. Besides it was all likely a little too late. I started using my time between customer calls to clean up my LinkedIn profile, wracking my brain for synonyms for 'efficient,' 'hard-working' and 'completely screwed.'

***

"You're looking tuckered out," observed Uncle Martin. He was maneuvering a toothpick around his mouth with his tongue. I suppose this was one method for showing off his oral dexterity, but I wasn't convinced it would impress the ladies.

"Sorry?"

"Tuckered out. You know, tired." Martin leaned in over our usual table in the cafeteria. "Been…shaking the sheets all night, have we?" Martin winked, his head tilting in the direction of the kitchen doors where Lila could often be seen coming and going through on the weekends.

I shook my head, not because I didn't know what my uncle was talking about, but because I was not in the right headspace to respond any other way. I indeed was 'tuckered out.' The month was nearing a close and not knowing whether I'd have a job was giving me insomnia. I couldn't stop crunching the numbers; couldn't stop trying to figure out how long I could go before I would no longer be able to pay my rent.

Martin's eyes twinkled, not at all concerned with my bank balance, as he looked off into the distance and started reminiscing. "Employed in the service of Venus, we used to say."

"What? That's…an interesting phrase." I ran my hands through my hair and decided I might as well come out with it. "I'm stressed about work. They're laying off staff and I'm pretty sure I'm on the chop block."

I wondered if Lila would be disappointed when I lost my job. I could imagine no other outcome and it was one of the questions keeping me up at night. The only reason I'd stopped bringing up my layoff fears with her was because I sounded insanely insecure even to myself. Besides, between school and work and parenting she had enough on her plate.

If I lost my job it would affect absolutely everything, including the fantasy I'd been spending a lot of time thinking about: Lila and Quinn moving in with me. I didn't want to scare Lila off; we'd only been dating a few months. Still, how great would it be? It made perfect sense: they'd get out of the basement suite. *Who wouldn't want that?* I'd pay the bills and she could quit the 'Nest cafeteria job. Lila could study all day or leave for service calls that were an expected part of her funeral service apprenticeship and not worry about bills or meal prep or childcare. I could cover all that.

I'd never lived with a kid before, but I couldn't stop thinking about how wonderful it would be to hang out with Quinn and Lila on a more regular basis. I imagined Quinn and I spending Saturdays playing video games with our feet propped on the coffee table. We'd eat cereal and chips all afternoon, then pick up three phos for dinner.

I'd almost suggested it several times, but now I'd have to wait and see what happened with these layoffs. As long as I didn't lose my job it might still be possible.

I looked up to see a worried look on Martin's face.

"They won't let a smart, well-educated man like you go."

I shrugged. "Everybody's got a degree these days."

"There's always the postal service. Good job, being a postie. Have you considered a change in career? I still know a few good people around there."

"I don't know, Martin. I've heard they've stopped hiring as many people too. You know, all the automation these days."

He sighed. "True. The boss-class is always doing away with good jobs cause of these computers. But they don't run themselves. They'd be crazy to get rid of you! Everyone around here knows they've just got to ask and you'll set up their new devices just right."

"Er…about that. I saw the new poster. On the bulletin board." Martin had started advertising my services, making what appeared to be an official volunteer position out of me. 'Smart phone expert,' it read. I flushed, thinking about how proud Lila was of me. I couldn't very well admit I'd been annoyed about the whole thing, could I? "If it's a 'women only' session, you know you can't attend, right Martin?"

"I'm your assistant!"

"Well…that's true. But I think it might defeat the purpose. You know, considering what you wrote on the poster? 'One-on-one, personal and individualized support?'"

Martin grimaced. He knew I was on to him. My uncle always had an endgame in mind. And the endgame almost always involved a woman. "Are things not working out with Clara? I thought you were happy."

"I *am* happy! It's just...I'm not sure Clara is." An unusually pained expression crossed my uncle's typically carefree face. "Seems preoccupied. Always wants to play chess but not interested in...well, in anything else if you get what I'm putting down. I hate chess!"

"Maybe she's interested in someone else?"

Martin's shoulders scrunched up around his ears and his teeth were clenched. Ahhh. Not used to being jilted, now was he? "Competition from Herb?"

"Not him." Martin looked highly uncomfortable and didn't elaborate further. I decided to be merciful and let it drop.

"So anyway," I continued, "it's the job keeping me up at night. Or the worry about losing my job. Everyone's in overdrive, trying to keep their numbers up so the company will keep them."

"What do you think it'll take to stay on?"

"Not sure. Most people think it'll come down to seniority and customer-service quotas."

Martin pursed his lips around his toothpick and narrowed his eyes. "Nothing you can do about the seniority. It is what it is. The customer service though...what you need is the old postie one-two."

"Sorry?"

"The postie one-two. We used to help each other out when it came to bonuses. See, there's nothing more the boss-class likes than a happy customer. All kinds of people will call in with complaints, but it takes a real special situation for a person to report excellent customer service, see what I mean?

"We posties used to send in positive customer service cards for whoever's route we lived along. We had to be creative, mind. Use the wife's name. Document how the postie went above and beyond with a patch of ice or difficult dog, you get what I mean. Then bam! Bonus time."

"Sure. Makes sense. It's just..." My words petered out before I admitted my number one flaw. I was the everyday generic man.

The one who didn't leave an impression, either good or bad. "It's hopeless. I'm not. I don't know…memorable?"

"Come now, a nephew of *mine*? Course you are. You managed to turn Lila's head, didn't you? And after months of watching I'd almost given up hope."

I spluttered on coffee. "What? That was just spur of the moment. Unplanned. I certainly wasn't…" My voice trailed off as Martin sat back and folded his arms, the toothpick still gripped loosely between his teeth. "You knew? All that time?"

He chuckled. "I've a damn sixth sense about these things."

***

The week of the layoff deadline rolled around, and with that a heightened sense of desperation permeated the office. The mass of cubicles in the complaints department looked bare. Gone were personal items. My desk, like many others, had slowly de-cluttered. I'd secreted away my personal items in a box under my desk in the event that I would be laid off. Nothing was left but a bottle of antacids next to my computer screen.

The one exception was Janice's workspace. Spider plants hung over the walls of her cubicle. A cat calendar and various porcelain felines decorated her desk. As for Janice herself, she was methodically filing her nails when I walked past Monday morning.

"Morning, Janice."

"Good morning, Chad," she trilled. "Nice weekend?"

"Sure, just me and my favourite job search engine."

False sympathy blossomed on her face. "Oh dear. It must be hard scrambling around for what's left after us senior staff are secured. I'm just so thankful not to be playing that game, you know what I mean?"

"And what about your weekend, Janice? Do any…reading?" I gave her the sweetest smile I could manage. I enjoyed watching Janice's doughy face pinken in embarrassment. Who was this new Chad?

I sat down and clicked on my office email to see if there were any new announcements about the layoffs. Would they just email people if they were gonzo? Or maybe they'd be meeting in person with those who would be out of work? I didn't know, but like everyone else I'd find out soon enough.

There were two new internal auto messages in my inbox. I steeled myself and clicked on the first message.

"Congratulations Chad MacEwan. You've received a customer commendation:"

"Never had a good experience with your company until last week. Chad from Complaints Department settled my cellular problems. Walked through the set up and explained how to make the font larger. A stellar guy.
— *Herb, customer.*"

I didn't remember the situation, but I was not about to kick a gift-horse in the mouth. I tapped on the second email.

"It's awfully nice to have a young man explain the wifi to me. Now I can look at animal rescue listings on my phone anywhere! EVEN Tim Horton's.
— *Rosie, happy customer.*"

Rosie. Herb? *From the Eldernest?* The Wi-Fi conversation was definitely familiar. It had taken most of a Thursday evening, but it hadn't occurred on the complaints phone line. It had occurred in the social room at the Eldernest Assisted Living Lodge. Why had Rosie called my work? How did she even know where I worked?

And Herb. It was true he had a wireless plan through our company, but I'd only found that out by accident. He barely used his phone; for one thing he couldn't hear. For another he could hardly make out the text messages his daughter sent. That had been a simple fix; I'd enlarged the font size and he was now a texting fiend. It was probably coming in handy with his New Zealand 'friend.'

I picked up my desk phone and slowly dialed my Uncle's number. He answered on the second ring.

"Martin! Did you...have anyone call my work?"

"Good morning, lad. It's a fine day for the postie one-two, wouldn't you say?" Martin dropped his voice. "Is this call being recorded?"

"No. I don't think so. Martin, I'm not sure this is a good idea—"

"What do you have to lose?"

"Customer phone calls are usually traceable."

"Don't worry. Just leave it to me."

"Martin, I appreciate-"

He cut me off. "It's coffee time. I'll see you Saturday and don't forget the Brylcreem." Martin hung up the phone.

No further automated messages or announcements from management arrived in my inbox that day. There was nothing to do but answer complaint calls and wait it out.

By Wednesday we were all on high alert. Would they wait right until Friday to tell us who would be laid off? It seemed a bit heartless and I was starting to wish they'd not given any notice at all.

After lunch I opened my email to find another automated internal message.

"Chad's a whiz on the 'net. I was thinking 'bout closing my wireless account but decided against it because of him.

– *Harold, customer*"

Right. Who hadn't my uncle spoken to? I opened the bottle of antacids and ate two.

It was Thursday afternoon before they started pulling people one-by-one into the supervisor's office. I didn't have long to wait before I received a call.

"Chad McEwan? Can we see you in the boardroom?"

"Right. Of course. Right now?"

"That's correct." My stomach plummeted as I hung up the phone. Out of the corner of my eye I saw a flurry of fuchsia and purple. Without looking up I knew it was Janice, popping over the cubicle wall. Watching. Listening. Wondering what I'd been told.

I pretended I didn't know she was there and rubbed my armpit; lifted my fingers to my nose and sniffed. I heard a quick indrawn breath and looked up in time to see a look of horror on her face before she plopped back in her chair.

You couldn't say I'd learned nothing from my uncle.

***

Imran was one of the last to be called. I waited around until he was walking back down the cubicle corridor and immediately knew he was safe by the way he was practically bouncing on the balls of his feet.

"Good news, I take it?"

"Oh ya! Moving up to sales! They say I've got what it takes. I wasn't about to argue, you know what I mean?" Imran grinned, his head moving side to side like he was about to break out some dance moves. I could tell he was trying to speak in a hushed tone in respect to everyone else, but his body language was practically shouting success.

He rested his forearms on the top of my cubicle and tried to pull his face into a straight expression. "And what about you? Your meeting was before mine."

"Well, I've still got a job." I tried to smile, but I could feel the stiffness in my face. "That's good news, right?"

"Of course! Still in Complaints?"

"Right. About that." I rolled my shoulders and tried again to look as though I'd an ounce of the excitement Imran oozed. "Back in Complaints as soon as I get a small task out of the way." Imran waited. He'd find out soon enough. Everyone would. I might as well get it over with. "Something about the algorithms. I'm popular with customers in the sixty-five plus age group. It's a growing demographic, you know. Baby boomers. They've got special needs what with advances in technology."

I'd already texted Lila the news. She'd said she was proud of me. An opportunity to showcase my skills. I was pretty sure I would prefer to stay un-showcased, but I was relieved I would not be unemployed as of tomorrow.

"Special needs?" prompted Imran.

"Confidence building with tech. Simple solutions. You know. That kind of stuff." I cleared my throat, feeling panic stricken as beads of sweat ran down the back of my neck. "It's a bloody staff training video." I rubbed my forehead, ran a hand through my mussed-up hair. "They want me to work on one of their customer service campaigns. I'm supposed to, you know, get everyone pumped and adept at working with seniors." My face was on fire and I was talking a mile a minute. We all made fun of the schmucks on those internal videos. Now it would be me. "It's just, I really don't want to be in the training video, you know?"

Imran no longer cared about offending our potentially laid-off colleagues. "I can't even," he choked, bent over, holding his knees. Laughing, crying and generally trying not to piss himself. It was shortly after he wiped the tears of hilarity off his face and said goodbye that I noticed Janice.

She was carefully packing spider plants into a cardboard box. Seeing her blotchy, tear-stained face didn't feel nearly as good as I would have imagined.

In the end I carried her boxes down the elevator and waited with her for a taxi.

"What will you do?"

"Call you for advice? I'm as old as dirt, you know." For once it was Janice putting on a brave face and trying to crack a joke. "I think I'll take early retirement. It's only a few years earlier than I'd planned." She blinked, her eyes swollen and red-rimmed. "Maybe I'll find somewhere to volunteer. Do you think someone would want me?"

I nodded. Bit my tongue. Damn if the Eldernest bulletin board didn't come to mind. Cause right beside the Smart Phone Basics for Women poster had been another advertisement. A volunteer was needed to run a book club. Janice, unfortunately, would be perfect.

Quinn: Little White Lies

Quinn fidgeted as her mother read her school journal. There was nothing she could do but stand and watch and wish they'd never come to Student Showcase Night. When Ma managed to peel her eyes away from the journal, her face pressed into that plastic-pleasant look she used when she was irritated but didn't want strangers to know. This was not good. Definitely not good.

"*Why on earth* are you writing about us, sweetheart?"

Us. That's what Ma said. *Why are you writing about us?* But Quinn hadn't written about *us*. Us meant *Ma and Quinn*, didn't it? But somehow *us* had become Ma and Chad.

At first, when her mother had started 'hanging out' with Chad, Quinn had worried. Things might change, and she might not like it. But things hadn't changed. Not that much, anyway. Chad liked Clue and had good video games he let Quinn borrow. Ma even seemed happier since she'd met him. Still, Quinn didn't like that *us* no longer meant, well, *Us*.

She couldn't tell Ma that, not in the middle of her grade three classroom, with other families swirling around, admiring their children's artwork like they were supposed to be doing. They weren't supposed to be interested in things like Monday Morning Journals.

This was all Mrs. Chou's fault. She'd practically steered her mother to it the moment they entered the classroom.

"I believe you'll want to take a look at this," she'd said, a big cheery expression smeared across her face as she tapped her finger on the Quinn's journal. Just like the other student's journals, it had been sitting on top of Quinn's assigned desk, right next to her indoor sneakers. But unlike everyone else's, Quinn's was no longer a Monday Morning Journal. It was the Dating Diary.

Her mother had walked straight toward the journal like

127

a paperclip being pulled toward a magnet. She'd opened the notebook and started reading, paused, flipped a few pages and read more before looking up and stabbing Quinn with the *us* question.

Quinn clutched at her mother's hand and tried to pull her toward the art board. "Let's check out my artwork 'kay Ma?"

"Give me a sec." Ma broke eye contact with Quinn. It was a relief—to be out from under her laser-beam stare—but the relief didn't last. Ma continued flipping through the journal, stopping at random pages, reading entries and looking back at Quinn with narrow, questioning eyes.

Ma flipped back to one of the first pages. It was an entry from when Quinn first changed the Monday Morning Journal into the Dating Diary. "I don't have a—" she paused and cleared her throat. "A hot pink dress with a slit, Quinn."

"True. That's definitely true. You can see it would look good though, can't you Ma?"

Ma didn't answer. She was too busy reading.

Monday, October 3rd
Date: Friday Night Movies
Chad: Black sweater and jeans
Mom: Hot pink dress with a slit. Very HI heels

Then a drawing. Every time Quinn looked at her drawing of the pink dress, she felt triumphant. "That's totally cool," Winona had said, tapping the image of the bright pink dress with the long slit and only one shoulder strap. It was the first time Winona had said anything nice about anything in Quinn's journal. Before the hot pink dress Winona had never wanted to partner-read with her. If Mrs. Chou made Winona work with Quinn, Winona would scowl and shrug and look off into the distance as though Quinn wasn't there. Or she would wander out of the classroom and spend a long time in the girl's washroom. The Dating Diary had changed all that.

After the picture came the descriptive paragraph.

Chad and Mom had a special date this weekend. Mom spent hours getting ready. She tried on three different necklaces and asked me which one looked the best. I said the one with the biggest diamond. Then Mom and Chad went to the movies and Mom said it was very special. I think they are falling in love.

Ma was using her pointer finger to follow along with Quinn's writing. When she got to the end of the paragraph her finger stopped moving and slowly tapped the paper. Quinn could practically taste the silence hanging over them. She was glad Mrs. Chou and the other families were all on the far side of the classroom. "You've...spelled everything correctly I see."

Wow! Quinn took a breath for the first time in what felt like four minutes. That wasn't too bad. "Can we look at the art board now? I've got something to show—"

"I'm not quite done here, Quinn." Ma flipped through a few pages before stopping on another entry.

Monday, October 24th
Date: Saturday night hang-out
Chad: Jeans (no holes) and Spiderman shirt
Mom: Silver dress with spaghetti straps. Hair in bun

Her mother reached up and tucked her chin-length hair behind her ear. It wasn't quite bun length. Not really. Quinn couldn't remember her mother's hair ever being bun-length.

Mom and Chad went on a date this weekend and it was 'low-key.' Low-key is the word for a date that happens at home and you don't leave the house. It's OK for kids to be around on low-key dates. We played Clue together (my favourite game!!!!!). We ordered pizza. We watched a movie. Low-key dates are nice because you can veg-out on the couch.

Ma closed the Dating Diary. "Let's talk about this at home."

***

"It feels weird, Quinn. I'm not entirely comfortable with you writing about my relationship like that at school."

They were sitting side by side on the couch, Ma looking at Quinn and Quinn looking at the television. She couldn't tear her eyes off it even though Ma had muted the sound. It was much easier to look at the TV than at her mother; it didn't stare back at her trying to get glimpses inside her soul.

The thing Quinn's Ma didn't seem to remember about school was how hard it was if you didn't have friends. It wasn't only learning that kids had to worry about; they also had to fit in. Fitting in meant people *wanted* to partner read with you and it also meant you had friends to play with at recess without even thinking about it.

"I'm just confused," Ma continued. "Can you help me understand why you're…documenting my relationship with Chad? And the fake clothes…you know life's not a fairy tale, right?"

"I know."

"And you know there's no guarantees, right? Sometimes dating is just that—dating. Lots of the time people don't end up staying together." Ma gently tugged on Quinn's chin, so Quinn had to turn and face her. "There are no guaranteed happily ever afters. Even with like, the best clothes. Sometimes it works. Sometimes it doesn't."

"I *know*, Ma."

"Good. Cause honestly, Quinn, you've kind of scared me. I like Chad, I really do. He's a great guy, but I don't want you to get too attached. I've no idea what will happen. Dating doesn't work like Disney, you understand?"

Quinn's face flushed. She wished she could float right into the muted television. She knew all this already. Ma had told her plenty of times. Anyway, her Dating Diary wasn't about wishing for some other kind of life…or at least not how Ma was thinking about it.

The Dating Diary was a friend magnet. It was dating Jessie and Ella and even Winona wanted to know about, and it was only Quinn who had an up-close point of view.

On Mondays when everyone else wrote about their hockey tournaments and ski trips, birthday parties and visits with non-custodial parents, what was Quinn supposed to write about? There were only so many times you could write about playing Clue or about going to the T & T to grocery shop with your grandfather. No one else had a mother who worked on weekends and everyone else seemed to have loads of money to do all kinds of fun stuff.

At her old school Quinn was invited to birthday parties and

to her friends' homes after school. She hadn't been invited to any parties or to anyone's home since moving to the new school. And as for non-custodial parent, Quinn didn't have one of those. She didn't even realize that was a problem until this year.

But that was all behind her now. The Dating Diary had made Winona and Ella and Jessie argue over who would get to partner read with Quinn first. The Dating Diary has made her almost part of the squad.

When Quinn first asked Ma what a squad was, her mother said, "You've got to be kidding me. A squad? Is that a thing?" It was. It definitely was. Winona and Ella and Jessie were in the squad, but it was Winona who made the decisions: in or out. Right now she was deciding about Quinn. Ma didn't understand about the squad and she didn't remember what it was like not to fit in.

"Do you have any questions, Quinn?" Ma squeezed Quinn's knee, trying to get her attention. "Because you know you can ask me anything. Any time, right?"

"Nope. No questions."

"Alright. From now on I'd like you to keep my personal life out of your school assignments. That's fair, isn't it?"

Quinn nodded so it looked like she was agreeing, but really she was nodding at the TV.

"I didn't know you were so into fashion. All those cool clothes… are you saying you don't like the clothes I wear in real life?" They both looked down at her mother's knee where it stuck out of the hole in her jeans. Wai Po hated those jeans.

Ma chuckled. "Holes are cool. Some people pay money for these."

Quinn smiled. She knew this was Ma's way of dropping the horrible conversation about the Dating Diary. Finally! She hoped it would never come up again.

***

On Monday Mrs. Chou told the class, "Pull out your Monday Morning Journals. Let's get some thoughts down on the weekend and then we'll split into small groups to partner read."

Quinn pulled her journal out from her desk, still wishing her mother hadn't read it, but at least it was over. There was no reason for Ma to read it before the end of the year, and maybe it could just magically disappear beforehand…in the recycling bin. For now,

Quinn still needed it.

> Monday, November 5th
> Date: Friday night dinner
> Where: Spaghetti Factory
> Chad: Plaid shirt and jeans
> Mom: Off the shoulder sweater with sleeves that end in a point on the back of her hand. Lots of bling.
>
> Chad got a promotion at work and on Friday we celebrated with Chad's family! Chad's family is his uncle named Martin. Martin has very white hair and Xtremely straight and shiny teeth. We went to Spaghetti Factory because it has a nice menu and not too much background noise. Mom says background noise isn't good for old people. Besides, quiet restaurants are more romantic. We made a toast to Chad and Mom gave him a kiss. It was a quick kiss, but still a public kiss. They must be in true love to public kiss.
>
> Chad's Uncle smiled a lot and said Chad was a very lucky man. I agree. My Mom is beautiful.

Quinn read over her descriptive paragraph and then erased the period after beautiful. She added *and very, very smart*. If her mother did end up reading the journal again maybe that would help.

"Your Mom sure has a lot of nice clothes," Ella said.

Quinn nodded. "Ya. She's into fashion."

"But it's strange," said Winona. "How come she never wears that kind of clothes when she drops you off in the morning?" Her eyes narrowed as she tapped her pencil on the desk.

"Oh, dating clothes aren't for every day. When you're dating you buy all new clothes just for going out." It had come out of Quinn's mouth easy, just like knowing dolphins were grey or that ten times ten was a hundred. "What you've seen is my mom's school clothes and those are like *completely* different. They don't even go in the same closet."

Ella and Jess nodded. It made perfect sense.

"Your mom's in school?" quizzed Winona.

"Yup. College." Quinn folded up the Dating Diary and turned to Jess. "Your turn."

Questions were nice but sometimes too many questions could be difficult. It was hard to keep the answers straight.

Clara: Heart on Fire

The Eldernest Rom Com Book Club

First Tuesday of every month
1:30 in the Fireside Lounge
(All puzzlers have been asked to respect this time
for the readers!!!!)

We will start promptly at 1:30 leaving plenty of time to enjoy the Tuesday Chowder Lunch Special.

Serious readers only!!

Members are asked to make book club a priority!!! If you miss more than 2 meetings you will be asked to leave the group!! We are a FUN group and our reading selections will include: Chick-Lit, Historical Romance and Rom-Coms (that's Romantic Comedies).

We will *NOT* be reading murder mysteries, westerns or crime related materials.

The volunteer facilitator: **Janice Shultz** has over twenty-five years' experience in the telecommunications industry. An avid reader, she has been an active member of the RRFC (Romance Readers Fan Club) for ten years! She has attended many book signings and author readings and will share **exclusive** information about local romance-genre book signings with Eldernest Book Club members.
Be in the know!!!!

Read books now!!!!

Clara read through the poster hanging on the Eldernest bulletin board for a third time. She had a terrible feeling of *déjà vu*. It reminded her of waiting with those fluoride trays crammed in your mouth at the dentist, with one small difference. There was nowhere in the lobby to spit. No mechanism for suctioning up the bitter taste in her mouth. Clara had no option but to swallow and face the truth: she had been replaced with a rampant exclamation-point-user, rom-com reader, fan-clubber named Janice.

It was agonizing. And yet she couldn't walk away. Couldn't tear her eyes from the poster.

Rom-com. *Was that even a word?* And bragging about being a member of a fan club? Where had the social director found this Janice? And why, on God's green earth, was Janice preferable to herself, a retired librarian and avid reader of *actual* literature?

It was her the social director had approached in the first place. "Call me Barbara," she always said upon introduction; it didn't seem to matter if you'd already met the woman. "I've a new programming idea I want to discuss with you, Mrs. Cardinal. Everyone raves about your computer class. And with your background in the library…this will be right up your alley." Barbara squeezed Clara's arm in excitement and grinned. Her unnaturally long eyelashes caused her to blink sluggishly and Clara wondered if their weight strained Barbara's eyelids. Trying not to stare, she looked down at her skirt and pretended to remove a stray piece of lint.

"It certainly sounds like something I would enjoy."

Clara spent an afternoon strolling through the bookshelves at the public library, writing down titles, then on second-thought scratching out some and circling others. She chose classics which would be sure to generate meaningful discussion and wasted no time in depositing the finished list in the social director's mail slot. She asked for feedback as a courtesy but knew she wouldn't receive any. The list was good. It needed no improvement.

When Barbara tracked Clara down in the social room to discuss the list, Martin had winked from across the chess table, and she'd flushed with pleasure when he announced to those around them, "Clara's helping start a book club for the 'Nest."

***

The social director's cubbyhole office was papered in posters of active seniors wearing brightly coloured pantsuits with matching headbands. The outfits were long out of fashion, but the posters looked as crisp and bright as though they'd been pinned up yesterday. Clara chose a worn, upholstered chair and sat down while Barbara perched on the edge of her desktop. In one hand she held Clara's list and with the other she tapped a purple marker against her track-pant covered knee.

"I see you've gone to a lot of trouble, Mrs. Cardinal. This is certainly a serious reading list you've proposed." She cleared her throat and leaned toward Clara, her eyes as wide as her false lashes would allow. "Here's the thing. People have requested titles that are *lighthearted*."

"Surely Anne of Green Gables then—"

"Lighthearted *and* adult content."

"Adult? Let me assure you, these are all very much worthy of the adult mind."

Barbara nodded agreement. "So true. Absolutely. I'm a huge fan of...Fahrenheit 451. Who isn't, right? It's just the folks I've chatted with are hoping for something...well, entertaining. A bit of escapism from the everyday. You've heard of beach reads, right?"

"Beach reads?" Clara looked left then right as though she would spot someone else in the office wearing a floppy hat and sandals. The beach, with its uneven surfaces could be a dangerous place for seniors. "I'm not sure anyone around here...goes to the beach?"

"I'm talking about the *feeling* of going to the beach." Barbara grinned and started waving her arms in a hula dance imitation. Clara blushed on the social director's behalf and tried not to look at the quivering flesh of her underarms. "Why don't you go back over your list with these principles in mind, hmm?"

Barbara took the lid off the purple marker and beside Clara's carefully constructed list of literary greats she wrote: Romance. Escape. Lighthearted. Humour. She added 'Beach' in quotations in case Clara forgot she'd meant a metaphorical beach, and underneath a happy face for good measure. "It would be ideal if the selections were available in a variety of sources—large print, audio. Sound like a plan?"

Clara picked up her tarnished list and left the office.

In a short five minutes she'd gone from being a well-respected, albeit retired, librarian to the compiler of cheap bodice rippers *slash* beach read paperbacks.

No. She would not put an updated list together. Instead she filed her rejected offering in the gray metal filing cabinet she kept in her room, under P for 'prose.' That evening when Martin asked how the meeting had gone, she shrugged. "I've decided to give it a pass. I'm just too busy volunteering with the computer class." Martin accepted her explanation and didn't press further. That was the last she'd heard about the book club until seeing the announcement on the bulletin board.

"Sure looks interesting, doesn't it?"

Startled, Clara looked down to see Rosie had sidled up beside her without her noticing. Clara had still not managed to tear her eyes off the poster.

"I bet you're excited—a book lover like yourself." Rosie rubbed her hands together in anticipation. "I can't wait to find out what wonderful stories we'll get to enjoy."

"I usually read more literary fiction. This..." Clara pointed to the poster. "Historical Romance. Rom-Com. Not my cup of tea, I'm afraid. Chicklit. What is chicklit?"

"Oh, it'll be fun! You won't want to miss out."

Clara shrugged and managed a small upturn of her lips. She wouldn't be going.

***

In the coming days there was no avoiding the book club chatter. The Eldernest residents were like children the day before Halloween, eager for the program to begin. Clara felt bitter and envious and told herself she didn't like candy anyway.

"Who's going to book club?" Rosie asked whenever she entered the social room. "I love the outside volunteers. Fresh ideas—like your nephew, Martin. He's just ace on the smart phone."

Martin smiled. "So true. I'm afraid I won't be going to book club though. Not that I don't like a bit of romance," he winked at Clara. "I'm just not much for reading."

"I'm going to suggest we read something spicy." Felicity said with a sly grin.

"Spicy?" said Herb. "Don't think cookbooks are allowed, Felicity. And they've outlawed suspense too! I don't know what they've got against suspense." A frown wrinkled Herb's forehead. "It's almost like they don't want men to join."

"Men can join," said Felicity. "But we aren't reading any of those Tom Clancy's. You've got to accept the book club is going to be working through a certain genre of literature."

"Literature, you say?" Clara didn't bother hiding her eye roll.

"My, my. Edgy, are we?" Felicity smiled sweetly at her and Clara felt her body temperature rise. "Perhaps you should try a multi-vitamin. Something good for moodiness."

Clara forced a smile onto her face, unwilling to give Felicity any more ammunition. "I'm sure those formulaic reads are enjoyed by many, but I'm afraid I'm just not a fan." Then she riffled through the stack of magazines on the coffee table, in hopes of finding a distraction.

"Oh Clara, won't you change your mind?" Rosie asked, her forehead wrinkled in concern. "You might be pleasantly surprised! Try at least one meeting before making up your mind, won't you?"

Clara smiled noncommittally. Her mind was made up as surely as Felicity's forehead had received a recent shot of Botox.

***

Linus had been a reader. Martin was not.

Which was fine. *Of course* it was fine. Martin had his men's health magazines and the newspaper. He kept himself busy. She kept herself busy too.

Martin had his regularly scheduled visits to the barber and that nephew of his—always needing some cheering on and encouragement.

She had the computer class, her facetime with the grandkids and emailing her son who was overseas on a work contract. And twice a week she read to Linus.

She stuck to his favourites: political thrillers and Soviet espionage affairs. Not because Linus asked for them—he wasn't able to do that—but because they were the type of stories he'd always chosen for himself. Reading was the one thing they'd done together; their pillows propped against the headboard, bedside

137

lamps on. It had been their nightly ritual, spent in companionable silence, for decades.

That had ended, like everything else, with Linus's stroke.

Since things with Martin had extended beyond, well…beyond chess, the bi-weekly reading to Linus was a constant reminder everything wasn't quite what it should be. Paragraph after paragraph, guilt edged in on her happiness, anchoring her to the past. If only Linus could give her the go-ahead. The absolution. But that wasn't something he could do.

She'd thought being in a relationship with Martin would be a one-time decision: a person makes a choice and that was the way it was. But no. It involved repeating the decision day after day. Spending alone time with Martin. Reading to Linus. Balancing one night against the next. At first the excitement and warmth that came from spending time with Martin had been enough to silence any guilt, but as the weeks went by Clara's feelings of culpability grew.

The comfortable, everyday moments with Martin were marred. They'd be squeezed beside each other on her twin bed and a sudden thought would scuttle across her horizon; she was not a loyal person. Or in the cafeteria. A warm touch of Martin's hand on her shoulder drew backward glances from the caregivers and she could see the judgement in their eyes. Clara was a callous and uncaring wife.

A clean break would've been better. Easier.

But what kind of person wished for something like that?

***

It was the guilt that drove Clara to the inaugural meeting. She needed a distraction, that was all. She wouldn't actually *read* their romance fodder. All Clara was doing was sizing up the new volunteer—finding out who this Janice was—and for a short while distracting herself from the dilemma she was in.

She chose a seat in the back.

"I thought we would start with some rules." The volunteer, Janice, smiled at the group of assembled seniors like a grade one teacher in September. Her lipstick was an exact match for the bright magenta of her sweater set. "They're just to keep things fair and focused." She looked down at the paper she held in her hand, and Clara could see her fingers fumbling with the edges. "Number one: Read the book. That's simple, right?" Janice looked up and smiled at the group of seniors seated before her. "Number two: To each their own. We might not all agree, and that's okay. Number three: Let the group leader—that's me," Janice paused and touched the space between her throat and her ample bosom, "know if you will be away, for any reason, whatsoever. We've got to have a full group for full discussions, don't we?"

Clara stifled a sigh. It was as though the volunteer thought she was Moses reading the Lord's ten commandments on Mount Sinai.

And Clara had to listen because against her better judgment, she was there. She'd had to do something to avoid the guilt. She bit on the edge of her thumbnail and winced. There was nothing left for her teeth to grab on to. When had this nail biting gotten so out of control?

***

If it were difficult for Clara to avoid book club chatter before the first meeting, it was impossible to avoid the reading-fever that swept the Eldernest afterward. Janice's first selection was entitled Heart on Fire. The cover featured a dehydrated looking man, his arms hairless and tan, standing beside a barbeque. He wore an apron over his trousers and no shirt.

Rosie, her body folded into the social room couch, gasped. "You can do that?" she asked no one in particular, her eyes never leaving the page in front of her. She'd spent the day reading at breakneck speed.

"Do what?" said Felicity. "What page are you on?" She picked up one of the copies sitting on the coffee table and started flipping through.

"Could you pipe down, ladies?" Herb picked up the remote control and pointed it vigorously at the television set, but the volume was already as loud as it would go. "I can barely hear the sports over your hollering."

***

Clara couldn't sleep. She didn't like using pills, but her anxiety was keeping her up more and more frequently. Her son's recent email had left her restless. He held out hope, had asked if there

139

had been changes in his father's vegetative state. She didn't blame him, regardless of the straight facts the doctors had laid out for him. Any good son would keep on hoping.

Clara had written a short response back, *No change. Seems content.*

Linus might be content, but she wasn't. She had yet to mention anything to her children about Martin and didn't know if she should. She didn't want to. She feared what their reaction would be.

Her circular thoughts weren't helping her sleep; they only made her feel more anxious. What she needed was a distraction. Something mind-numbing. Lying in bed she thought of the book. Might there be a copy someone left in the social room? At this time of night there would be no one to see if she happened to flip through it, reading a few pages here and there to help her sleep.

Pulling herself out of bed Clara put her housecoat on over her night clothes and slipped her feet into her warm slippers. The Eldernest hallways were deserted but the social room was not. In the soft lamplight sat Herb, reclined in his favourite armchair. He was wearing a pair of reading glasses and in his hands was an open copy of Heart on Fire.

She cleared her throat. Startled, Herb dropped the book as though it were a hot potato.

"Can't sleep." He said, a blush creeping up his neck. Clara couldn't help smiling. "Nothing much else to read around here," he added. Neither of them looked at the bookshelves spilling over with second-hand novels, or the magazines stacked on the coffee table.

Clara tightened her housecoat belt and took a seat on the coach across from him. "Fill me in, won't you Herb? I couldn't get past the first page. What's all the excitement about?"

"It's got more sauce than a rack of ribs, that's for sure."

Herb was having trouble making eye contact with her and sensing his desire to change the subject Clara searched for something else to say. She didn't share his love for football and didn't know much else about him. She bit her lip. Should she ask? She wasn't sure, but what else was there to talk about? And it wasn't like anyone would overhear them. "Martin mentioned the online dating. Any luck?"

Herb snorted and slapped his hand down on the armrest. "He did now, did he? Figures." He shook his head. "Well, Clara, to tell you the truth it's a bit tough these days. A difficult market. And besides, I miss my Annabel."

Clara's eye's widened. "Weren't you divorced?"

"Sure, sure. You can miss someone even if you're divorced, can't you? Nothing's ever as black and white as they'd make you believe."

Wasn't that the truth.

Herb picked up the copy of Hearts of Fire sitting on his lap and tossed it onto the coffee table between them. "I say, Clara, don't give up on it yet. Page 135 seems rather interesting if you catch my drift."

Clara laughed but shook her head. "Oh, I don't know, Herb. I'm more of a—well, I'm not sure a person who admires the classics would enjoy a guilty pleasure read. The two just don't seem compatible in the same person."

Herb eyed her for a moment. "I don't see why not. Though you've got to answer that for yourself, I suppose?"

They sat quietly in the glow from the lamplight, neither interrupting the other's quiet contemplation.

***

She told Martin in the cafeteria. The tables around them were empty, giving the feeling of privacy which was hard to come by at the Eldernest, especially during the day time. "I'm not built for this, Martin. This shifting and balancing. This…ambiguity." Under the table she clutched her hands together in a firm grip. "Maybe it's not right. Otherwise why haven't I been able to tell my son?"

Martin nodded, barely a worry showing on his face. "You know what I've always said. We can always go back to just playing chess. No problemo. And when things change—"

"Thank you, Martin." A huge weight lifted from her chest, and Clara couldn't keep the relief from her voice. "That's what I need, I think. The chess. For now."

A feeble smile touched the corners of Martin's mouth. "Of course, my dear. Of course."

Rosie: Night Search

How could this have happened? Rosie had been extra careful; always double checking and triple checking her door was tightly closed whenever Mr. Terrance visited. Not only had she let the PET-ition die (at least until she could figure out what was the best strategy for moving forward) but not one cat-related word had passed her lips in weeks. As for Mr. Terrance's mealtimes, she'd curtailed those too. Now she only fed him after nine at night when most of the other Eldernest residents were sleeping.

But somehow, some way, her door was open a smidgen and Mr. Terrance, who she could've sworn was curled up at her feet, was nowhere in sight.

She hadn't meant to drift off. She'd been sitting in bed, propped up by pillows, reading the latest book club selection. It was feeling the paperback slip from her hands that made her eyes fly open. How long had she been drifting off?

Too long. That darn door! Rosie groaned. Normally she gave it a firm push of the handle until a little click was heard. Otherwise it had a way of easing open on its own. Had she forgotten to do that?

"Terry!" Fear made Rosie's voice a hissing whisper. "Mr. Terrance, where are you?" On shaking feet she climbed out of her raised bed and looked underneath. Not there. She swished the long curtains away from the wall, but he wasn't there either. It was possible he'd leapt onto the windowsill and returned to his wild domain, Dear Lord she hoped he'd done that, but with the door to her suite open…Rosie wouldn't be able to rest knowing Terry could very well be rambling through the Eldernest hallways.

If anyone saw Mr. Terrance the consequences would be devastating; dark possibilities spun through her mind at a sickening rate. If Director Knightly was feeling lenient Rosie might be assigned a room on the second floor: the unit where people could no longer care for themselves. Their windows didn't open more than an inch or two and there would be no way for Terry to visit.

If Director Knightly was feeling less than lenient the consequences could be much grimmer. It would be the animal shelter for Terry. The shelter that euthanized cats no one wanted. Sure, some were adopted, but an old stray like Mr. Terrance? He didn't stand a chance. A rising sense of panic stuck in Rosie's throat and she shivered.

And an old stray like Rosie? She didn't stand a chance either.

Swallowing her panic, Rosie slipped on her housecoat and sturdy runners then peeked out the door. The dimly lit hallway was deserted. There was just enough light for Rosie to tell no four-legged animal was waiting conveniently within sight.

She looked to the left then the right; the hallway stretching in both directions. Which way would Terry have gone? He was in a strange place. An unfamiliar place where he had been yelled at and chased. He didn't have any friends here except Rosie.

She had no time to waste. She went with her gut and headed toward the common rooms. As she passed by closed bedroom doors Rosie heard snoring and the occasional hum of a lone television. The forced air through the heating vents whirred and rattled.

As she searched the long corridor Rosie's mind tossed around plausible excuses in the event she crossed paths with anyone. Walking the halls at night wasn't prohibited, but it also wasn't encouraged. The staff would gently and firmly guide residents back to their rooms, reminding them they needed their rest; of the importance of sleep. If Rosie didn't comply it might be reported. Could it be used against her?

Rosie looked down at her worn terrycloth house coat. The blue material had been snagged in several places by Mr. Terrance's sharp claws causing loose threads to unravel. A warm blush crept over her skin as she recalled what Director Knightly had wrote in his annual client-subsidy report. Unkempt. Possibly declining.

At times confused.

A concern to be watched.

Reading the report had been a terrible upset, but apparently not for her daughter. Kathleen had been nodding her head as though she agreed with every line!

Rosie had balled her shaking fists under the table. She'd wanted to tell Director Knightly it was a bunch of B.S., but she had also been scared. What would be the consequences of acting out? So instead she'd swallowed her anger and tried her best to stay under the radar.

She had to find Mr. Terrance.

Turning a corner, the social room doorway came into view. Light spilled out into the dim hallway and she could hear the low murmur from the television. Carefully, heart racing, Rosie made her way to the entrance and pressed herself into the wall just outside the doorway. No one was shouting or indicating in any way they'd seen a stray cat. That was a good sign, wasn't it? But if Terry were minding his own business, curled up on some bookshelf or under the puzzle table while some person watched television, Rosie would have a dickens of a time trying to get him out unseen.

Rosie curled her fingers around the door frame, then leaned forward so she could peer into the social room like a spy.

It was deserted except for Herbert. Or Herb, as he liked to be called these days. He sat in his favourite recliner near the television, his walker within arm's reach. By the way his chin folded toward his chest she guessed he had drifted asleep.

That was lucky. It was hard to notice an intruder, even a shaggy ginger one, if you were sleeping.

Rosie scanned every surface in the room: the puzzle table. The bookshelves. The stacking chairs and coffee station. Mr. Terrance wasn't in sight. Could he be on the couch across from Herb? Rosie tiptoed into the room until she had a clear view of the couch, but it was empty.

"Mr. Terrance," she whispered. "Come here, Mr. Terry," but nothing.

Herb was all alone. He'd be better off with a cat curled up

beside him. Rosie knew it, but what could she do? She had tried her darnedest.

Where to now? The cafeteria? That made sense. Rosie crept back out to the hallway and decided on the longer route to the kitchen. She took the long way to avoid the nursing station.

A quick pull on the double doors revealed the cafeteria had been locked for the night. At least that was one place ruled out.

Where to look now? Rosie's panic was turning to dread in her stomach, and without a better plan she decided to return to her room and check if Terry had returned on his own. Her mind made up, Rosie turned and ran smack into a starched uniform.

"Uph!" Nurse Bernie reached one hand out to steady Rosie and with the other clutching her round stomach which Rosie had just rebounded from. "Nearly winded me, Mrs. Dylan. Are you alright?"

Rosie tried to look natural but found it hard to breathe with her heart racing so fast. "Never better!"

"Whatever are you doing up so late?"

Rosie had never come close to a full-on heart attack before, but she imagined this was exactly what it would feel like. Her heart pounded so hard it was difficult to pull air into her lungs. She walked over to the wall, resting her hand on the handrail that ran along all the hallways in the facility.

Nurse Bernie frowned. "I'm sorry, did I startle you?" The nurse placed her hand on Rosie's shoulder, her firm grip massaging Rosie's shoulder through her terrycloth housecoat. This could be trouble.

Nurse Bernadette was a new hire. She'd only been here a few months, a replacement for Harold, the previous night nurse. Like many other new hires, she was known to be a stickler when it came to the rules. They all started out that way. Most of them relaxed with time; a few became increasingly tyrannical.

Rosie peeked at the nurse's face, looking for clues the woman had been chasing a feline through the facility. Her expression was relaxed, perhaps concerned for Rosie's welfare, but there was nothing to indicate she was on an unexpected wildlife hunt. Rosie calmed a fraction.

"Why don't we get you back to your room? It's rather late, and rest is important for our health."

"Right. Okay." Rosie nodded and started shuffling up the darkened hallway. Bernie walked along beside her. "I can go back on my own."

"I'm sure you can, but these hallways can be confusing. They all look the same at night, don't they?"

It was a question, but it wasn't a question. Nurse Bernie grasped Rosie's hand in hers and placed it in the crook of her arm as though Rosie needed a guide back to the East Wing. "I must say, I'm surprised to see you up at this hour. You aren't usually one for night wandering, are you?"

Rosie's face flushed, and she twisted her head to look at Nurse Bernie. Bernie winked back at her as though they were sharing secrets. But what secrets? Rosie's mind raced for a cover-up story. "I was having trouble sleeping. Thought I'd watch the late shows with Herb for a bit."

The nurse's eyebrows rose like two hairy birds. "Herbert? Well, I must say. A lucky man to have such fine company."

"Oh, he fell asleep. And the television wasn't helping so I turned it off and thought maybe I'd go back to my room and read a book. All alone. Just me. No one else."

The nurse placed her free hand on top of Rosie's fingers where they rested on the crook of her arm and gently squeezed. "It can be lonely, can't it? I think Herbert might be more attentive during the daytime hours. Maybe try then?"

"What? Oh. No. I mean. He's fine enough but I don't like football that much. You know, I think I'm feeling ready to sleep now. Good night."

Rosie smiled so as not to appear rude and pulled her hand away. Her bedroom door was in sight. If Mr. Terrance had made his own way back, Rosie didn't want him to pop out at the sound of voices.

She walked swiftly to her room and firmly closed the door behind her. In the darkness she leaned her back against it and listened to Nurse Bernie's receding footsteps. When she could no longer hear them, she crossed her fingers and counted out twenty slow seconds before turning on her lamp.

"Terrance," she hissed, "Mr. Terrance." She carefully got down on all fours and looked under her bed, under her chair, behind the curtains and before pulling herself back up. Terry had either come back to the room and left out the open window or he was still roaming the halls of the Eldernest.

What was she going to do? Rosie rubbed her hands together trying to stop them from shaking. She had no choice. She had to keep looking and pray she found him before anyone else did.

She opened her bedroom door and for the second time that night left her room. She would try the opposite direction.

Wait. What was that? It sounded like yelping or hissing or, or...

Rosie picked up her pace and hurried 'round the corner. Standing in the middle of the hallway was Martin, an orange ball of fur wrapped around his leg.

"Get off!" he yelped, stomping his foot on the linoleum in a frantic effort to shake the cat.

"Calm down, Martin!" Rosie raced forward, making soothing sounds to Terry. "Hush now, kitty. Hushhhhh!" She put her hands around the hissing cat, and one-by-one untangled each claw from Martin's thigh.

"That's no kitten, Rosie. It's an asshole tomcat. Tried to tear my leg off." Martin might have been whispering but his tone was as hot as sausage sizzling in a frying pan. Tear drops had formed in the corners of his eyes and he rubbed his leg with shaking hands. "I didn't do anything to it. He just attacked me."

As for Mr. Terrance he burrowed his giant orange head into Rosie's neck, his claws retracted as though he were an innocent. "Oh, Martin. Please don't tell. They'll take him."

"I've probably got the friggin' rabies and you don't want me to say anything? My damn leg is bleeding!" A pin-drop of blood had seeped through his trousers.

"He's not got rabies. He's bitten me before and see, I'm just fine." Rosie nodded her head and Martin starred at her; his jaw hanging open.

"Says who?"

"I won't let him back inside the Eldernest, Martin, I promise. It's just if they take him—"

Loud footsteps sounded from down the corridor. They were coming from the same direction as Rosie's room. A look of panic passed between her and Martin. Would Martin tell or would he help? She had no time left to argue. Cat in hand Rosie hightailed it in the opposite direction of whoever was approaching.

But where to hide? She turned the corner, onto another long hallway of closed bedroom doors. She was on the edge of panic when Martin caught up to her, grabbed her elbow and pulled her toward one of the closed doors. He knocked rapidly. Paused, knocked again.

"Come on..." he said.

He raised his hand a third time when the door creaked open. There stood Felicity.

Felicity's hair was set in neat rows, one curler after the other. Her face was void of make-up; her signature arched eyebrows had vanished. She gave Martin and Rosie the once over before her eyes narrowed on the cat.

"Good God."

"Please, Felicity," said Martin. "It's an emergency."

Felicity glared at Martin even though it was Rosie holding Mr. Terrance. The footsteps were getting louder, closer by every second and Felicity must have heard them too because she sighed, stepped back and allowed them to squeeze in. Quick as lightening Rosie closed the door.

Had they made it? Would they escape detection?

In the hallway the sharp footsteps slowed outside Felicity's room. Rosie met Felicity's eyes, met Martin's. In the silence Felicity reached for the light switch and turned it off, plunging them into darkness.

They heard the door handle squeak as it turned, the door swinging open smoothly on its hinge. Nurse Bernie's silhouette filled the doorway. She flicked Felicity's light on and looked at each of them in turn before her eyes settled on Mr. Terrance.

"Give. Me. That. Cat."

Felicity's voice was steel. "Pardon me? I don't believe you knocked."

Martin cleared his throat. "Which cat? This one?" He pointed at Terry as though there were more than one cat in question. "He's mine. I brought him in for my lady love."

Felicity scoffed. "Wrong room, if that's the case."

"This cat is a living demonstration of my love. Although... it's turned out to be, er...a poorly though-out decision. Rosie is helping get him back outside, isn't that right?" Rosie looked from the nurse to Martin and nodded weakly. Martin, for his part, didn't take his eyes off the nurse. He looked remarkably put together for the middle of the night, not one strand of hair out of place, and he flashed a debonair grin. Rosie could tell he expected it to work. It always worked.

"I've had enough of your gallivanting, Martin. You must have me mistaken with some other nurse. I'm writing this incident up and the report will be on the director's desk in the morning." She pointed at Rosie. "This is a confused, lonely woman and you aren't helping matters. You're making it worse."

The nurse reached for the cat. Terrance lunged toward her hand, exposing a set of sharp, yellow fangs. The nurse jumped back. "You've got to be kidding me." A deep red burned Nurse Bernie's cheeks. "I'm calling for backup. You." She jabbed a finger at Rosie, a look of profound disappointment on her face. "Step back with that nuisance so I can get by."

Rosie shuffled further into Felicity's room letting the nurse edge over to Felicity's emergency call button. Bernie pressed the brightly lit red square and immediately a voice spoke over the intercom. "This is the nurse's station. Can I help you, Felicity?"

"This is Bernadette," said the nurse. "I need some assistance in room 14B A-sap. We've a pest on the premises."

For several moments' static passed on the intercom before the voice responded. "What type of assistance do you need?"

"I don't know! A box? Gloves! Just get down here." She let go of the call-button, and muttered, "I'm not paid enough for this shit."

Martin coughed and spluttered as though covering laughter. Bernie glared at him before turning her back and walking back to the hallway. "None of you move."

Martin might find the situation funny, but Rosie did not. She sat down on one of Felicity's upholstered chairs and stroked the top of Mr. Terrance's head. Tears and snot streamed down her face and she didn't care. Martin tried to offer her a Kleenex from the box Felicity kept on her glass coffee table but stopped when the cat batted his claws at him.

"They'll take him to the shelter," sobbed Rosie. "He'll be euthanized." It had taken weeks, dozens of weeks before Mr. Terrance would allow her to touch him. Now he was cuddled under her chin, purring like a baby with no idea what terrible things were in store.

Felicity sighed. "No one wants him, Rosie."

"I want him."

Felicity rolled her eyes and walked over to the bay window. "You know the rules. You've been told the rules." Even through her tears Rosie could see that Felicity's room looked nothing like hers. It was though it existed in a completely different building. It was double the size, furnished in cherry wood and thick carpets.

"It's completely *outrageous* that you've implicated me in this. That cat *smells*. Can you not smell him, Rosie? He's probably been rolling in the garbage. Or worse. I've been saying for weeks there was something that smelled in the East Wing. Something wild." Felicity moved toward the window and opened it as wide as it could go. "I need some fresh air."

Felicity glanced back toward the nurse. She was standing in the doorway, her back to the room, waiting for the first sign of backup. Gently and without making a great deal of commotion, Felicity pushed the latch that released the window screen. It was like she had done it a hundred times. The screen dropped into the garden shrubs with barely a sound.

Rosie couldn't believe it. Felicity? There was no time to consider. She popped up from the chair and kissed the top of Terry's ginger head. Within moments she'd dropped him out the ground-floor window and Felicity slammed it closed behind his bushy tail.

"For shit sakes!" Nurse Bernie yelled and charged toward the window, but it was too late.

Quinn: Wedding Bells

Ella's eyes lit up as she clasped her hands together. "Do you think they'll get married, Quinn? You'll be a flower girl *for sure*. I was a flower girl in my cousin's wedding last summer!"

Quinn felt a sharp jolt in her stomach but didn't have time to say anything before Winona sighed dramatically. "Can we talk about something else for once?" Winona opened her lunch bag open. "Gross! Yogurt." She pulled a container of strawberry yogurt out of her bag and set it on the carpet in front of her. "Anyone want it?"

"It was so fun," continued Ella, as though she hadn't been interrupted. "I got my hair done and I even wore lipstick."

Quinn fiddled with her lunch bag. She hadn't thought about marriage. Besides, how could Quinn explain that Chinese weddings had tea ceremonies and twelve course meals in restaurants filled with circle tables and flower girls were a sometimes thing, not an always thing.

She wasn't ready for marriage. She was definitely not ready for marriage.

"Will you call him Dad?" asked Jessie. Jessie had both a real dad and a stepdad who was married to her mom. Her mom made her call her stepfather, Dad.

"Dad?" Quinn gulped. "No. I'll call him Chad."

Winona looked up from her lunch. By now she'd pulled several matching purple containers out of her bag, sorting them into two piles: foods she liked in one pile. Food she didn't like in another. Her eyes settling on Quinn. "Where's your dad, anyway? Does he live in a whole other country or something?" Quinn felt Winona's eyes crawl over her non-white skin, her non-white eyes, her lunch that Wai Po had made. Today it was soup with tofu, cabbage and bok choy, packaged carefully in a reusable margarine container wrapped in a plastic bag. When Wai Po made her lunch, it was never a sandwich on white bread or stacks of cheese with circle-shaped crackers.

Quinn loved her grandmother's food, but she did not like the way Winona's nose curled up and said it smelled. More than anything she wished she had little matching purple containers instead of the yogurt and margarine tubs her Wai Po used.

She'd tried talking to her mother about getting regular food. Food like everyone else. Ma had shaken her head, said "I know it's tough, not having the same as everyone else, but trust me. That processed food is garbage. It'll preserve your body from the inside out. Besides, why do you want to be like everyone else, Quinny? It's good to be your own person. To be unique." But unique made it impossible to fit in.

"Or maybe your Dad's got a new family." Jessie took a bite of her sandwich and nodded the way people did when they wanted someone to agree with them.

The truth was Quinn didn't know anything about her father. She didn't know where he lived or what he did for a living. When Quinn asked about him—which was almost never because honestly, she didn't think about him that often—her mother would shrug and say, "We never planned to stay in touch."

Winona had finally started eating. She'd opened a small container of vegetables and an even smaller container of white dip. She dipped a carrot into the ranch sauce and before popping it into her mouth, said, "He might be dead." The other girls looked from Winona to Quinn, their eyes big and round like mama marbles. *Was he dead?* Quinn didn't think so only because her mother would have said. Ma had no problem talking about death; she talked about it all the time. *But maybe she didn't know he was dead.*

Winona swallowed her carrot and smiled. "It won't be long until your mom and her boyfriend have their own kids. They'll want their own family now." She dipped another carrot into the ranch and went on eating as though this were any other conversation. Quinn wanted to crawl under the nearest desk and never come out, but instead she sat unmoving, forcing her face to stay as still as stone. "Anyway," continued Winona, "I'm tired of talking about this. Who wants to know where I'm going for Christmas?"

Jessie pulled her gaze off Quinn and looked to the squad leader. "Sure...where are you going, Winona?"

"Disneyland! Isn't that amazing?" Winona adjusted her scrunchie. "Come on, I don't like it here on the carpet. Let's go over to my desk and finish our lunch. Then I'll tell you all about what we're going to do in California."

Quinn knew Winona wasn't inviting her. She was only inviting the true members of the squad: Ella and Jessie. Winona collected her lunch containers, stacking each one back into her bag, then walked away. Jessie scrambled to follow, shooting Quinn a look that said she was sorry, before racing after Winona.

Sudden tears threatened at the corner of Quinn's eye. She bit her lip and turned to Ella who had yet to pack up. She was methodically digging raisins out of a homemade cookie, piling the shriveling purple things on a napkin. "Aren't you going with them?"

"Nah." Ella squinted, searching for any more hidden raisins in her cookie. "I hate raisins." The cookie seemed to finally meet her approval and she took a bite. "Do you want to be science fair partners?"

A wobbly smile surfaced on Quinn's face, relief spreading across her chest. "I'd like that."

It wasn't until after out of school care was over that Quinn was able to ask her mother the question that had burnt in her mind since lunch. She'd felt nervous and anxious ever since and wasn't even sure how she wanted her mother to answer. Still, she needed to know. The words tumbled out before they'd even rounded the first corner on their way home. "Are you going to marry Chad?"

"Whoa!" Ma stopped mid-step and looked at Quinn. "Where is that question coming from?"

Quinn shrugged. "I'm just wondering." She continued walking so her mother had no choice but to stand on the street by herself or hurry to catch up.

Ma hurried up. "I don't know, Quinn, I'm not actually a fan of marriage. It's like, super permanent." She rubbed her forehead as though she had a headache coming on. "Why are you asking me this? It seems...so left field."

"I just need to know." Quinn swallowed, a mix of emotions rising in her belly. Was she relieved? Disappointed?

"Wait a sec!" Her mother grabbed Quinn's shoulder. "You didn't go and write in your journal that Chad and I got married, did you? Tell me you didn't do that."

"Ma!"

"If you did, you better have put me in a really amazing dress. Red of course. Not one of those fluffy white ones with the big skirts."

Quinn's face coloured. She'd been planning exactly that kind of dress. Anyway, she hadn't actually done it yet, she'd just *thought* about it. "I didn't write about you getting married."

"Right. That's good. I was just checking." Her mother let go of her shoulder and then pointed down a side street that was a detour to their regular path home. "Come on, let's get some hot chocolate."

They'd almost reached the coffee shop before Quinn's ma said anything else. "Okay so right now Chad and I are dating. I guess you could say we're a couple but that's it. Maybe, way in the future, we might still be together and want to, I don't know, be closer. That could happen. It's not happening right now, you understand?" She stopped walking and put both hands on Quinn's shoulders until Quinn looked up at her. "Nothing is going to happen without you and I talking about it first, okay?"

Quinn nodded. She felt her shoulders drop and she was able to relax for the first time since lunch.

"Any other questions?"

Hmm. There was one. "If you marry Chad, like sometime way, way in the future. Like not now, but some other time, I'm wondering, would he do his own laundry? Cause I'm not sure I want his clothes mixing with my clothes." Clothes were personal, after all. "And also, I think he should clean the bathroom too. I don't want to clean the bathroom all the time."

Her mother bit her lip. "The bathroom...honestly, it's just

you and me for now, kid. You're stuck on bathroom duty." She ran a gentle hand over Quinn's hair, smoothing the fly-aways by tucking them behind her ear. "Let's get some hot chocolate."

And that's exactly what they did.

Chad: Dinner Party

Everything had fallen into place. It was a bit miraculous, really. I still found myself waking in the middle of the night, my body restless and ready for hours of worrying. But no matter how I compartmentalized my life, I couldn't figure out what to worry about. Surely there was something wrong? Some nugget I'd overlooked; a part of my life on the brink of misfortune. But no. Everything was…good.

I was employed; had avoided being laid off. Even the project I'd been assigned wasn't nearly as painful as I'd anticipated. It gave me a break from the phone lines and the film crew was easy to work with. Strangest of all, a little part of me seemed to enjoy being visible. After making a handful of cameo appearances on the company's internal vlog (my most popular episode 'Simplifying without Antagonizing' had over 800 views!) other employees had started to recognize me. At first it was a head nod in the elevator, then a question in the photocopy room. Last week had been an introduction by the urinals. That one had felt, well, odd, but overall, I was flattered.

Then there was my uncle. When I visited Martin at the 'Nest, I couldn't help but feel a powerful sense of gratitude toward him and the few who'd helped me out with the 'one-two.' I felt…cared for. Like I was part of a community who had each other's back.

And by far, the best thing in my life was Lila. There'd been none of the drama or screw-ups or frantic requests for clemency that characterized my previous relationships. Maybe it was because Lila was such a straight shooter. I found her to be keenly honest to the point of being refreshingly blunt. I loved that about her. It meant I didn't have to guess what she was thinking or agonize over what I should do.

I'd changed too. I was finally adept enough at relating to another human being that I wasn't constantly screwing things up. We were two competent people, on the same page, who got each other.

So now, when I woke in the middle of the night, I would roll onto my side knowing everything was right in my world. In fact, if I didn't know better, the world seemed to be conspiring for me. About the only thing that could've made it better was if Lila were lying on the bed beside me. I would picture that sweet spot, that concave space where her neck sloped into her shoulder, and I would go back to sleep.

***

"So…," began Lila during what had become one of our regular phone chats, "my parents want to meet you. Why don't you come over Sunday night?"

"Wow." I switched the phone receiver to my other ear. I let my head fall onto the back of my couch, a grin spreading across my face. "That's big, right?"

"It's just dinner. You can say no."

"Are you kidding? No way. I'm in. What should I bring? Maybe some wine? Or like dessert or something?"

Lila laughed. "I don't think so. Just your appetite and maybe…" Lila paused, as though she were thinking. I scrambled for a pen and an old receipt sitting on my coffee table so I could write down whatever she suggested. "Don't be nervous 'kay, Chad? It's just dinner."

My pen was poised above the receipt, waiting for something practical to write down. Something easier than charm or charisma. "Okay, dinner. Will this be a vegetarian affair?"

"Nope. My parents are meat eaters."

"In that case I can't wait." I had a rapid pounding in my chest. That's excitement, I reminded myself. Not panic that I'd mess it up. Lila's parents wanted to meet me. How great was that? Everything, after all, had fallen into place. Why wouldn't this too?

My mom had never said it, but the way she'd acted had always made it clear: meeting the parents was a big deal. It might have been the way she changed into one of her nice sweaters or wrapped a silk scarf around her neck the few times I'd invited a female friend home. Or maybe it was how she pulled out her favourite recipe book, stained and dog eared, and made something other than the five staples we normally rotated between: spaghetti, tacos, tuna melts, mac and cheese, or take out.

I'd say things like, "It's not serious, Mom," and she'd smile and nod. Then she would run a vacuum over the living room carpet. I'd say, "Seriously. We're just working on a group project," and she'd step out to the grocery store and buy the kind of snack foods we didn't normally keep around the house.

She was my mom. She knew me. I could pretend all I wanted my heart wasn't on the line, could say I only wanted a good science mark, but she knew better.

We never talked about it. Not even afterward, when my guest had left. Mom would go to her room and change back into one of her old and pilling sweaters. Then she would curl up in an armchair and watch one of those Victorian television dramas she loved.

A wave of homesickness rolled over me. I would never take Lila and Quinn home to meet my mother. Instead I would meet Lila's parents. I was not going to be nervous. I was going to look forward to it.

I didn't need directions to Lila's parents' home; I'd walked past their front door dozens of times already. Normally I walked briskly past the front entrance on my way to the side door that led to Lila's basement suite, a smile plastered to my face in case her parents happened to be looking out their front window. I often worried my smile was too big, that it made me look like some kind of creepy horn-dog hoping for action. And yet I couldn't help it. The smile crawled up my face and stretched from ear to ear. Today was no different. My giant smile was in place, but this time I didn't walk to the side door. I waltzed right up those front steps, heart hammering, and rang the doorbell.

Nothing happened. I rang the bell two more times before deciding to knock. That's when I heard someone running and then the interior wood door flew open, its hinges squeaking in protest. Without waiting to open the screen door Quinn turned her head away from me and yelled, "He's here!"

"Sure am." My chest swelled with pride. Quinn and I had hit it off pretty good. Still, to be greeted with so much enthusiasm was a pleasant surprise. Hopefully Lila's parents were listening.

"Finally!" Quinn added. "What took you so long? I'm starving!" She turned and ran back to where she'd come from, my ego shrinking to its typical size. Should I open the screen door and let myself in as though I belonged? Or wait on the step like a respectful guest? Thankfully Lila rounded the corner and opened the door for me.

"Hey babe," she leaned up and gave me a kiss. "Glad you're here."

"Me too." Here goes nothing. I stumbled out of my shoes and followed Lila into the kitchen, taking in my surroundings. The room was steamy and filled with the smell of spicy ginger and roasted chicken. Her mother stood over the stove, her back to me, several pots on the stove in front of her.

"Ma. This is Chad."

Lila's mom peeked over her should at me. "Awww." she said, her mouth spread into a wide smile and she nodded toward me.

"I'm pleased to meet you Mrs. Leung." She'd already turned back to the stove and I was talking to the back of her head. But still. That hadn't been hard.

Quinn had slipped into a seat at the table and an older man, Lila's father, had just placed an electric rice cooker at the far end of the table where we would be able to reach it easily. He looked up at me and because Lila's mother was busy cooking, I thrust the flowers I was carrying in his direction. "Thanks for having me over."

He gave one slow nod of his head and took the flowers, a small smile curving his lips. I bobbed my own head, copying his movements. It was like a mini bow. I'd seen those on films before. Was I doing it right? Was I supposed to do that? I should've asked Lila for some cultural directions or something. "Please," he pointed toward the table and chairs. "Sit down. We eat soon."

As Lila's father looked through the cupboards for something to put the flowers in—he settled on a Molson Canadian beer glass—I tried to look around the kitchen without making it look like I was looking around the kitchen. It was a busy place. Anyone could see that. Like my own home growing up, it was probably where everything important happened. Various papers were stacked beside the home telephone—when was the last time I'd seen a corded home phone? Even Martin didn't have one of those! The fridge was covered in children's artwork and pictures of Quinn as well as two younger looking boys in front of a large expanse of water. They were likely Lila's brother's kids.

Quinn and I sat at a table that had been pushed into the corner of the room. The rest of the adults were busy transferring food from pots to serving bowls and setting them on the table. A large plate of green leafy vegetables with a thin, dark sauce. Chicken, the scent of ginger wafting in my direction. A bowl of fried egg in a bright red tomato sauce and a large, steaming fish I hoped someone else would cut seeing as I had no idea the proper way to do so. I adjusted my collar, wishing I hadn't buttoned it up all the way. The kitchen was warm, humid, but it would be weird if I started unbuttoning my clothes, wouldn't it? I'd worn a Martin inspired button-down, something I would normally have reserved for weddings and interviews, and I was easily the most dressed up person in the home.

"So..." I said, looking at Quinn. "That's a nice costume," She was wearing a kind of one-piece furry thing, a mane down her back and a rainbow tail extending out the rear.

"It's called a *onesie*." Her eyebrows lifted as though she were imparting very technical information. "Everyone has them."

"Right. Of course."

Her forehead crinkled with concern. "Are you sick? You look sick."

"Sick?" I adjusted my collar again. "No, not at all."

"Your face is all red."

Out of the corner of my eye I could see Lila glance over at me.

"I'm just a bit warm, that's all." Lila's parents were in sweaters and slacks, Lila—gorgeous as usual—was rocking a black tee and jeans. Weekend clothes for everyone but me, the whitey. No one else seemed to be hot or sweating buckets in the warm kitchen. I wasn't going to either. I was fine. Please, don't sweat buckets I pleaded with my body.

Lila said something short and quick in a language I didn't

understand. It must be Mandarin. I knew that was what they spoke at home, but I had never heard her do so before. This was a whole part of her life I knew nothing about. Whatever Lila had said, her father nodded, walked over to the window, and cracking it open several inches. Lila winked at me, and I gratefully nodded, wishing I'd worn one of my short-sleeved shirts.

As Lila helped her mother, they spoke little to each other. They didn't seem to need to. Occasionally her mother would point with her chin toward a particular pot, say something, and Lila would respond.

Maybe I should be taking language classes? There was so much to know, so much I hadn't thought about before. Why hadn't I?

"Here. For you." Mr. Leung handed me a small white bowl, a set of chopsticks and a fork.

"Oh, thank you." I did another quick head bob. He picked up another stack of bowls and a handful of chopsticks and gave them to Quinn who proceeded to set the table. No forks for anyone else, I noted.

And then, when everyone sat down, we ate. I'd spent the last several days worrying about how best to describe my career as an 'up and comer.' I'd thought about how I might mention my credentials in a way that wasn't bragging. What I should have been worrying about was how to eat as though I weren't a bloody idiot.

I used the fork only when absolutely necessary. This turned about to be quite often. The chopsticks were friggin' torture, my hand cramping up painfully as I tried to follow along, taking pieces of chicken and fish and the leafy greens Lila called Chinese broccoli and adding them to my tiny bowl one morsel at a time. The food melted on my tongue with the most vibrant flavours, my desire to eat hindered only by the painful stitch developing in the pit of my hand.

***

"I bet there's YouTube videos on how to use chopsticks."
"It's okay. You're good at other things."
"Ha. What things?"
"Things like making me happy." We were sitting on opposite ends of Lila's couch, my feet on the coffee table and her feet in my

lap. Quinn was in bed, showered and bag packed for school in the morning. While Lila had helped her daughter get ready for bed, I'd sat on the couch in an emotional fog, dissecting each part of the dinner.

"I should've practiced. Why didn't I think of that?"

Lila sighed. "Because you don't need to be good with chopsticks. It's not important."

I appreciated Lila's loyalty, but I'd already decided to do something about it. I could eat my breakfast everyday with chopsticks until I was proficient enough not to embarrass myself. "Your mom's cooking is amazing. Those white buns with the pork inside—can you make those?"

Lila yawned. "Nope. Not unless I have to. Meat, remember? Not my thing. But I'm sure my mom would teach you. You know, down the road." That stopped me. Lila often spoke about the present but rarely commented on the possibility of our future together. I pictured Mrs. Leung and I working side-by-side, her shouting instructions at me in a language I didn't know, and I grinned, looked at Lila, and for the first time noticed how tired she looked. "I should be doing homework," she said.

"You look exhausted." I picked up Lila's foot and gently massaged it. "Maybe you should just relax. Cuddle on the couch with me. Just enjoy how good everything is."

Lila gave me a funny look. "Ha. Spoken like a guy who doesn't have an assignment due tomorrow and a kid to get off to school before eight in the morning."

I chuckled. "True. How can I help you then?" I massaged her foot, trying to work out the tension. I sometimes forgot how much she was juggling. I'd been done school for several years and it was easy to forget what it was like having assignments hanging over you all the time.

"And Christmas," Lila groaned and put her hand to her forehead. "I'm going to have to find time to shop. Gawd. I hate shopping."

"I can help with that, no problem."

"You can't shop for Quinn for me. That'd be…"

"Sure I can. Just give me a list. What does she want?"

"Thanks, but no. It's really something I should do." She racked her fingers through her hair. "Sometimes I just wish there was a little bit less to do, you know?"

I nodded, thinking about the empty hours I spent in my apartment, traveling to and from work. I didn't honestly know what it was like to be as busy as Lila. But I could help; more than anything else I wanted to help. Maybe now was the right time? Without overthinking it I presented the idea that I'd been secretly fantasizing about.

"You and Quinn should move in with me." Life would be so easy. Peaceful images flashed through my mind of what life would be like. I'd make Kraft dinner with broccoli, the noodles served in bowls at the table and not eaten from the pot over the stove. "It would be great. I'll help with everything. Your parents could come over whenever they wanted, or we could come here. They could even rent out this basement suite for extra money."

Images of Lila's dead people textbooks stacked on my coffee table floated through my mind like cotton candy. The second bedroom would be Quinn's. I'd help her paint the walls any colour she wanted.

I smiled and squeezed Lila's calf, imagining the amazing life we could have together. It was in my power to do it. I was the kind of man I'd always wanted to be. A provider. Resourceful in the face of adversity. Not anything like my own father who had up and disappeared without a thought for anyone else.

Lila pulled her foot out of my hands, swung her legs over the side of the couch and stood up. From my state of euphoria it took me a moment to realize the sudden shift in energy.

"Why would I want to do that? Move in with you?" Her voice was flat. Her face showed little emotion, but her arms were folded tightly across her chest. "You can't be serious."

Whoah. "Er...well. Kinda?" I rubbed the back of my neck and sat up. "I just sort of thought it would make things easier?" I searched for an answer that put my feelings and positive endorphins into the right words, but all I managed to do was open and close my mouth a few times. What had I said that was so wrong?

"Look, Chad. I was just saying I was tired. I wasn't asking you to solve my problems." She was giving me the stony stare normally reserved for problem-patrons in the 'Nest Cafeteria.

"We've only been dating, what? A few months?"

Six. It had been six almost perfect months.

"Besides, I've got an obligation to my parents. Did you think I'd just walk out on them?"

"I...right. Right. Sorry. Dumb idea." The world had just pile-drived me into the couch. A smarter man would have shut his mouth and tried to recover. But I wasn't a smart man. The dream that had materialized in my mind, in the middle of the night when I couldn't sleep because of a lack of worries, was too strong to let go. I only needed to explain it better. "I guess I was thinking life would be easier if you could quit the Eldernest and focus on finishing your apprenticeship."

Lila nodded; her arms still folded as tight as ever. "Maybe easier, but then I'd have no money."

"I would cover all our costs until you're done school."

"So...I'd just depend on you, my boyfriend of a few months, to take care of my child? No. That's just crazy." She left the living room and I could hear her moving stuff around in the kitchen. After a few minutes not knowing what to do, I followed her into the kitchen. She was sitting at the table, her schoolwork spread out in front of her. The way she leaned over her books, refusing to even look at me made it clear: this discussion was over.

I fumbled through my goodbye, off-kilter and rejected, and let myself out the door. What. Had. Happened?

***

I didn't sleep that night. Not much, anyway. I dragged myself through an entire day of work, only too aware that I'd yet to receive even one text from Lila. After work I couldn't bring myself to go home to my empty apartment, so I stopped for an impromptu visit at the 'Nest. I'd searched just about everywhere for Martin when I came across Grant sitting on one of the couches in the hallway.

"Any idea where my uncle is?"

"He's gone to the library with Clara." He looked down at his wristwatch. "I'm sure they'll be back soon."

"Mind if I sit for a bit?" I didn't honestly have the energy to do much else.

Grant nodded, "Of course, make yourself at home...just not too at home, if you catch my meaning. The damn nurses might try and trim your toenails." He winked, in case perhaps I hadn't realized he was joking.

A gave a weak laugh then collapsed onto the couch beside him. "You look a bit worn down, kid."

"I'm worn down alright." I'd been blindsided by my own confidence. I rubbed the back of my neck. "And how about you? How's your online dating going?"

Grant smiled and folded up his paper. He looked like he was carefully weighing his words. "I think I may need to widen my search."

I nodded. "All the way to New Zealand for you too?"

Grant let out a bark of laughter. "I don't think so. Can't afford the phone bills! Anyway, no need to limit myself to older women, is there? The younger crowd may want a piece of this too." Grant patted his belly and laughed. I chuckled along politely, all the while wondering if I should say anything. Feeling off kilter in my own relationship I could think of no better thing to do but give another lonely person a hand in the right direction.

I cleared my throat and jumped in. "You know, there's some other apps out there. Sometimes they can be more effective for, you know, widening your search."

Grant wrinkled his forehead.

"If...like let's say a person was looking for something different then...well, what Herb or Martin were looking for, then I might try an alternative." Grant's expression didn't change. I hoped I hadn't misunderstood the situation. It was possible, of course that was possible, but my gut didn't think so. "I've heard there's this one called Grinder. You could just search for it on the internet, you know?" I rubbed the back of my head and pretended to be very interested in the mountain landscape in the painting across the hall from us.

Silence stretched between us and I was just about to fill it with some comment about the painting when Grant spoke. "Thanks for the tip. I'll...look into it. I admit though, not sure I'm up for another app, I miss the old-fashioned way. It seems to have worked for you and your girlfriend."

I swallowed. "Girlfriend?"

"Come on now. That fine woman from the cafeteria. Pours a

mean coffee."

"Right. Ya, I guess. My girlfriend, but you know. She likes her freedom. Not that I'd take that from her. She just…doesn't want to be tied down on anything. So to speak. Not literally. I mean hell, we've never talked about anything like tying down. I'm just saying."

My voice petered out as silence settled around us. I was probably better off not speaking. Better off not expecting some kind of solid relationship in life. Really, what did I have to offer anyway? I was good enough for a boyfriend, someone to have fun with, but not to live life with. I was a fumbling baboon who couldn't even get through a conversation without sounding like an idiot.

"And you think I need an alternate app? Gawd, kids these days. Tying down and hanky panky like that…" I smiled, knowing Grant was trying to make me feel better. "I haven't seen her around so much lately."

"Oh. She's busy with school right now. But she'll be back. Definitely intends to work. A do-it-all kind of person, you know?"

"Oh yes, a modern woman. What's she studying?"

"She wants to be a funeral director. And an embalmer. She's really passionate about it."

"That's…just." Grant grimaced. "It's unusual."

I nodded, glad for the change of subject. "There's a whole subculture, you know? Online chat rooms and traditional learning. Besides, she says there's a steady flow in business. No sign of becoming obsolete."

"Practical, I see." Grant cleared his throat. "All the same, I hope I don't meet her anytime soon. Outside the cafeteria that is." He elbowed me in the ribs, and I gave another weak laugh.

It was true. Lila was practical. It was me who was the romantic. Lila was self-sufficient, living her life, not in need of some kind of bullshit hero. She didn't, in fact, *need me*. Me on the other hand…I wasn't sure I would get far without her. What had I been thinking?

We sat in our loneliness, me too tired to stand up and Grant, well, I didn't know what kept Grant on the couch other than he was there first. Life was hard. Love was harder.

Martin: Distraction

Goddammit, you think this would be easier. His nephew was a grown man and not an adolescent in need of constant supervision.

If only he hadn't made that promise, Martin could roll his eyes and say, "to each their own." But no. Just like his sister had been able to do all their lives, she'd scuttered the promise out of him and it was too late to back out now.

His nephew was slumped over the cafeteria table like a damn P.O.W. and for no good reason whatsoever. He lived in a free country, had food to eat, a job to go to—thanks to the postie one-two—and yet here he was: shoulders rounded, head down, hang-dog expression. What was more, he was still wearing those kiddie t-shirts covered in cartoons. If ever the lad had needed to pull himself up by the bootstraps, it was now.

"Look here, Chad. There's plenty of fish out there."

"I'm not online dating, Martin."

"What? I'm saying *there's plenty of other women*. This ain't a damn desert."

Chad scowled and Martin tried not to roll his eyes. Who got their heart involved this early? It was a rookie move. And maybe that was the problem. He nephew was, after all, pretty much a rookie.

"We aren't *technically* over. It's just...not looking good." Chad rubbed his head, mussing up his hair. "Everything was going so well and now it's just...getting more strained every day."

"Right. Well, can I at least ask what happened?"

Chad took a quick look around the cafeteria. Was he checking to see if someone was eavesdropping on him? Newsflash sonny, no one would be that interested. Or maybe he was seeing if that lady love of his had popped out of the kitchen doorway with her pots of coffee? Finally Chad cleared his throat and said in a voice void of emotion, "I asked her to move in."

"Okay." Martin nodded, waiting for his nephew to expand on his statement. When it was clear he didn't intend to, he asked a question of his own. "And what about the kid? Would she move in too?"

"Of course the kid too!"

"Wowzers. Big commitment there."

Chad glared at Martin as though *he* were the enemy. For the life of him, Martin couldn't understand why. He'd only stated the damn truth. "Don't leave me hanging. What did she say?"

Chad sighed and again scraped his fingers through his thinning hair. It worried Martin; the way Chad treated what was fast becoming a nonrenewable resource. He would have suggested his nephew be less vigorous considering the delicate follicles, but the lad didn't seem in the right mood for advice. He'd also have to get the young man onto some products if he intended to keep what hair he had left. But one thing at a time, one thing at a time.

"She said, 'Why would I want to do that?'"

Martin winced at the pained look on his nephew's face. "These women…hard to keep happy sometimes. Did you try the fire and ice?"

"Martin."

"Just an idea. Just an idea." Martin felt for him, he truly did. If he were sitting a little bit closer, he might even give his nephew one of those manly-type pats on the shoulder. "Back in our day we didn't want to look too interested, you know? We played 'hard to get.' We didn't do this vulnerability thing you're so fond of. Although…might be working a bit of magic with my Clara. Moving in the right direction, anyhow."

Chad managed a small smile. "That's great, Martin. I'm happy for you."

"Not out of the woods yet, mind you. But I'm hopeful. The trick is patience, I reckon. Time and patience." Martin leaned across the table. "Have you tried expressing *your feelings*? The ladies love that stuff."

Chad answered with a non-committal lift of his left shoulder and then let it drop. "We aren't talking enough to express much of anything right now."

Martin was at a loss. He'd need to find a way to get the young buck's mind off his troubles. Give him time to heal, to come up with a plan. Perhaps a solution would materialize all on its own.

It had taken him a lot of imagination to help Chad the last time he'd looked so hang-dog, but that time around Martin had been operating entirely on guess work. He'd assumed his nephew was having one of those middle-aged crises the young people were so fond of. After months of looking like a worn-out doormat he'd finally come clean. He and the common-law had broken up and it explained a lot, it did.

This time around Chad had come clean about his woman-troubles right away. It must be a sign Martin was doing something right. Taking care of his herd; earning his nephew's trust. Martin's chest puffed with pride. His sister would've been pleased about that.

Now that he knew the problem, Martin could come up with a plan of attack. He just needed to keep the lad distracted until his lady love had time to miss him.

Missing someone was underrated these days. The way his nephew was constantly on that damn pocket phone, texting and messaging and what-not, he'd no doubt the woman felt bombarded. A person needed to miss their lover in order to truly appreciate them. At least that's the way Martin saw it.

Hadn't that been just the case with his Clara? She'd asked for space and what choice had Martin had but to give it to her? It hurt his pride, his ego, but he'd done it. Backed right off and returned to their platonic state. And now look; all the signs were pointing in the right direction. And he was a man who could read the signs, alright. It was only a matter of time before they would return to their special relationship, he was sure of it.

"You know, Chad, back in my day you'd see this pattern all the time with the posties. One would get weary of the daily grind, would be dying for a desk job, you know? But when they got the indoor gig it'd be all pressure and pencil pushing. Sitting on their ass without pavement beneath their feet...I can tell you the poor fools would have a change of heart. They suddenly could appreciate the door-to-door for what it was: a piece of heaven, I tell you.

"She'll come around, Chad. She'll have a change of heart if you only give her some space. A chance to miss you."

Once again Chad responded with a shoulder shrug. "Sure." He said. "Sure." He pulled his phone out of his pocket, glanced at the screen then put it back.

Good grief. It was worse than Martin had thought. If he were to help Chad help himself Martin would need to get him off this moping and instant messaging.

What Chad needed was a distraction. A hobby.

And some sharper shirts, but some things were easier said than done.

***

Martin adjusted the shoulder strap of the taxi's seatbelt. He'd begun accompanying Clara on her weekly trips to the public library. It wasn't his cup of tea, but she seemed pleased when he'd asked if he could tag along. Now it had become what the younger crowd called 'their thing.' Today he was updating her on the recent chat he'd had with his nephew. "I'm worried about him, Clara. Seems at odds with himself." Martin let out a low whistle and shook his head. "And his woman friend doesn't seem to be helping matters. Sending mixed messages from what I can see. Interested one day, pushing him away the next."

Clara raised an eyebrow. "She has *a child*, Martin. I can understand her not rushing into living together. Personally, I think she's putting her child first, and that's what you've got to do as a parent. Especially as a single-parent."

"Right. Right." Martin gently rubbed his thumb across the back of Clara's hand. He liked holding her hand, but it only happened when they were away from the 'Nest. Otherwise Clara pulled away. She said she didn't want people to stare, to whisper. "That's exactly what I told him." Martin made a mental note to tell Chad that. Take things slow. Single mother. He'd meant to say it; he'd just needed the reminder.

"If it's meant to be—" Clara started.

"It'll be." Finished Martin and winked at her. Que Sera Sera.

"That reminds me…have you had a chance to talk to your son? About us?"

Clara pulled her hand away. "Not yet." She patted Martin's knee to take the sting away. "But I will."

Martin wasn't sure what good telling her son would do. It sure wasn't his idea. "Well—take your time. I know this hasn't been easy for you." Anyone could see how it weighed on her, prevented her from enjoying their time together. In truth, he hadn't been altogether surprised when she'd wanted to return to an amicable yet unromantic friendship. He'd gone with it, played 'the good guy,' because he knew that was the ticket to returning to their previous state of affairs.

But it was exhausting; didn't come natural to him, playing 'the good guy.' He'd thought it would take a week or two, but the situation had dragged out for several weeks now. A celibate man at his age—he was turning into a statistic! "You know dear, I've been thinking on it. Are you sure talking to your son is the answer? You shouldn't need to answer to—"

Clara stiffened. "Martin. I've abandoned his father." Her eyes narrowed and she lowered her voice. "You know how I feel about this, Martin. It feels like I've betrayed my marriage vows. I thought I'd come to terms with it, but it was a constant struggle." She put her hands on her forehead, massaging her temples. "It still is."

Martin ground his teeth and tried to rein-in his frustration. Linus could outlive them both—if you called what he was doing living. Martin needed to tell his nephew to pull the plug if he himself ever got to that state. End it before Martin could no longer care for himself. No longer run a razor across his face or see to his own toileting. That would be one day too long.

"Look Clara—"

"Shhhh." She glanced ahead, locking eyes with the driver in the rearview mirror. Caught, he averted his gaze back to the road.

"Clara," Martin began again, his voice as soft and soothing as he could make it. He reached again for her hand, but she pulled away. He sighed but pressed forward anyway. "I've been thinking about this, doll. I really have. And the way I figure, everyone's going to have an opinion, your son included. What if he doesn't agree? Are you just going to walk away from a good thing?"

Clara didn't answer. Her gaze was glued out her window, her head turned away from Martin. Still, he had to try.

"Here's the thing, maybe no one else's opinion matters. Maybe not even mine—or yours, you bloody eavesdropper!" Martin shook his fist at the taxi driver who had again been caught watching in the rearview mirror. "Look Clara, the only opinions that matter should be yours and Linus's. And have you ever wondered what he would want you to do?"

"Of course I've wondered! Don't be daft, Martin."

Martin reached over and massaged her shoulder the way he would a skittish colt. "I doubt a loving husband would want you to be lonely."

Clara pulled away from his hand and turned toward him so Martin could see her face was red and angry. That hadn't been what Martin expected. He was only trying to...well to show her the way.

"What would you know about being a husband? For the love of—you're just like everyone says." She rubbed her clenched fist across her reddened cheek. "You're selfish, Martin. And presumptuous." Silence danced between them like a live wire.

Good lord. Now what? He wanted to defend himself but that *never* worked. Not with the ladies. It would only make him look guilty.

"You just want what's easiest for you. Consequences for me be damned." Clara leaned between the two front seats. "Excuse me, driver—"

"No, Clara. You're right. Let's not ruin—"

"Driver, please turn around. I'd like to go home."

***

Martin's telephone rang in the silence of his darkened bedroom. He fumbled for the bedside lamp, then pounced on his telephone like a drowning man on a life raft.

"Clara, my dear. I'm so very—"

"Martin, that you?" The voice was panicked and breathless.

Martin swallowed his disappointment and answered as best he could. "Yes, it is. Can I er, help you, Rosie?"

"We are a go. Operation Re-Home is a go. I repeat—"

"Got it. I'll be over in a jiff." He hung up the phone and sighed.

He'd likely ruined things with his Clara; misjudged the situation like the old fool he was. Maybe she was right. He was selfish. Knew nothing about what it meant to be a loving spouse. Heck, he'd never even been a spouse.

He kicked his legs out from under the covers and maneuvered himself into a sitting position. He'd need to get a move on. No more time for wallowing now. And at least he'd found a distraction for his nephew. The distraction was, perhaps, a hell of a lot wilder than Martin had been on the lookout for. But wasn't it true the best distractions were those that crawled up your pant leg when you least expected them?

He dialed Chad and was pleased the lad picked up rather than letting it go to the voice mail. He explained the situation as best he could, but it took some convincing. "Come on. You've gotta take this cat. I've promised Rosie."

"Rosie." Chad's sigh was audible across the phone line. "How many women is that now? Your dating needs are—"

"What? I'm not dating *Rosie*! Me and Rosie—you can't be bloody serious!"

"I sure as heck can."

"Clara's all I need. I've told you. Found my muse." The pain of it caught in Martin's throat. Found and lost. "Anyway, this isn't about me. The cat'll be euthanized if we don't find him a home. Given the needle. Rosie's beside herself. Can't you just take the cat then maybe find it a home?"

"Look, Martin, I'm not even a cat person. I'm ending this call—"

"It's a damn crisis, over here, Chad. Have you no compassion?" His voice rose in frustration and he had to take a breath to calm himself. "Now get over here. Take a cab." Martin hung up the phone, grabbed the cardboard box he'd been storing in his room and snuck over to Rosie's.

The handover was quick. When the taxi pulled up to the curb, Chad limped out of the passenger door in a pair of jogging pants and wrinkled sweater to collect the box. "You've got to be kidding me, Martin. I don't even like cats!"

"I'm sorry, lad. I really am. But you wouldn't want to see it put down, would you? It'd kill Rosie. Just kill her. Besides," Martin leaned in toward his nephew and said very emphatically, "Kids like cats. They all do. Maybe this cat might be a bit of a draw..."

Chad's eyebrows lifted as he looked down at the box. The cardboard shook and hissed. Martin was damn glad it wouldn't be him opening the thing. Gingerly, Chad picked up the box and without another word got back into the waiting taxi. Martin watched the taxi's taillights fade into the night before returning back inside. He hoped this wasn't another of his mistakes.

As he shuffled back to his room, a hand on the hallway railing to help keep the weight off his bad knee, Martin felt old. Tired. And more unsure than ever.

Rosie: Aftermath

When Rosie thought on it, she had trouble remembering the order of things. It didn't use to be that way. She used to know things. About what happened before and what happened after. Now she knew most things, but sometimes she didn't always remember what came first and what came second.

At some point there had been that meeting in Director Knightly's office. She remembered Kathleen, face white and expressionless, sitting ramrod straight in the upholstered chair. And there had been Martin, standing in the middle of the room, his face grim with disappointment.

"Not in all my days—and I was in the civil service! The things we'd see; *the things we'd hear*. But such coarse language. Even for me…" he'd paused as though he couldn't bear the thought. "Shocking. And with ladies present." He'd shook his head at the memory of Nurse Bernie, flustered and angry in Felicity's room. "I'm prepared to write a statement on the situation. A documentation so to speak."

Director Knightly had cleared his throat, his left pointer finger rapid-tapping on his desk top. "It shouldn't be necessary, Martin." The nurse had already received a stern warning for using offense language in front of the residents and for entering a private bedroom without announcing her presence. Felicity had seen to that. Outraged, Bernadette had left her name tag on the nurse's desk and none of the residents had seen her since.

Still, it seemed Director Knightly was more unhappy with Rosie than with the nurse! He had murmured the words 'repeat offense,' Rosie was sure of it. But in the end he had pressed his lips together, glanced at Kathleen, and not said anything else.

There had been the Eldernest board meeting too. Had that been before or after the meeting in the office? Rosie wasn't sure.

She was pretty sure it hadn't gone the way Director Knightly had anticipated.

"You've seen that video on YouTube, right?" The youngest looking board member with the full beard had looked so earnest after Rosie presented her facts. He looked around at the other board members, nodding solemnly at each of them. "The one from the Netherlands? With the chickens in the senior's facility? You know, they raise the hens, sell the eggs. It's like a social enterprise plus a mental wellness win-win. We should be doing that, right?"

It sounded like a darn good idea to Rosie. She'd clasped her hands together and cheered. Kathleen had put a firm hand on Rosie's knee and suggested to the board that the Paws and Pals program might be a more conservative option. She even suggested Rosie as chief volunteer! Every week Charlie, a handsome golden retriever, and his handler would visit the Eldernest. The residents had access to a therapeutic animal, the eager young board member was appeased and Director Knightly could sleep at night without fear of a dozen egg-laying hens making their home at the Eldernest.

Kathleen and Director Knightly had gone to dinner to discuss the details. Rosie wasn't sure what all had been discussed at the dinner, but that wasn't a memory problem. It was because she hadn't been invited along.

As for Rosie, she no longer felt quite so alone. In fact, she was a lot less alone. She had Charlie. And she had friends, even Felicity, who would help her in a pinch.

Even at the costume shop she wasn't alone. A brand-new assistant had been hired. Her nephew wanted Rosie to train him. "Train him up good, alright? He'll be here with you all the time. Same shifts. No need to move heavy stuff, you hear?"

Rosie had nodded. The assistant didn't seem to need much training to her. He knew how to use the cash machine and the debit card reader. He knew almost as much as she did about the classic cosplay line but disagreed with her on whether the

Minecraft costumes were overpriced. Still, he was nice; listened to all her stories when the store wasn't busy.

***

Mr. Terrance didn't scratch at Rosie's window for what felt like ages. But eventually, he returned. She'd been in bed when she heard his familiar meow outside the window. She got up, secured her door by wedging her chair under the handle, then removed her window screen. Mr. Terrance looked at her for a long time, then jumped through the window and settled himself on the carpet.

From her bottom dresser drawer she pulled out his dish. For the last time she filled it with his favourite dinner: turkey and halibut in gravy. Then, as planned, she phoned Martin.

"We are a go. Operation Re-Home is a go. I repeat—"

"Got it. I'll be over in a jiff."

As she watched Terry eat, Rosie let her tears trail down her face without wiping them away. This was goodbye. She only brushed them away when she heard Martin tapping on her door. She let him in; a cardboard box in his hands. Terrance hissed and spat and made an awful fuss, but together they managed it. Within minutes Martin had a dozen new scratches and an angry tomcat inside a vibrating cardboard box.

"He's gonna be fine," Martin placed a hand on Rosie's shoulder and squeezed. His shy nephew could use a companion. "He'll get Mr. Terrance dewormed and micro-chipped and if this here damn cat gets picked up by the authorities, they'll have to return him to my nephew and not euthanize. You can even visit if you want, Rosie."

***

Rosie didn't end up visiting. She didn't need to. Sometimes, late at night, after most of the Eldernest residents were sleeping, Rosie would hear a scratch at her window or sometimes a loud meowing from the ledge. On those nights she would get out of bed, disoriented but not confused. She knew what to do.

First, she secured her door. Then she opened her window and removed the screen. Mr. Terrance would be sitting there, looking as ferocious as ever. He wasted no time hopping over the windowsill and into her room.

Unlike before she no longer fed him; he was fat and hefty from regular meals at his new home. Instead he'd curl up on the bed, pressing his great orange head under Rosie's chin. She would leave the window open and the door firmly closed. In the morning he would be gone.

Chad: Respite

"I don't know why you're so salty," Imran leaned against my cubicle partition wall, careful not to wrinkle his spiffy work attire. He'd gotten into the habit of visiting on his morning coffee break, returning to the complaint-line trenches to remind himself how good he had it in sales. "You've got your own space. You can do whatever you want: order pizza at midnight, lie around in your boxers on the couch. You don't even have to do the dishes unless YOU feel like it."

I rubbed a hand over my face. "Right. You're right." I tried to look like I was fortunate to be living the bachelor life. In truth, I was a hurting unit of rejection, convinced catastrophe was about to rain down. By all accounts Lila and I were one step away from breaking up. It had happened to me before and I knew the signs: stilted texts. No phone calls. Too busy doing laundry to hang out. I was positive the dreaded end-of-relationship conversation was hurtling toward me, and there was nothing I could do to stop it.

"I'm a reject." The words slid out despite my attempt at male bravado.

Imran's eyes squinted. After a moment of consideration, he said "Nah. I wouldn't go that far." His gaze roamed around my cubicle until it settled on the papers stacked on my desk. The words SCRIPT were boldly printed across the top of the page. "How goes the old people vids?"

I shrugged. "Not bad." When I was 'performing' with the crew I was too busy trying to get my lines right to worry about anything else. "It's actually a pretty good distraction."

"Hey!" Imran slapped the top of the cubicle wall with his palm. "I've got an idea. Why don't you come out to the community centre tonight? We could use another volunteer for our youth basketball program."

"Right…" my voice trailed off. Imran had asked for my help months ago, but I'd never gone. I'd been too absorbed spending time with Lila. "I don't know, Imran. I'm not in the mood."

He raised an eyebrow. "Come *on*, man. It's better than crying in your apartment, waiting for a text. I'm throwing you a life-line here."

He had a point.

***

I ate my orange Kraft Dinner sans broccoli but dosed with hot sauce in silence, a fork in one hand and the handle of the cooking pot in the other. In the silence of my apartment I couldn't help but re-play the night I'd sprawled on Lila's couch and innocently asked her to move in. The conversation stayed on constant repeat, looping itself around my brain. My bravado. Her scorn. It was torture. For the life of me I couldn't understand what kind of Greek-god-confidence had consumed me.

Why hadn't I understood? They were the family unit; I was the add-on. I was the virtual tail of a salamander; capable of being cut-off without any real harm to the reptile. The tail on the other hand? Worthless on its own.

I put the empty cooking-pot down on the coffee table, determined to push Lila out of my mind. I had another major problem to deal with anyway. A problem that was watching me from the top of the bookshelf.

"How goes it, Mr. T?"

As usual, the cat didn't answer. He stared back with ambivalence, probably wondering why I was sitting on what he deemed his couch. Certainly, it was no longer mine. Mine had been a slightly worn but comfortable piece of furniture. That couch no longer existed.

The couch I now sat on was shredded. I traced a finger over an open tear in the armrest. "You know Mr. T, you're a real jackass."

Why *on earth* had my uncle saddled me with this cat? Sure, it needed a home, but how had *I* been deemed a capable savior? Of all people I was not competent at relationships—not with humans, not with animals. I wasn't even a cat person.

What kind of person was I, anyway? Not, apparently the living together, supporting your girlfriend kind of person. I picked up my phone and looked to see if I'd missed a text. Nothing.

"Any advice?" I asked the cat.

He didn't bother responding.

Yes, I was a man willing to take advice from a cat. A cat who seemed to despise me.

I wasn't sure why. I'd spent a small fortune purchasing several tins of cat food before finding one he would eat. It turned out to be the overpriced, small tins of gourmet beef and rainbow trout, so that's what I bought him.

He seemed to know what the litter box was for, thank God, but he yacked up hairballs on my carpet with alarming frequency. He was a roommate from hell.

As a first-time cat owner I hadn't a clue of what I was supposed to do and so I checked with my good friend, Google, for advice. Apparently, I could prevent him destroying my furniture by trimming his nails with clippers. I should also be rubbing his teeth with a Q-tip to prevent plaque build-up. I couldn't even pick the damn cat up without getting attacked. There was no way I'd be trying to insert a Q-tip in his mouth.

My phone pinged and I immediately looked down at the screen. Not Lila. It was Imran, texting the address for the community centre.

I really didn't want to go, but I also didn't know how to get out of it without looking like a depressed man hiding at home. As I considered possible excuses my phone pinged again. This time my heart skipped. It was Lila.

How goes the cat?

Fingers twitching, I tapped out a response. *Still wild.*

Okay, Chad. Play it cool. This was the first time she'd initiated contact in over a week. I put the phone down and walked the empty pot to the kitchen, putting it in the sink and filling it with soapy water. Then I raced back to the couch to see if she'd responded. Nope.

Nothing. Five minutes went by. She was probably busy—of

course she was busy—but still I felt sorry for myself. I let my disappointment out in a moan. I had to try *something*. So I broke the unwritten code and texted again even though she hadn't responded yet.

Hope he'll be okay on his own tonight cuz I won't be home.

No immediate answer. I swallowed my pride and kept going.

I'm volunteering at this youth thing with Imran. I deleted *thing*. Replaced it with *program. Say hi to Quinn for me.*

See? I had a life. I was a community volunteer. And a cat rescuer. I was wanted…and not at all insecure. No sir. My phone pinged again.

Cool. Have fun.

Shit. It wouldn't be fun. It would be total shit. I didn't even like basketball. More than anything I just wanted to hang out with Lila, doing nothing more than sitting side by side on my clawed-up couch, starring at our phones and drinking coffee in companionable silence.

I looked at Mr. T who had stalked his way onto the coffee table and was now only a few feet away from me. His demon-yellow eyes were full of loathing.

Imran was right. I needed to get out of here. *Thanks* I texted back to Lila and stood up to get my joggers. The cat pounced onto the couch as soon as I was off it, his front paws stretching out in front of him, his claws spreading out like weapons of destruction.

***

When Imran said it was a community basketball program for kids, I'd pictured a bunch of gangly adolescents. I hadn't pictured the future NBA line-up. The gym was packed with growth hormone hardened teenagers.

"I thought you said this was a *kids* b-ball thing?"

Imran looked up from his phone, "Hey! Good to see you, man! Just give me a sec and I'll get us set up." Imran continued to dribble a basketball in one hand and scroll through his Insta feed with the other. He looked like a version of himself from an alternate universe. Gone were the slim fitting trousers, tucked in patterned dress shirts and carefully styled hair I was used to. Business Imran had been replaced by a backwards hat wearing, hoodie layering, shiny white Nikes, basketball dude.

I was out of my league. Imran walked over to the side of the court and dropped his phone into a gym bag, then started tossing the ball from one hand to the other with about the same ease I had when toggling through the Netflix menu. Here was a man as relaxed on the court as he was on a sale's call. If ever I had been impressed with his skills, it was now.

"Everyone, gather round," called Imran.

He gave the kids thirty seconds or so and without any further reminders everyone did what he'd asked. There was a bit of shoving and joking amongst a group of older boys, but it was easy to see my friend had the respect of both the youth and the few adult volunteers scattered throughout the crowd.

"Tonight we'll be working in small groups on our passing. Afterward we'll play some three on three, cool?" He continued to toss the ball from hand to hand, his eyes roving around the crowd. "Before we begin, I'd like to introduce you to a new volunteer whose joined us tonight. Everyone, this is Chad, a friend of mine." He nodded his chin in my direction and everyone's eyes turned toward me. I tried to give a chin nod back, as everyone size me up. "Go easy on him or he won't be back, a'right?"

The kids were looking away, already losing interest. "No worries," I stammered. "Lay it on me." *Come on, Chad. You could do better. Besides, who cares what they think? It's not like I was planning to be back here.* But I cared. Of course I did. How did a person stop caring? Stop trying to make a good impression and just say: this is me, whether you like it or not.

***

It turned out volunteering wasn't that hard. I didn't need to be a basketball expert or know how to lead skill-building drills. Imran took care of all that.

I just needed to play basketball with kids. What surprised me most was the hardened teenagers assigned to my group weren't all that hard. I saw it in the way they glanced over for my approval when they made a basket. The way they hunched their shoulders when they missed a pass. I knew those feelings; understood those needs better than I understood the rules of basketball. These were just kids who needed the same kind of things I needed: someone to celebrate the small wins and to commiserate the lost opportunities.

Before I knew it, the program was over. The kids in my group banged on my back, not worried about the sweat causing my shirt to stick to my skin. I smacked them right back on their equally sweaty, oversized XXL shirts that hung loose over their skinny frames.

I had managed not to trip over myself, had even managed a few baskets here and there.

"Hey," said the oldest kid from my group and threw a chest pass at me. I caught the ball, it's roundness already feeling more comfortable. His face was carefully guarded, not revealing any emotion. "Coming back next week?"

I didn't overthink it. "Ya. Why not, right?" The exercise was good for me. And even better, for ninety whole minutes I'd found respite.

***

I got home, sore but proud, and flicked on the lights. The first thing I saw was my living room lamp, the glass base shattered across the floor. I froze, for a split second believing there'd been a break-in. Then Mr. T whizzed past, sending an angry hiss in my direction.

It hadn't been a break-in. It had been the bloody cat.

Damnit, my mom had bought me that lamp. I pulled my heavy jacket off, threw it on the counter, then punched Martin's number into my phone. I didn't bother with pleasantries when he picked up.

"You've saddled me with a *freaking demon*." I said, choking on my frustration. "He's destroying my apartment."

Martin coughed. He was not sick. It was a cough intended to conceal laughter. "He likes to be outdoors. That's what Rosie says. Just let him outside for a bit."

"I'm on the second floor, *Martin*. The damn thing will drop to his death."

"He's a cat; has almost ten lives. Besides, you said it yourself: he's demonic. He's probably unkillable."

I was taking a few deep breaths, trying to calm down, when I spotted it. For shit sakes! "I think he's taken a piss on my wall! For the love of—"

"Nonsense. Couldn't be that." More coughing. There was nothing funny about this "Have you, uh, introduced the cat to Lila and her daughter yet? That was part of the reason you got it, wasn't it? Kids love furry animals."

"That was your idea, Martin, not mine. You're the one who foisted the damn cat on me." Sure, his idea had *sounded* like a good one. At first. The more I thought about it the more I'd convinced myself it wasn't. If I invited Lila to my apartment, she might think I was pressuring her. That I hadn't taken her 'hint' she didn't want to move in. Maybe she'd say 'no' simply because she didn't want to get my hopes up. And so I'd chickened out, fearful it would make things worse.

I wasn't in the mood to discuss all that with Martin though. I was tired. Annoyed. And not interested in listening to seven ideas for improving my love-life. "Anyway, I can't invite them over when there's a strong potential they'll be attacked."

"Hmm. That's what you're waiting for?"

"Of course that's what I'm waiting for!"

I hung up the phone, cleaned up the broken lamp and washed down my wall. While taking a shower I considered my uncle's advice. Maybe he was right, and I should just let the cat outside. What was the worst that could happen? After I toweled off and got dressed, I slipped out the balcony door and quickly closed it behind me so Mr. T couldn't follow me out. I looked around. Could a cat get down from here?

The only route off the balcony seemed a crapshoot. I pictured the ginger cat launching itself from my balcony to the overgrown poplar tree that had probably been planted too close to the building when it was a sapling. It was close but far enough away that it appeared unrealistic a cat could jump several feet, land on a branch and make his way down to the ground without getting injured.

It was no use.

I was angry but I wasn't quite ready to cause a living thing to plummet to his death. I'd have to keep the windows locked tight and the patio door closed. I'd already discovered I couldn't let fresh air into the apartment because the asshole cat had torn the screens. I sighed in resignation. The 'Nest guy, Knightly, had probably been right. The cat was not fit for human co-habitation.

Halfway through the night I woke because of a sharp stabbing pain in my big toe. I yanked my foot up and, in the darkness, saw a shaggy ball of fur hurtle itself off the bed.

"That's it!" If no one else was worried about the cat being outside, why was I? "Go. Just go," I yelled while stumbling into the dark living room. I unlocked the patio door and slid it wide open. The damn cat didn't give me time to pull open the screen and jumped through a tear he'd made sometime in the previous week. He got stuck, his head and front paws on the outside, his lower end still in the living room.

I was so tired of the ungrateful beast I pushed him from the backend until, plop, he landed on his feet on the balcony outside. He turned and looked back at me, his eyes glinting from the streetlights below. Whether he was giving me the evil eye, locking me in his memory for future bloodletting, or if he was thanking me for freeing him, I couldn't guess.

"Good riddance," I told him, "You're a bloody menace." My toe was throbbing and tingling in a very uncomfortable way. I should have kept him in the damn cardboard box that first night and taken him to the vet for a rabies shot. Now I had no idea if I'd be foaming at the mouth in a few hours.

Mr. T had enough of looking at me. He jumped up onto the ledge of my balcony and flew over to my neighbour's balcony with more grace than I'd imagined a giant cat could possess. I wished him well making it to the ground, then slammed the sliding door closed.

I went back to bed. In the darkness I stared at the ceiling. The minutes ticked by. I knew I wouldn't sleep. Guilt was clawing at me, keeping me awake. I limped back to the balcony door, wondering if the cat had plunged to his death.

But no. He was in the tree. I'd worried and overthought it for nothing.

Chad: Small Steps

My uncle set his coffee cup down on the table and cleared his throat. "You've got to hang in there, man. I've found out the hard way there's no point rushing." I shrugged. As far as I could see, my uncle and I were as far apart as you could get when it came to dealing with women. "Seriously. You're doing the right thing. Staying busy. Focus on this basketball thing you were telling me about. And you've got the cat." He was working hard to keep his face straight and I gave him a dirty look. "I'm glad he made it back alright."

He had. The morning after I'd let Mr. T outside, he'd been sitting pretty on the balcony. I'd opened the sliding door and he'd sauntered over to his dish. Like the man he knew I was, I had filled it to overflowing thankful he too hadn't left me.

I'd only exchanged random, very short texts with Lila for the rest of the week. She hadn't even made it to Sentry on Thursday night. She texted that she had a final the next day. I took it as a further sign that she was slowly and surely disengaging herself from my life.

Now it was Saturday. With nothing better to do, I was visiting my uncle in the festively decorated cafeteria. I'd spilled my guts to Martin over three cups of burnt tasting coffee and now he was trying to console me.

"I've made the same mistake before. Been too needy."

"Needy? You're pep talk isn't making me feel better."

"I know," continued Martin as though I hadn't spoken. "Hardly seems my style, but sometimes, when you really like someone…"

A sad look crossing his face. "Anyway, it's been the death of many a flirtation. Just look at Herb. Scared Maggie off, he did. That's why he needed to do the online thing."

As Martin went on, *and on*, I scanned the cafeteria. Red bows and little lights hung on the walls. Little plastic poinsettias dotted the tables and bowls of festive red and green jello were in the self-serve display case, but no Lila.

"Take me, on the other hand." My attention was drawn back to my uncle, his voice louder than before. "Clara wants to slow down. I slow down. I'm not going to pressure her or make demands. No no, kid. I wouldn't do that."

"Sure," I said. "But I hadn't meant to demand. Or pressure. It's just—"

Martin cut me off. "I know. Believe me, lad, I know." He tilted his head to the side and seemed to be considering something. "Are you sure she's the right one? Don't get me wrong, Lila seems a very nice young woman. But this mortician-ambition thing…it's a little strange."

I laughed. "That's the least of my worries. It doesn't bother me at all."

"Alright, just a thought." We sat in silence, each stuck in our own heads. "You know what you've got to do. Be patient. And be confident in yourself."

"I know, fake it till I make it."

Martin's shoulder's slumped. "Don't fake it. *Be* confident. Where has all this faking come from?"

Confident. I wasn't sure that was possible for me. It had nothing to do with Lila, my ex, Kate, or any of the other women who'd lost interest and left. It wasn't even about my dad who hadn't stuck around long enough to see how I'd turn out. It was me. Maybe I just wasn't meant to be the rock star Imran and my Uncle were. I was just one of those kids on the basketball court, looking for acceptance.

***

On Sunday morning I was still in bed when I heard my phone ring. It was the particular ring I'd programed to indicate someone was buzzing my apartment from the lobby downstairs. Slowly I got up, in no rush to find out whether this time it was the Jehovah

Witnesses or a census taker.

I found my phone when it rang for the second time. It had been where I'd left it, on the coffee table. Sitting beside it was the beast. I'd let him out again last night, this time leaving the balcony door open six inches so he could squeeze back inside if wanted.

"So, you've come back."

He shifted his gaze toward the food dish. It was almost like he was communicating with me.

I picked up my still ringing phone. It was 10:00 am.

"Hello?"

"Hey! It's us. Me and Quinn. We were in the neighbourhood. Thought we'd stop by."

It was the first time I'd heard her voice in a few weeks. In shock, I cleared my throat, trying to think of something to say. "You're not working?"

"No way! It's Christmas holidays. I took a few days off while Quinn and I have time off school. We're living it up." I could hear Quinn giggling in the background. "So..." I could hear a moment of hesitation in her voice. "You goin' let us up?"

"Of course." I buzzed them in then raced to the washroom. I managed to brush my teeth, apply deodorant and put on joggers and a shirt before I heard them knock on the door.

"Wow!" I said in greeting. "Come in." I ran a hand through my messed-up hair and gratefully took the Timmy's coffee Lila was holding out for me. "It's great to see you." She looked amazing. Old jeans that fit perfectly and a toque framing her beautiful face.

Lila gave me a slow smile. "You too."

Quinn pushed in between us and held a shiny object toward my face. It had shimmering bits of ribbon attached to a long stick like some kind of crazy fishing rod. "Look what I got your cat."

"Er, thank you," I said. "You have to be careful, okay? He's a bit of a...jerk sometimes."

She raced into the apartment, leaving me and Lila at the door. I heard her calling "here kitty, kitty," as she swished the cat toy through the air. I knew I should be supervising, readying myself to remove Mr. T at the first sign of trouble, but I was having trouble taking my eyes off Lila.

She gave me a nervous smile. "Sorry to drop in on you like

this." She'd pulled her hat off, and she was trying to tuck the flyaway pieces behind her ear. "I didn't know…I mean…I'm not sure you want us here?"

"Of course I do. Why wouldn't I?"

"Look Chad—I'm sorry. Honestly. I didn't mean to hurt you."

"No. I'm sorry. I overstepped." I led her into the apartment, and we sat down by the kitchen table where we could watch Quinn and Mr. T. I took a sip of my coffee. My heart was pounding and not only from the caffeine. Unsure what to say, I kept my eyes on the cat.

Miraculously, he seemed to be enjoying the toy. Quinn was waving the stick in the air, causing the ribbons to dance. Mr. T jumped and leapt at them, appearing to be a normal, if somewhat mangy, cat.

"My parents are there, you know?" I looked back at Lila when she spoke. Worry creased her forehead. "And Quinn. I can't just rush into things without considering…"

"You don't have to explain. Honestly. You're a family."

She continued on as though I hadn't interrupted. "I can't just leap. Can't just jump in and not think about everyone else. And it's not just convenience either; being near my parents. I *want* Quinn around as many people who love her as possible. Do you understand?"

"Yes." I did. What good parent wouldn't want that?

We drank our coffee and watched as Quinn continued to play with the cat. It was oddly hypnotic. The winter sun was low on the horizon and it shone brightly through the balcony doors so interior lights weren't needed. The brightly coloured ribbons twirled in the air, Quinn turning in circles and praising the cat every time he leapt for them.

When he'd had enough Mr. T jumped onto the kitchen table, making himself eye level with me. For once he wasn't hissing. Instead he was making a weird sound like an idling car engine.

"Wow!" said Lila. "He really likes you."

I scratched my chin and laughed. "You think? It's been hard to tell. I think he just wants his breakfast."

"No. He definitely likes you. He's purring." Her hand inched closer to mine where it rested on the table. Tentatively she entwined her fingers with mine. "Maybe he's just the kind of cat who needs to take it slow. Baby steps rather than, you know, jumping straight in. Doesn't mean he doesn't like you."

My chest expanded with light. Tension, my constant companion, eased.

"Hey, Chad!" Quinn called. I turned to look at her. She was still swirling the cat toy in the air, making giant figure eights even though Mr. T had lost interest. "Do you like bowling?"

I grinned. "Love it."

Felicity: Comfort and Joy

"Is this chair taken?" Felicity looked up from her magazine to see Grant's hand resting on the back of the upholstered dining chair. She closed her magazine and slipped it into the large handbag she carried with her.

She nodded at Grant. "Enchanté, darling. Do sit down."

With a flourish he pulled out the chair and sat down. "Aren't we festive today," Grant said, eyeing her low-cut sweater. A rather stretched Rudolph stared back at him. Felicity had ordered the sweater online as a holiday gift to herself. She'd been pleased with how well it fit, and although Rudolph's face was a bit pulled out of shape across her bosom, his wide-eyed grin and cherry nose was the happiest part of her Christmas season thus far. "You're practically bursting out of your sweater, my dear."

"Thank you." Felicity winked. "I thought it might brighten the place. Annoy Clara. Cute tie yourself."

Grant patted his tie. A mini string of holiday lights was sewn onto the black fabric. Little bulbs of red, yellow, green and blue twinkled. "A gift from David, some years ago."

"Oh yes, I remember. You wore it last Christmas." Felicity pulled out two packets of Sugar Twin from the plastic container holding various sweeteners and laid them on the table beside her empty teacup. "Do you find it hard getting through the holiday without him?"

Grant shrugged. "Christmas was never our thing. David spent holidays with his family." He slid one of the empty coffee cups sitting in the centre of the table toward himself and flipped the cup right-side-up in its saucer. "Let's talk about something I've been curious about. Is it hard to get those fake eyelashes to stay put?"

"Watch it. A woman never tells." Felicity batted her lashes, her augmented black fringe waving heavily back at Grant. "They look good, don't they?"

"Like a fawn. You're the spitting image of Bambi."

There was something easy about being around Grant. Maybe it was his dry sense of humour or perhaps it was because there was clearly no game that needed to be played between the two of them. She was the only one at the Eldernest who seemed to realize Grant was as gay as the day was long. It was right there for anyone to see if only they'd care enough to look. But they didn't look. Not past what they thought they already knew.

"How are you really doing, my dear?"

Felicity's shoulders stiffened. "Whatever do you mean?"

Grant nodded his head toward Martin. He sat with his most frequent visitor, that lanky nephew of his. Felicity relaxed her jaw with effort. She wasn't about to let on—even to Grant—that Martin's rejection had stung. He'd chosen Clara. Over her. While it was certainly true that Clara was even-keeled, polite to the staff, Miss. Manners at all times, she was also as bland as oatmeal without sugar.

Felicity loathed oatmeal. It irked that a cold bowl of oatmeal had displaced her in Martin's heart. Months had passed yet Felicity's rejection was a scab refusing to heal.

"Bhah. What do I care? If he wants to spend his time with a bore, then he's done well. I hate chess."

"You like tennis."

"No. I like watching sweaty, agile men play tennis."

Grant smiled. "You would have loved my David."

"He played tennis? Then there's no doubt."

A cafeteria attendant approached their table. Without needing to ask their orders she filled Grant's cup with decaf coffee and Felicity's with hot water, before setting a basket filled with individually wrapped tea bags on the table.

Grant nodded his thanks, but Felicity's nose crinkled in distaste as she sorted through the assorted selection of teas. "Licorice?

Peppermint? You think this place could stock decent tea. I bet the staff," Felicity paused to glance at the young woman standing at their table, "are drinking all the good black tea in the back. Leaving all this damn Licorice Spice for the old people, aren't you?"

Grant's cheeks pinkened; Felicity's did not. She tried not to roll her eyes as his mouth opened and closed without finding any words to say. Not that the young woman cared. She hadn't even bothered acknowledging either of them. Instead, she tucked her black hair behind her ear, turned and walked to the next table.

"Did you see that? Ignoring us in our own home. We pay their wages. You think they could show a little more respect."

Grant shifted in his chair. "Don't take it out on the help, my dear."

"What?"

"You know what."

Felicity tried not to blush. Grant was probably right. Of course he was right, but she was too angry to change her behaviour these days. She covered her embarrassment with a loud sigh. "Fine. Always the gentleman, aren't you?"

Grant took a sip of his coffee and graciously turned the conversation back to the original subject matter. "Have you considered setting your sights elsewhere?"

"I've nowhere else to set my sights."

"What about the Garden Wing?"

"The Garden Wing! You've got to be joshing me. Too geriatric." Felicity fished out a lone packet of Earl Gray and set about steeping her tea.

"And how about Christmas? Do you have any plans?"

Felicity sniffed. "The family has been pandering me to foot a family ski trip to Whistler. I'll not be going."

"Why not?"

"Why not? I've told you before, Grant. That damn daughter-in-law has brainwashed them all into thinking I've got suitcases of money just waiting to be spent."

"But you do, don't you?"

"Damn if I'll give it away that easy. They can wait till I keel over." She pulled the tea bag out of her water and plopped it down on the saucer creating a brown puddle around the base of her teacup. "How about you? Any plans?"

"Nothing major." Grant leaned across the table, as if imparting a secret. "I am, however, conveniently missing the 'Nest family night on Christmas Eve."

Felicity raised her eyebrows. "Really? Do tell."

"There's a poetry reading at the library. You should come with me."

"Poetry?" Felicity pursed her lips. "Not my thing."

"And kids and cookies are? Come on, there'll be meeeennnn."

"Straight men? I highly doubt it."

Grant chuckled. "There's got to be a few, hasn't there? They'll be the lonely ones. Who else listens to poetry on Christmas Eve?"

Felicity eyed her friend. "You've got a point."

***

"Felicity, you can't be serious! You can't miss the family Christmas party!" Rosie wrung her hands as though missing the party was actually a big deal. "You'll miss cookie decorating and the Santa visit. And Charlie will be here too. He's going to wear an elf costume!"

"I don't do cookies, Rosie, and I'm certainly not sitting on *that* Santa's knee." It was Martin who always volunteered to wear the Santa costume.

Rosie was the one person genuinely excited to decorate the social room with the Eldernest's tacky decorations. She was an odd duck. With her frizzy hair, thick glasses and secondhand sweaters she wasn't what Felicity would call inner circle. She'd even broken the Eldernest rules with that damn feral animal.

But watching Rosie lose that cat had been heartbreaking, even for an icy dame like herself. Felicity crossed her arms and sighed. "Give Charlie a scratch for me, won't you Rosie? He's sweet, as far as crotch-sniffers go."

Rosie nodded, a smile brightening her face. "I've got myself a matching elf hat too. Me and Charlie will work together handing out the presents, what with him not having any opposable thumbs."

"Er…sure. That sounds. Just lovely." Gawd, what to say to that? "Take a picture, won't you?"

She glanced over at Grant who was elbow deep in the

Christmas decoration box. He winked at Felicity as if to say, "See? That wasn't hard, was it?" He was a better person than her; a better person than most. He didn't have a swarm of grandchildren that would be visiting, and yet he seemed the least annoyed with Rosie's decoration dithering. He followed her around the room, tape dispenser in one hand, and yards of tinsel garland in the other.

Clara looked up from her novel. "And what will you be doing on Christmas Eve instead of the party, Felicity?" she asked. "Going out with family?"

"Gawd, no. I have plans. With Grant." Felicity dropped the little nugget of information into the churning waters of the social room and watched the ripple effect. Several pairs of eyes swiveled back and forth between herself and Grant. Sure, she'd made her announcement louder than required, but it was only polite when around the hearing impaired, wasn't it?

If these old goats couldn't figure it out on their own, that Grant wouldn't be interested if she were the last person on earth, then let them ponder. Let them think what they wanted. There was an upside to this poetry thing that had absolutely nothing to do with poetry.

"I'll be pulling that tinsel down if it interferes with the television screen, Rosie." Herbert's face was red with indignation. "I'll be pulling the damn thing down, ya hear?"

"We'll tack it up with tape, Herb," Grant said, soothingly. "No point getting your shorts in a knot."

Felicity watched as Clara looked up yet again, her eyes on Grant this time, before returning to her book. The tension between herself and Clara was at an all-time high, even if on the surface they maintained a polite demeanor. The woman had set up one of those Hanukkah candelabra things in the windowsill where Felicity kept her plants. She'd moved her violets—*without asking*—to the bookshelf, as though candles needed more light than living plants!

She wasn't going to let it get to her, though. Not on the outside at least. Waste of energy.

Felicity glanced at Martin, wondering if he'd overheard her declaration about Christmas Eve from where he sat at the card table with Herbert. She'd been careful not to pay him any attention when she'd announced her plans. It had been hard not to look over, but she'd been principled. Out of the corner of her eye she was pretty sure she'd seen him raise his hand and adjust his hearing aid, but she couldn't be sure.

She had not been alone with Martin since that day months ago when she'd dragged him out of the cafeteria. Felicity had chosen the bench at the back of the garden, the one overlooking the tennis courts by the lilac shrubs. It was furthest away from the walking path. Furthest away from intruding voices and the curious eyes of Eldernest residents and their guests.

"Is this really necessary, Felicity? My nephew is visiting, and he was just telling me some very serious news."

"What? That your cologne company is going out of business? You bought the whole vat and there's nothing left?"

Martin's brow furrowed and his nostrils flared as though he were trying hard to smell something. "Indeed. You've always been one for dramatics. If it bothered you, you could've told me."

"What, and rob Clara of the opportunity?"

An angry heat pawed at her chest. She'd let the cat out of the bag, without meaning to. Martin tilted his head to the side and pursed his lips in that pretentious way of his. Gawd. "So that's what you're on about. Look Felicity, your anger isn't charming."

"Your infidelity isn't charming!"

Martin raised both hands as though to ward off an angry bull, "Whoa now. We were never serious, you know that. We are ill suited."

"That is not what you were moaning a few months ago. Or maybe that was just that giant bottle of Viagra you carry around with you."

Martin flushed. "That's a medical condition, Felicity. It's not a joke. Besides..." he paused. Adjusted his collar and then continued. "I was still figuring it out a few months ago. Look, Felicity. You are very much overheated about this."

"Don't talk to me like a child, Martin. I know what this is about. We all know. You get bored and you move on. You've probably lived your whole life like that. Well you've messed up this time. You aren't going to find my equal around here." Felicity touched her immaculately groomed hair with her manicured hand. Most people around here weren't even fighting the aging process. Besides Martin. She'd thought they were a perfect match. They looked good together—everyone said it. What's more, she'd felt it.

He'd made her laugh.

He'd made her feel beautiful again.

She needed to know. She couldn't keep on guessing and wondering and not knowing. "What was it? Just tell me the truth."

He'd looked at her then back at the tennis courts before answering. "Your unhappiness is hard to be around."

Felicity's heart squeezed. It was practically the same thing her son had said when she'd demanded to know why he didn't visit more often. He only stopped in when he needed money. The truth was she was an inconvenience. She'd been left in this Nest-prison and only remembered when it was necessary. Her pain must have shown on her face, which was a feat in and of itself given the Botox sheen, because Martin cleared his throat. "I'm sorry I've hurt you."

There was nothing more to discuss. They sat in silence watching the staff on their lunch break, lobbing tennis balls back and forth in their blue and green scrubs, laughing whether they hit or missed. Everyone else seemed happier than her. Living in their happy little bubbles. And here she was on the outside.

But that had been months ago. The grass had still been green and the tree branches heavy with leaves. Now the snow lay thick on the ground. Tinsel wrapped the social room as the patrons got ready to celebrate the festive day with cafeteria-made turkey, instant mashed potatoes and tasteless wafers the staff passed off as diabetic-friendly baking.

She watched as Grant helped Rosie pin up the last cardboard cut-outs on the wall. It surprised her; did Rosie even have grandchildren? She had that mousy daughter who rarely smiled, but Felicity had not seen children visit. Yet here Rosie was, hopping around in her sensible footwear, taping images of snowmen on the wall. Cheap, cardboard snowmen at which Felicity's own grandchildren would turn up their noses.

"I'll meet you in the lobby at five, Grant. Does that sound about right?"

Grant glanced up from the box of decorations and smiled at Felicity. "Sounds just right, *my dear*." She felt rather than saw several heads swivel in their direction, but she didn't allow herself to look at anyone but Grant.

Despite everything, she had one true friend. She couldn't have asked for a better one than Grant. Gratitude ballooned in her chest. Finally she allowed her eyes to drift over to Martin. Sure enough, his eyes were like saucers. When she caught his gaze, he quickly dropped his eyes back to his cards. Perhaps it was just curiousity. Perhaps it was something more. She didn't know, and maybe, she didn't need to care quite so much anymore either.

Martin: Reconciliation

"Happy New Year, Uncle." The young buck clapped Martin on the shoulder, grinning from ear to ear as though he'd won the Lotto 649. Martin didn't need a glass ball to see a weight had been lifted off the lad's shoulders.

"You're in high spirits." He pointed to a table in the far corner of the cafeteria, away from the other patrons. "Come on. Let's go over there where it's quiet. I'm sick and tired of all the noise around here."

"Martin! You're sounding like an old man."

Martin swatted the air as though trying to shoo away a house fly then marched over toward the tables in the far corner. He got halfway there before allowing himself to look back over his shoulder and see if Chad was following him. He was, and Martin felt a little better for it. It had been a tough few days and he was feeling irritable, tired and…well, lonely.

"Here," Martin tapped his knuckles on a table along the back wall. "This'll do." He sat down and waited for Chad to join him before prying open the can of the worms. "So let's see, kid. Last time we chatted you appeared to be in the depths of despair. But now? You're walking on cloud number nine. I take it you've resolved your row with the lady-friend?"

"Ha! What row? It was a simple misunderstanding." His nephew leaned back, draping his arm over the back of the empty chair beside him. "Thank God! I haven't screwed it up yet."

"Simple?" Martin leaned forward. "Spill it then. I want the details."

"Well Martin, I hate to say it, but once again you were right. Time and patience. That's all that was needed." He paused, taking a second to bask in his good fortune.

"Bah! I said I wanted *details* not philosophizing."

Chad's face lit with a smile; not the slightest bit irritated by Martin's mood. Good gracious, at least one of them had hope restored.

"I can't help but notice you look a bit rough." Chad pointed at his uncle's wrinkled shirt. "That's not like you. Were you up late last night? Maybe ringing in the New Year with a lady friend?"

"Ha. Aren't we funny? Nope. I had a quiet night." Martin rubbed a hand over the stubble on his jaw. "An early night."

Chad leaned across the table, a twinkle in his eyes. "Why not try the fire and ice? Hmm?"

Martin scowled. "I thought you just said there's no point rushing things, remember? Patience is underrated in your generation. Always rushing in..."

"Right, *my* generation." Chad raised his eyebrows waiting for his uncle's comeback, but Martin didn't have one. That was okay. Even though Martin's mood was on the dark side, it was good seeing the lad having fun; it was definitely worth taking a bit of ribbing.

"You're a good kid. Visiting your old uncle on New Year's Day. I appreciate it, you know that?"

Chad's forehead creased. The look of humour washed off his face and his eyes roved over Martin as though looking for signs of the end times.

"I'm serious, I appreciate you stopping in. I'm not sure a selfish old man like myself would've done the same."

"Selfish? That's not true. You've gone out of your way to help Rosie, and you've been a big help to me, too. Remember? The postie one-two? Plus enough relationship advice to write a book. Where would I be without you?" Chad folded then unfolded his hands on the table. "How are things going with Clara?"

Martin sighed, then grit his teeth. There was probably no avoiding it. He might as well get it out of the way. "They're strained. More than strained. Downright frozen stiff, but let's not dwell—"

"Strained? I could put a good word in for you, how about that? A postie one-two for your rela—"

"What?" Martin cut in. "Not on yer life! That's a bad idea if I've ever heard one."

Chad raised his eyebrows. "Have you thought about volunteering? Maybe something to get your mind off it. Sure helped me." Martin sighed and rubbed at his jaw. This wasn't a simple misunderstanding he was in. He didn't even have the energy to answer his nephew. "Looks like…you've got your heart involved," Chad said.

The lad was right. How the hell had that happened? It was the one thing Martin should've known not to do.

Chad pointed to the group of people sitting near the window at the far side of the cafeteria. There was a middle-aged couple Chad was unlikely to recognize. The couple were sitting with two Eldernest residents, the first a woman—back straight and hands folded on her lap—and beside her a frail looking man. As usual Linus was propped in a wheelchair at a relined angle, a safety strap across his chest. "Isn't that Clara over there?"

Martin didn't answer.

"Who's that she's with? Doesn't seem very stiff competition for a sly fox like yourself."

"It's her husband."

Chad's face turned white, his eyes round and unblinking.

"Disappointed in me?" Martin winced, cleared his throat and continued. "I never meant to hurt the man. Not when he was down like that. It's just…like I said, I'm selfish."

If this were the movies Clara would turn and glance at him and the nephew, but it wasn't the movies. She didn't turn, she kept her attention focused on their guests. Still, Martin would wager she knew he was there. There was no avoiding anyone for too long at the 'Nest.

"It doesn't look like her husband's in a good way."

"Stroke. Could happen to any of us. I should have been more understanding. It's a difficult position for Clara to be in, ya see? It's just…time. I can feel it, ticking away. My clock—her clock— could be outta juice before we know it." Martin's throat thickened with emotion, but he wasn't giving in to it. Not here. Not in this cafeteria. "Okay, enough of this bullshit." Martin rubbed his hands together. "I need some good news to cheer me up. What's the update?"

***

After the lad said his farewell, Martin wandered the halls. He needed a distraction. There were options—a small gathering at the puzzle table or the sports channel with Herb—but Martin wasn't in the mood. He couldn't shake his misery, and so he went back to his room, prepared for a quiet night of contemplation.

How could a man live his whole damn life, the vast majority of those years happy as a pig in mud, beholden to no one—no woman or man outside the postal service, that is—only to find himself in the twilight of his years insecure as a pimply faced fourteen-year-old? That wasn't the Martin way. If he'd been beholden to anyone during his lifetime, it *should* have been to his sister. She and the lad had been his only living family for years.

But he hadn't been. Not really. His sister had always had to ask twice; had to convince Martin of what was in it for himself in order to get him to do anything.

Father's Day event at the lad's school? Young unmarried teacher with slim legs.

Teach a young man to shave? A story to impress the ladies with.

Attend his nephew's convocation? More than a few divorcees in the crowd.

Why had it taken till now for Martin to feel sheepish? Aware of how self-absorbed he'd always been? It was like his greatest flaw had been scratched into the white walls of his bedroom with heavy, lead pencil and it'd taken Clara for Martin to finally see it.

It had been easy looking out for the Numero Uno. The one and only. But what difference had he really made to anyone? His weak joints, the tremor in his hand, it was all a reminder that he was an old man and running out of time to build any sort of legacy. When he was gone, would anyone miss him? Would he have mattered… to anyone?

A sharp knock on the bedroom door startled Martin. It was undoubtedly Grant or Herb, wanting to resurrect the poker games or some such activity. Martin sighed. Maybe another day, but not tonight. He couldn't bring himself to do anything tonight.

Using the chair's armrests to support himself, Martin pushed himself up. He was getting to be a geezer for certain. Maybe, when he was feeling a little better, he should play a little poker if only to keep his mind active...as long as that trash-talking, sore-loser Edgar wasn't at the table.

Pulling open the door, Martin was ready to say just that, but the words died on his lips. There was his Clara, hair in a braid draped over her shoulder, hands tightly clasped in front of her.

"My dear." Martin cleared his throat, adjusted the collar of his maroon robe and moved back to let her in the bedroom. He was thankful he'd never gotten out of the habit of picking up after himself. His clothing was already stored neatly in the laundry basket, his lamp illuminating a spotless bedside table. His one regret was the glass dish of water awaiting his dentures. Nothing killed romance like a denture dish.

"May I offer you a seat?" He gestured toward the chair by the window then sat himself down on the end of his bed.

Clara perched on the chair; her hands still tightly clasped together. Her shoulders rose with each inhalation, her forehead creased with worry. Martin's own heart was pattering away, from happiness or anxiety, he wasn't certain.

Clara exhaled, opened her mouth to say something, then closed it again. She unclasped her hands, stretching her fingers out, then clenched her hands into fists before finally looking at Martin for help.

"Did you enjoy the pot pie at dinner?" Martin smiled through his own anxiety and nodded encouragingly.

"It was a little bland—not the way I used to make it."

He nodded. "Could've used some salt. But a nice change from the stroganoff."

"True. Absolutely." Clara bit her lower lip. "Rosie was telling me—in confidence, you understand—about the cat. How you've been such a help."

Martin grimaced. "That lady needs all the help she can get."

"She's well meaning. Just...you know."

"I know." Silence settled around them like an itchy blanket and Martin searched for another topic. He'd just settled on asking her about her reading, when she spoke.

"I've come to talk about Linus." Her words rushed into the void and her face coloured a soft pink.

Martin squirmed. He didn't want to, *gawd he did not want to talk about Linus*. It wasn't the first time he'd been 'the other man,' but he'd always told himself it wasn't his problem. He just went where the energy was. He wasn't proud of it, but he didn't deny it either. Besides, he hadn't been the kind of man who wanted matching hand towels in the bathroom or grandkids on the living room rug.

"And I also wanted to apologize," continued Clara. "I'm sorry I've hurt your feelings. Some of the things I said—it was unkind. I shouldn't have said them."

Martin swallowed. "No, it's me that's sorry. You were right. I do think of myself first. Always have." Martin pulled on the sleeve of his housecoat, unsure how much to say but worried he wouldn't say enough. "But I see it now, and I'll change." He wasn't too old to change. He could make this work. "We can even play chess. I love chess."

Clara gave a shaky laugh. "I'd like that."

"I'd like that too."

"As friends." She added, then shifted in the chair; her expression once again serious. "You understand?"

A soft moan escaped Martin's lips. There was a dullness in his chest, an inability to fill his lungs properly.

"I should clarify why I'm here. I wanted to see how you were doing and to apologize. I…wasn't happy the way we left things. It's not what I wanted, to end on bad terms. You know that, right Martin?"

"I know," Martin stammered. "You were just angry with me—which is completely justified. I was only thinking of myself. From now on it'll be different."

"I'm sorry, Martin." She leaned over and placed her hand on Martin's hand where it lay lifeless on his lap. "I thought this would make me happy—"

"Please, Clara."

"I'm sorry."

***

It was the night that would not end. Hours after Clara had left,

Martin sat in the dark trying to breathe. He was unable to sleep, unable to turn his mind off. Switching the bedside light on, Martin picked up his telephone receiver and dialed. It went to voicemail three times before the lad picked up.

"Is that you, Martin?" His nephew's voice was full of sleep and worry. "Is everything okay?"

"I should have been around more when you were young, Chad. You know that, right? Know I regret not being around?"

His nephew didn't answer right away. Martin could hear rustling, as though Chad were sitting up or moving the phone to his other ear. Finally he heard him clear his throat, and say, "You were around, Martin. You never missed a holiday."

"Your mom made a mean roast, no way I was missing that." The damn kid was obtuse. Martin would have to spell it out. "What I'm saying," the emotion caught in his throat and Martin hesitated for a moment. "I'm saying I should've been around for the everyday sort of stuff. Not just the holidays."

"It's almost 3:00 am, Martin." Chad paused, then asked in a voice laced with worry, "Why are you thinking about this now?"

"I just want *you* to know—that *I* know—I'm lucky to have you around *now* even though I wasn't around *then*. I've come to a sort of realization, you understand? I wish I'd done things a little differently."

Martin leaned back against his headboard, the strength going out of him. He'd said what he needed to say, and he could now sit back and hear whether his nephew would accept his apology.

It was a few moments before Chad said anything at all. "You were around, Martin. You explained the difference between antiperspirant and deodorant, remember?"

Martin's breath caught at the unexpected memory. It was a sweaty memory, that was for certain. Chad's mother had been buying him the wrong kind, but Martin had seen to that. Given him the low-down.

"And there was that time Mom took the haircutting course. You can't have forgotten those home haircuts. I'll owe you one forever for getting me out of that."

Tears welled in Martin's eyes and he had to swallow hard so the lad wouldn't hear the emotion in his voice. "That's true, indeed."

211

He'd helped the boy not get crucified at school. "Thank you for reminding me on that. It seems, as you get older, you forget some of the details." He paused and cleared his throat. "I needed that tonight, trouble sleeping, but I'll be fine now. Good night. And I'll see you Sunday."

"About that, I might have to cut Sunday short. I've got—"

"Cut it short?" interrupted Martin. "But that's our time. And I'm outta talc."

"They don't make talc anymore. Remember? We've talked about this."

"Of course they do! And…some razors. See you Sunday."

Chad sighed but Martin could hear the laughter in his voice. "Alright. I thought you said you'd never finish that megapack of razors? Anyway, see you Sunday."

Quinn: New Year

Monday, January 3rd

This is my brand-new Monday Morning journal. I got it from Mrs. Chou. She says "it's a New Year. It's a good time for a fresh start."

During Christmas holidays Mom and I went to Chad's apartment. I got to play with Mr. T. Mr. T is Chad's cat. Chad named Mr. T after a famous man who was on TV a long time ago. Chad says the famous Mr. T was tough and had attitude just like his cat. 'OK…' I said, because I didn't want to argue. Chad's cat isn't tough. He's big and orange and he likes to chase ribbons.

After we met Mr. T we went bowling. It was Mom and Chad against me and Ella (!!! BFFs forever !!!). Mom asked the desk person to put our guard rails up so we wouldn't have so many gutter balls. I scored over 100!!! So did Ella. We ate popcorn. It was great.

February 14th

Today is a big day—Valentine's Day! We will exchange cards at school and have a class party.

Last Saturday Ella's family took me swimming with them. It was awesome!! We went to the wave pool and it had two waterslides, an orange one and a blue one. On the orange slide you can go down holding hands with your friends but on the blue slide you have to go one at a time. Ella and I like the orange slide best. We went down together 7 times.

Then on Sunday night Chad came over. He gave my mom a heart shaped box of chocolates. My grandparents gave me and Mom red envelopes with money inside because it was also Chinese New Year. I got $20!! Then we ate dinner. Chad is getting a lot better at chopsticks. I told him so and grandfather agreed.

March 7th

Mom says I can have Ella over for a sleepover to celebrate my birthday. My birthday isn't until April but that's exactly what I'm going to do. I will make an invitation for Ella and my mom will talk to her mom on the phone. We will watch movies and eat pizza and popcorn. We will set up our sleeping bags in my bedroom and it will be like indoor camping.

I asked Mom if Mr. T could come for the sleepover so Ella could meet him. Mom said no. She says Mr. T doesn't like new spaces or travelling in boxes and I have to respect his wishes. I think Mom is wrong. He would like the party because I have many shiny things to chase. Ella and I would keep him busy. I will keep asking and maybe Mom will say YES!!!!!

Chad: The Man Code

"Did you hear about the new forward for the Bruins?" Herb asked. He smacked the sports section of the newspaper down on the card table in front of me and jabbed at it with his finger. "Says right here in today's paper he's a *hom-o-sexual!*"

Flecks of Herb's angry spit spattered the table as he swung his face back and forth between my uncle and myself. It was a miracle his reading glasses didn't whip off the end of his nose.

I politely swallowed my irritation before it showed on my face. Whenever Herb got onto something, he was impossible to distract. I continued shuffling the cards in the slightest hope he would take the hint.

"They're taking over, they are." Damn. He was not going to go away. He leaned heavily on his walker, both hands grasping tightly around the handlebars. He seemed to be waiting for something. Perhaps some kind of astonished response to his news or an equally indignant rejoinder, affirming his opinion.

I managed a shoulder shrug. Uncle Martin had yet to comment. He'd pulled the paper toward himself and was reading the article.

I didn't know where Martin stood on the issue. He wasn't known for attending pride parades or sporting rainbow socks, not that I'd seen anyone else at the 'Nest doing so. This included the one resident I knew with some certainty was gay.

I kept my eyes on my cards, not allowing myself to glance over at Grant. He wasn't far away; he was sitting at the other card table, the one situated under the window, and was playing a game of crib with Felicity. I liked Grant; who didn't? He was a decent sort and did not deserve to be caught up in Herbert's righteous vendetta against gay hockey players.

I didn't know why Grant was 'in the closet.' Perhaps he was the kind of person who just didn't believe his personal life was anyone else's business. Or maybe he didn't feel it would be safe at the 'Nest. Whatever his reasons, it was remarkable he managed to maintain his privacy when living in the close confines of a rumour-swarming place like the 'Nest.

Herb was still standing over us, his breathing getting laboured. I should've offered him a seat, but I really didn't want to encourage the conversation. And my uncle was no help at all. His head was lowered as he read the newspaper article.

"Another round?" I asked Martin and tapped the deck of cards on the table.

"Seriously, can you believe it? A hom-o-sexual in the bloody *NHL!*" Herb's voice boomed, causing others in the room to look over.

I cleared my throat. "Well, um, sure. It's not too hard to believe, is it? A lot of people are gay…why not in the NHL, you know?"

"Why not in the NHL? *Why not in the NHL?*" Now I'd done it. Herbert's face coloured a vibrant purple. He turned his walker around and put the locking mechanism on the wheels. With care he sat down on his walker's seat, making himself at home at our card table. "They've only got the one dressing-room, Chad. Just the one dressing-room per team."

"I'm sure they'll work it out, Herb," My uncle said, and put down the paper. "Besides, it says here the players support him. No mention of a problem."

I turned to Herb, trying to change the topic. "Any chance you caught the game last night? I didn't see who won."

"A sin! A sin against the Lord and a misuse of the body. They should kick him out of the league, they should!" *Great. There was no distracting the man.* He was now vigorously shaking his head; spit shooting in various directions. "An abomination unto the Lord!"

I looked over at my uncle for help. I was sweating bullets, trying to figure out what to say, and mortified I'd unwillingly become involved in this conversation. I'd known Herb was an opinionated old man, but I had no idea he was a full-on religious asshole.

Herb continued to gripe, even though no one was encouraging him. "Kick him off the team. That's what they need to do."

"You can't fire someone because they're gay." Felicity said, her comment like a shot from across the room. "It's a human rights violation."

"Human rights? What about the rest of the team's rights? They've a right to change without worrying about a pervert."

"Herb, you need to watch your blood pressure," said my uncle. *His* blood pressure? I could feel my own hitting the roof. I hadn't experienced this much confrontation when my last relationship ended, and here I was on the verge of a moral battle with a man more than double my age.

I could finally understand why Grant might have chosen to fly under the radar. The Eldernest felt decidedly unsafe at the moment, and I was a straight, white guy.

I cleared my throat, trying to swallow my anger so I could communicate just the facts. "The paper says he's gay. There's no reason to assume he's a pervert, Herb."

"But it's unnatural!" Herb practically shouted, then ground his teeth together as though he were chewing on a piece of beef jerky. He pointed a shaky finger at me. "I'm surprised at you, Chad. It's almost like you're trying to tell us something about yourself. Hmm? Is that it?" A malicious smile curled the ends of Herb's mouth upward.

My uncle slammed his hand down on the table. "Watch yourself, Herb! Like I've told you before, my nephew was only *between* relationships, that's all."

All eyes in the social room were on me, including Grant's. Rosie, who I'd not noticed earlier, was looking at us from over the back of the couch, her round eyes unusually large behind her glasses. "What's going on? Can someone tell me what's going on?"

No one answered Rosie. I met Grant's eyes and knew I had a choice. It was either the man code—vehemently deny my gayness—or risk looking weak.

The air was dry. It whistled through my nasal cavities as I

breathed in. I cut the playing cards, shuffled them in a wide arc, felt them move freely through my fingers. My uncle's knuckles were white where they gripped his chair's armrests, and Herb stared at me, waiting for a response.

I smiled, refusing to give one. Instead I dealt my uncle and I another round of cards. The man code was obsolete.

Herb pulled himself up from the walker, unlocked the wheels and made his way over the recliner by the television. He picked up the remote control that sat on the side table and started jabbing at the buttons.

"Can't get this damn thing to work," he said, and began peeling off some duct tape.

"You aren't to press those buttons," shouted Martin. "That's why they're taped off." I jumped in my chair, surprised by my uncle's yelling. "Bloody dingbat," he grumbled. "I think I've had enough of this room. Let's get some fresh air, shall we?"

Martin didn't need to ask me twice. Leaving the cards on the table we left the room and made our way to the bench outside the front doors of the 'Nest. Thankfully it was deserted, and we sat down on its hard surface. A light wind blew across the parking lot and I squinted to keep the blowing dust out of my eyes.

Martin was steaming mad. He ground his jaw and I wanted to tell him to be careful not to wear down his dentures but kept my thoughts to myself. My own anger had dissipated, surrendering to an immense wave of hopelessness for humanity. If you couldn't find a safe space to end your years, then really, what hope was there when it came to tackling global warming or world peace?

"The nerve!" Martin spat, rocking back and forth on the bench. "What an idiot!"

"Definitely. But look, I don't care what Herb thinks of me—"

"Don't care? You need to care! What if Lila were to hear him say something like that?"

"I'm not too fussed about that either. I don't think most people my age think being called gay is an insult. Maybe it used to be, but not now." I turned to look at my uncle. "Look, maybe you should try and reason with Herb once he's calmed down. Do you think he would listen to you? He could really hurt someone with that kind of talk. Someone he doesn't intend to offend."

"You mean the staff?"

"Maybe. Or a visitor." I leaned back on the bench, feeling the winter sun on my face and closed my eyes. "Or even one of the seniors."

"Oh, that's pretty rare, in our age group, Chad. I would know if there were some gays around here, and there aren't any. They would stick out like a sore thumb."

I bit the inside of my cheek. "You never know. If they think loud-mouths like Herb are going to discriminate against them—"

"Discriminate! Come now, Chad. Herb was being an ass, but discrimination...that's a pretty strong word, don't you think?"

I shrugged, picturing Grant in the corner playing cards and minding his own business. How many times would he be forced to listen to Herb talk about sin and abomination today? I knew enough about Herb to surmise he'd likely accosted everyone he'd seen since reading the article. "No. I don't think it's too strong a word. Who cares if someone's gay anyway?"

"Well, sure. But...AIDS, Chad. Maybe you're too young to remember, but that was definitely linked to the gays."

"We don't say 'the gays' anymore. Besides, as long as you use your condoms, you're fine." Not that he'd asked me to buy him anymore. It seemed the old man was slowing down. "All I'm saying is people should be mindful. You wouldn't want to unintentionally harm someone, would you?"

I felt Martin shift around on the bench beside me, but I didn't open my eyes. It was one of those beautiful end of winter days where the snow was melting so fast you could hear water trickling off the roof and down the gutters. Where the sun was warm on your skin and it made you realize you'd forgotten how amazing that felt over the course of the winter. It was, in fact, the first time I'd been outside without a jacket in months.

"You remind me of your mother, Chad. And that's a compliment. She was always pretty adamant about stuff like this."

"She was."

"Didn't laugh at off-colour jokes."

"That's true." I'd forgotten about that. A smile spread across my face; I was proud of the person she'd been.

"She'd have given Herb a good telling-off just now." We both chuckled. It was entirely possible.

"He's usually such a great guy," Martin continued. "A bit tenacious about the sports mind you, but a great guy. I didn't realize he could be such an asshole."

"Can you be both great and an asshole?" I wondered aloud.

"I don't know. I don't rightly know."

***

Lila and I went for a drink while Quinn was at the dojo. Even though the weather was cool for sitting on a patio, we both agreed it was by far the better choice to sitting indoors. It felt downright tropical compared to the winter we'd just had.

I'd given Lila a play-by-play of the fiasco in the social room. It was still top of mind, irritating me like a mosquito bite that wouldn't stop itching. "It was really terrible, you know?"

"I'm sure, but I've heard worse at the 'Nest. They're very entitled people."

"I guess." I rubbed the back of my neck. "But I can't help but worry about some of them. I like some of them."

"I know, I get it." She squeezed my hand where it rested on the table. "Did you always know you were going to have so many old people friends?"

I laughed and took a sip of my beer. I would not have guessed in a million empty nights at home that I would one day have a group of people forty years my elder as friends. "No. I definitely didn't know."

We picked Quinn up after her class was over. On the walk home we voted for which board game to play when we got back to their place. Quinn and I easily outvoted Lila, agreeing that Settlers of Catan was probably the second-best game in the modern universe. According to Quinn nothing would ever move Clue out from the top-spot and I nodded even though it was like agreeing the sky was brown. Some debates didn't need to be won.

I felt peace. I had people around me. Family. Old people, young people; communities of people to care about. It had been years since I felt this a part of something; this at ease with my life.

Early the next morning my cell phone rang. I'd spent the night at Lila's, and I rolled away from her warmth and reached for the phone where it lay on her bedside table. It was Director Knightly.

Uncle Martin had passed quietly in the night. An unexpected heart attack in his sleep. There was nothing that could have been done.

"I'm sorry, Mr. McEwan. Your uncle will be missed." I didn't hear anything else. It was like a massive wind had blown through my life and taken the ground with it.

Chad: Supplies

It was a day before the funeral when I received a second call from Director Knightly. He was sorry for my loss but needed my uncle's room vacated. The first of the month was around the corner, and there were people on the Eldernest wait-list. As Martin's sole remaining relative it was my responsibility to clear his personal effects. "Otherwise we just send housekeeping in. They bag it all up. Send the clothes to Goodwill and the rest goes in the waste compactor."

I agreed to go down to the Eldernest and take care of my uncle's effects as soon as I could. That would not be until after the funeral. I hung up, unwilling to negotiate the timeline.

I had never felt so disconnected. I was without any kind of steady anchor. I was without family; without anyone committed to me simply because of shared DNA.

"Are you sure you want to do it on your own?" Lila said and squeezed my hand. We were huddled on the couch, a blanket over us more for comfort than warmth.

"Ya, I'll be fine." I squeezed her hand back. "Anyways, you've already done so much." Quinn had spent the day with her grandparents while Lila and I met with her funeral director boss, going over all the odds and ends that needed seeing to. She'd taken care of all the relentless decisions and details that were too confusing or meaningless to matter much to me. "Maybe while I pack Martin's stuff you could do something with Quinn. Something fun, like the zoo or the water park. Something she would like."

"Knightly's a douche. He could've waited till the funeral was over before calling."

I couldn't help but smile. "Still. I've got to get Martin's stuff. It's not going to get any easier if I wait. How much could he have in his room anyway?"

"You'd be surprised."

***

The day after the funeral I called into work and told them I needed an extra day off. Then, before I could put it off any longer, I caught the bus, an empty cardboard box in each hand. With every bump in the road and turn of the bus wheels I said goodbye to the route that had become so well-known.

When I arrived at the 'Nest, there was Grant, sitting on the bench outside the front door. He stood up as I approached.

He pointed at the boxes. "Can I give you a hand, Chad?" I handed him one of the empty boxes and he fell into step beside me. I had developed an immediate lump in my throat, and I could only nod my thanks.

I hadn't expected anyone's help, and up until now I'd thought I didn't want any. But Grant was assuming in a very unassuming way and his quiet presence was easy to be around.

It didn't take long to weave through the halls and find Martin's room. We opened the door and stood side by side looking at the dark space. The curtains were drawn, blocking out the natural light and the scent of Jovan Musk gently wafted over us in greeting.

"Doesn't seem real, does it? It feels like he's just out and about, socializing with the ladies." It was easier to picture my uncle walking down the corridor in a navy button down, every white hair in place, then it was to believe I'd never see him again.

But of course, that wasn't the case, and I had the cardboard boxes to remind me I was here to do a job. I stepped into the room and Grant followed, walked over to the window and opened the curtains. Warm sunlight streamed into the room.

We set the boxes on the bed, and I got to work. It didn't take long. In less than two hours we'd sorted through my uncle's personal effects: keep, pass on, throw out. That was it. That's all the time it had taken to clear up a person's life. I didn't keep much. Just a framed black and white picture I found of Martin and my mom. In the picture Mom was a child about Quinn's age. She sat on a wooden swing; her hands tightly fisted around the ropes that held the swing to a tree branch overhead. A teenage version of my uncle stood behind her; an arm propped nonchalantly against the trunk of the tree and a wide grin revealing Martin's characteristic swagger even back then.

Holding the framed picture in my hands, I looked around the room. Two boxes to donate. A small pile of odds and ends to toss. Otherwise we were done. It took a few minutes of taking the emptiness in before I trusted myself to speak. "Looks like we're done."

Grant pointed at a cupboard inset into the wall behind the bedroom door. "There's one last cupboard."

I opened it expecting more clothes, or maybe Italian leather dress shoes. But instead what faced me were stacks of unused hygiene products.

Red jars of Brylcreem and unopened packages of razors promising the closest shave ever. Dark Temptation scented Axe shower gel and male nutritional supplements piled neatly on top of a dozen or so GQ and Men's Health magazines.

I blinked rapidly but it was no use; my eyelids couldn't keep up. Tears trickled down my face and I swiped at them with my sleeve.

Grant stood quietly beside me. He held a half-filled cardboard box and did not fidget or shift his weight or comment one way or the other. I appreciated it immensely and years later I wished I'd told him.

After what my uncle might have considered an unmanly amount of time, I gave my face a last wipe against my shirt sleeve, cleared my throat and squeezed out a few words. "I can't believe he didn't use this stuff."

Grant also cleared his throat before responding. "He used the condoms."

"Right."

"And that damn cologne."

I laughed, again the tears managing to escape down my face. "That was some strong shit."

"Very much so."

I was practically howling, my eyes still streaming, and I had to sit down on the edge of Martin's bed until I could stop. I was a freaking mess. I tried taking some deep breaths, tried to calm myself down, but my body was apparently as confused as I was. It took several more minutes before I had pulled myself together. "What the hell? Why did he keep sending me on all those errands if he didn't actually need all that shit?"

While I'd been trying to get a hold of myself, Grant had put the box he'd been holding on the floor and sat down on the one chair in Martin's room. "I think he just wanted to see you. Maybe it was a good excuse, you know?"

"I would've come by anyway."

Grant nodded. "Maybe it's easier to say you need soap than to admit you're lonely? And loneliness…I see it all the time around here."

Around here. Around everywhere. The basketball program was full of lonely kids, the Sentry full of adults eager for connection. I myself had spent months after Kate left where the only activity that broke up answering the complaint line were my weekly visits with Martin. I'd probably needed the visits more than he did.

"And maybe it was a bit of fun too," continued Grant. "On Martin's part. He couldn't wait for your visits. He used to say, 'let's see what the nephew brings this week.'"

"What?" I spluttered. "He requested those things! I only brought what he'd asked for."

Grant leaned forward and picked up one of the Men's Health and Fitness magazines. The pages zipped through Grant's fingers, their glossy pages crisp and polished. "You never said no? You never said, 'maybe next week?'"

"Why would I have done that?"

Grant rubbed his chin. "Your uncle was proud of you."

We packed up the supplies. The magazines went to the social room library. The unopened razors and soaps and hair products could be dropped off at the homeless shelter. Grant felt the unopened condoms could easily be added to the basket in the men's washroom; the health region had recently offered an education program onsite about sexually transmitted infections, but the basket of free condoms often ran low.

"What about all this protein powder?" I asked.

Grant shook his head. "I don't think anyone will use that here. What about you?"

I looked down at my skinny frame, at the Marvel Comics logo on my shirt. This was who I was. "Nah. I think I'm fine the way I am." I tried to think of someone in my life who enjoyed working out. Only one person came to mind. "Maybe Harold?"

Grant smiled. "We could always ask."

For myself I pocketed a half empty bottle of Jovan Musk which had been sitting beside Martin's toothbrush on the washroom counter. It was the only item I took besides the framed picture of Mom and Martin. I didn't plan to wear the cologne. I just wanted it. It would be a long time before I could open the bottle and smell it without tearing up. And that was okay.

Outside the front doors of the 'Nest I said goodbye to Grant, then loaded the boxes for the Goodwill into the back of a taxi and for the last time rode away.

***

Several months passed. My life had filled up with everyday happenings the way you never think it will after a tragedy. There was Lila and Quinn, and my job. With the video series now complete, I had evolved one quarter step up the complaints department ladder: section lead. There was the basketball group which I never missed and weekly dinners with Lila's parents. I enjoyed their company even though I hadn't been invited to help make dumplings…yet.

It was a Thursday evening, Lila out meeting with a bereaved family, when Quinn and I were at the library in search of a particular graphic novel. My heart skipped a beat when I saw a familiar woman with a braid of silver white hair in the adult fiction section. It was the first time I'd run into anyone from the 'Nest. I approached slowly, but a smile lit her face as soon as we made eye contact.

"How have you been, Clara?"

In the four months since Martin's passing his chess playing muse had barely crossed my mind. I felt a wave of shame at that. Would he have wanted me to check on her? Had she been lonely without my uncle's relentless pursuit?

"Oh, you know. Some days are better than others." She shifted the stack of books she carried to her other arm. "There's some new people who've moved in, shaking the old scene up a bit. That's been good. But…we miss Martin. Miss all that energy he had, if you know what I mean. And we miss you, too. We all enjoyed having you around." She smiled, her eyes searching my face.

"I enjoyed being around." It was the truth, after all. "What's been going on with everyone?"

"I've been helping Rosie with the Paws Program—it's a great deal of fun. And Herb's gotten hearing aids and it's made a world of difference for all of us. I'm thankful not to have to listen to the football announcer at quite so loud a volume!"

"Yes. I imagine that's a relief. For everyone."

Clara smiled, but it didn't quite reach her eyes. I had the impression she was thinking of something else, or some time else. I was thinking about something else too—what would Martin want me to say? I felt what had become a familiar ache knowing I would never again hear one of his old postal service stories or receive some unsolicited relationship advice.

Clara cleared her throat. "Do you still have that cat? The one of Rosie's?"

"I do. Against my better judgement. He's rather fierce, rather unloving as far as cats go. He only tolerates me, but he seems to like my girlfriend's daughter. He'll come and sit by her, let her rub his belly, that sort of thing. But only when he wants to. It's got to be his choice, you know what I mean?"

Clara laughed. "Sounds a bit like some of my neighbours at the Eldernest."

I politely laughed along and then it seemed we were both out of words. Neither of us made false promises we would see each other soon. Instead we said goodbye, turned away from each other, and moved on.

Martin: Leather / Prelude

"I'm surprised. A senior's facility? You aren't *that* old, Martin." Mary lifted her oxygen mask up to her mouth, inhaled and exhaled before letting both it and her hand drop back to the bed. Her voice was as soft as a whisper, broken up with stops and starts, and Martin had to listen carefully in order not to miss her words. "I always thought of you as independent."

Martin smiled and undid the cufflinks on his shirt. His sister's room was uncomfortably warm, and he could feel beads of sweat gathering at his temples. "There's a lot of older women at the 'Nest, Mary. I owe it to the ladies to keep them company. Help them not get too isolated." He winked at his sister then turned his attention to his shirt sleeves, folding one, then the other to just below his elbow.

"I never believed the day would come. My big brother—tired of living alone."

Martin smiled and nodded in agreement as though this visit were the same as any other they'd shared over Mary's kitchen table. He knew what was coming. So did Mary. Their mother's voice had been the same, hitched and broken before she could no longer talk at all.

"What can I say? I've finally seen the light." He picked up the plastic water cup that was sitting on the bedside table and guided the straw to his sister's lips. Mary took a sip of the icy water before mouthing the words *thank you*. Martin suspected she wasn't thirsty. She was letting him take care of her because she knew it made him feel better. And that, more than any of the physical signs or reports from specialists, told Martin his sister believed her time was short.

Martin set the cup back down and rolled his shoulders. Not that it helped. The tightness in his chest was persistent. It never quite left. "Between you and I—and seriously Mary, don't be telling that pretty nurse of yours that I said this—but I'm damn tired of all the yard work. I was shoveling the sidewalk last winter and I couldn't help but think, 'Why bother?' It's not like there's even door-to-door mail service anymore."

"An apartment maybe?"

"That's what I was thinking. At first. Somewhere trendy, you know? Maybe with a fashionable bar or pub close by, or even one of those coffee shops with a fireplace. But then I started thinking that wasn't quite right either. I've no wife or kids. No one to take care of me as I get older, so I might as well save myself the trouble of a second move. Might as well move to the old folk's home now, cause I'll eventually have to be there anyway, won't I?"

Mary offered her brother a weak smile. "I hope so, Martin. I dearly hope so," she turned her head to gaze out the window. The view offered nothing but gray, overcast sky and the roof of the hospital building that adjoined the cancer centre.

Martin swallowed, wondering how even *now* he could get caught up in his own situation. "Mary…"

"I'm serious. I hope you live a good long time. Get old, Martin. One of us has to."

He reached over and gently squeezed his sister's hand where it rested on the bedsheet. It was all the comfort he could offer. He couldn't promise her to get old. He didn't make promises he wasn't sure he could keep. Even if he promised her the bloody moon, what difference would it make if he couldn't deliver?

"There's something I need, Martin. Something I need to know you'll do." She made her request. It was simple and straightforward, and it wasn't altogether unexpected. It wasn't even very much to ask. But Martin would have preferred it unsaid. Unpromised.

"He's nothing like me, Mary. You know that. He's got his head buried in a computer all day, and it's not that I don't want to, but I doubt there's anything useful I've to offer him. I'd just be a burden." Why was it so damn hot in here? "Look, maybe I should find one of the staff. Maybe they should check your temperature, alright?"

Mary raised the oxygen mask back to her face and took a few more inhalations. She starred at her brother, refusing to break eye contact with him.

Martin shifted in his chair and looked away. "Me and Chad. I don't know." He shook his head. "He's not going to want an old man like me looking over his shoulder. He's a *millennial*. Has his own way of doing things."

Mary closed her eyes and lay her head back on the thin pillow. The wall clock ticked out the seconds, the red hand jerking forward inch by inch. Counting down until there would be nothing left.

Quietly Martin stood up. His sister's eyes had closed. She needed rest in order to keep her strength. Leaning over he gently kissed her forehead. Mary's skin felt tissue-thin and hot under his lips. Her eyes fluttered open and she looked up at her brother. Martin couldn't look away. It was just as it had always been.

He no longer saw the hollow cheeks or sharp bones pressing up around his sister's eye sockets. Instead he was peering into the bright green eyes of his sister as she flew down the slide. Her brown braids whipping in the air behind her as she raced on her bike. The scratched knees and dirty fingernails and summer happiness of little sisters who were supposed to be young and healthy forever.

Mary's gaze softened and her head tilted to the side. "I'm tired."

Untangling the elastic strap from her fingers, Martin replaced the oxygen mask on her face. The skin on the bridge of her nose was reddened and chapped where the mask rested, and he wanted to weep. Wanted to gather her in his arms and make everything go back to the way it was, but of course that wasn't something he could do.

"He's a good kid, your Chad. We'll work it out, him and I. You know I won't let you down, right?"

Mary's pale lips pressed into a smile. She lifted the oxygen mask off her mouth. "Yes, I know that."

She let the mask drop back over her mouth and Martin adjusted the elastic so it wouldn't rub the skin behind her ears. He remembered Mary's long braids whipping and dancing behind her. He remembered the way the two of them would run down the gravel road all summer, barefoot more often than not. The soles of their feet as hard and tough as leather.